A NOTE ON THE AUTHOR

STEPHEN KELMAN was born in Luton in 1976.
Pigeon English, his first novel, was shortlisted for the 2011
Man Booker Prize, the Desmond Elliott Prize and the
Guardian First Book Award, and he was also shortlisted for
the New Writer of the Year Award at the 2011 Galaxy
National Book Awards. *Pigeon English* is a set text on the
GCSE syllabus. Stephen lives in St Albans.

@stephen_kelman

MAN ON FIRE

STEPHEN KELMAN

BLOOMSBURY

LONDON · OXFORD · NEW YORK · NEW DELHI · SYDNEY

Bloomsbury Paperbacks
An imprint of Bloomsbury Publishing Plc

50 Bedford Square
London
WC1B 3DP
UK

1385 Broadway
New York
NY 10018
USA

www.bloomsbury.com

BLOOMSBURY and the Diana logo are trademarks of Bloomsbury Publishing Plc

First published in Great Britain 2015
This paperback edition first published in 2016

British Library Cataloguing-in-Publication Data
A catalogue record for this book is available from the British Library.

ISBN: HB: 978-1-4088-6546-0
       TPB: 978-1-4088-1825-1
        PB: 978-1-4088-4317-8
      ePub: 978-1-4088-4318-5

4 6 8 10 9 7 5 3

Typeset by Integra Software Services Pvt. Ltd.
Printed and bound in Great Britain by CPI Group (UK) Ltd, Croydon CR0 4YY

To find out more about our authors and books visit www.bloomsbury.com.
Here you will find extracts, author interviews, details of forthcoming
events and the option to sign up for our newsletters.

For Bibhuti, my pathfinder.

To Mum and Dad, for your courage.

To Uzma, the light I reach for.

My life is my message.

Mahatma Gandhi

I share my cell with a broken-down kid in a T-shirt that says 'Welcome to Fabulous Las Vegas'. He's coming down from something transformational and the tragedy of his return to earth is scratched into his face like a prayer gone cold. His eyes are empty and restless. He knows how close I came to killing a man. He can feel it coming off me and it's making him edgy.

I tell the Inspector I have to be somewhere.

'Where?'

'I have to go home. I'm dying. I haven't got much time left. You know I'm innocent. Let us go, we just want to go home.'

The Inspector mumbles something profane to himself and turns the page of his newspaper.

'You are dying?' my cellmate asks me.

'That's right.'

On hearing this he sways towards me, drawn in. I can smell the fight on his clothes. I know somehow that every day for him is a fight he can't win. His breath is hot and sweet and I need a drink.

'I also am dying,' he says. He looks very young when he says this. There's confederacy in his tone and it sickens me a little bit.

He puts his arms together as though he's handcuffed. The inner sides of his forearms are bitten and ravaged. He feels no disgrace in telling me he's a user of heroin. He says it's killing him but he can't stop.

'I need it too much. I have tried to stop but it is very difficult. My brother died from heroin also. He was nineteen years old. I am twenty-two. I have died twice before but each time I came back. When my brother died I was in college. I was studying to be an engineer. Now I am living on the streets. I steal and I beg. Sometimes I am selling books along the road but it is too much competition, the boys with limbs missing are always making the most sales, the customers are feeling sorry for them. I am just a junkie. They do not feel sorry for me.'

I reach out to touch his shoulder but then I quickly pull back in case he doesn't want the intrusion. I'm not sure why but it's important to me that he thinks I'm a good man, sensitive to the needs of others.

'Life is very hard. God has forgotten me. I know I have disappointed him. This is why he does not listen anymore. There are many other people who need his help before me. They should have it.'

His smile is disarming. He's as untouched by self-pity as I was enslaved to it.

I tell him God hasn't forgotten him. I surprise myself by believing it. But then I shouldn't be surprised, not after everything that's happened. I believe in you informally, like a recipe handed down. You're my bread now. Funny how my taste for you has come on like a fire in an airless room.

The kid hugs himself and shakes like a dog coming out of the rain. The boy he was is visible in the little tremors and the stamping of feet.

He asks me for money. Just enough for one night of comfort once he gets out of here. Then tomorrow he'll buy some more books and go out on the road again. The monsoon is nearly over and many things are washed away. He knows he can't get them back. Just enough for one night of comfort.

I tell him I can't help him. I say God is with him and he shouldn't give up hope.

He lies down on the concrete bench, curls up tight with his back to me. I listen for a warning of a coming rage but within moments his breathing is deep and he's still. I've stopped speculating about the contents of other people's dreams.

An hour goes by and you sit with me. You tell me that the world you made for me is a beautiful place, and it will still be beautiful long after I've left it.

What about earthquakes and volcanoes, I say.

Mostly beautiful, you say. And what horrors there are only pass through so beauty can have a new place to build its ministry. Grass grows from ash and birds from bone.

The horror I made is still fresh, and before I die I hope to be forgiven for it. I let myself smile. I'll miss India and the rain on my skin.

World Record Number 1: 43 kicks to the unprotected groin in one minute and a half (1998)

I achieved maiden World Record at the very first time of asking, at the home of my then employer and great friend Rajesh Battacharjee, who was at this time a local businessman and corporator of high esteem. He was among the four supporters who facilitated along with three of my students, having all landed the job due to their superior determination and belief in shared philosophy. It was quite experimental, as this was a record without precedent, therefore it was my honour to conduct attempt in my own preferred manner – with many thanks to good people from Limca for their kindness and understanding.

I chose the groin kick for my opening record because its danger and high skill level required would guarantee that it would remain intact for many years to come (this has since been proved correct as to this day of writing I remain unmatched in this area). When you are reaching for the heights you must stretch your arms to the furthest limit, this is what I have always believed since I was a youngster. My wife was not convinced but there was no deterring me. I had already my son, Shubham, who was six months old at that time, so my family was complete. Therefore if permanent injury grabbed me it would be no disaster.

During practice period I devised the perfect recipe for success: four supporters kicking me in turn could manage rate of one kick every two seconds or less, and I was sure this would be enough to set a respectable total. Rajesh Battacharjee was leading kicker as he was an important man in the community and also providing venue and refreshments.

'With your training you are well advantaged,' he told me. 'This will be the ideal platform for the skills the almighty has blessed you with.'

His words clicked with me instantly. My deep wish was always to lead the world in a great endeavour, something I alone could do. I had been searching high and low for many years for this outlet. Then on a strange impulse I purchased a copy of the famous *Guinness Book of World Records*. I found it by chance among the wares of a street seller on Marine Drive during my first lonely months in Mumbai – having arrived in the big city from my native place of Cuttack with high plans to make a name for myself and honour the dear ones I had left behind. I spent every spare hour between its pages trying to find inspiration and release from the toil of my days working as accountant in Rajesh Battacharjee's Everest Engineering factory producing cooling towers. But all records there seemed to me like a joke. Those captured by my fellow Indians especially. Longest beard. Longest fingernails. Most time sitting on pole. Most snakebites survived. Nothing matched my desire to branch out in new direction. I wished to make a fresh impact and when, some three years into my stint in Mumbai, Rajesh Battacharjee mentioned groin kicking as an untested area of achievement it sounded to me like the perfect example of this goal. I had not been so excited by this discovery since first I outstripped my friends in push-ups back in my native place as a young boy. Then I knew I was destined for great things and the feeling this time was one hundred times stronger. When I closed my eyes to introspect I saw a fantastic fire and emerging from this was BB Nayak with his arms up high in victory and gold medal of the World Record holder hanging from his neck.

'I will be the world topper in kicks to the groin,' I declared with great seriousness.

'Yes, BB, you will!' Rajesh Battacharjee agreed, and we embraced in spirit of joy and companionship. I was itching to go full steam ahead.

Period of training leading up to the attempt was quite enjoyable. It began with Rajesh Battacharjee and selected students overcoming unease at kicking me in unprotected groin. At first they were very afraid of hurting me and I had to build up their confidence with repeated assurances. Each time they kicked and I did not collapse they felt a little bit better until they were able to use full force with no inhibition. Then it was all plain sailing. First few days were sore but I kept this news from them to spare their concern. When I adjusted my breathing pattern and added extra meditation time into the warm-up it became fun for everybody. Every session produced better results and I was able to withstand more kicks with no ill effects, up to twenty continuously. When this milestone was achieved I was comfortable that success was in the bag.

Then a heavy drawback when Guinness people refused to recognise the event. I received fateful message only two weeks before the big day – as you can imagine this put me in a spin and I was gravely worried that my carefully laid plans would be all for nothing. The letter explained that due to extreme nature of this activity they were unwilling to encourage possible harm to my person. I respected their decision as they are organisation of worldwide esteem but it left me in state of punctured spirits.

'Perhaps it is a sign that you should abandon this course before you receive injury,' my wife told me. 'There are other records you can break if the desire is still strong, and they are less dangerous.'

Of course I did not listen to her opinion as it made no sense. We were at that time still quite newly married and she did not know how strong was my belief in these great moments. I could no more give up on this new goal in my life than a fish can stop swimming. 'There is another solution,' I told her. 'If the Guinness people will not ratify this record then I will get the support of Limca instead. They will be more than keen to jump on board, I am sure of it.'

If you are not familiar, the Limca Book of Records is the world's greatest collection after Guinness – and to make all the more satisfying is exclusive to achievers from my country. Limca are also more welcoming to aspiring record breakers with commitment to spreading word of Indian excellence to all corners of the globe. I received their full approval sans delay   the record was in my grasp again! One more week of intensive training and I would be ready to take first giant step into my future of dreams.

This final week was nail-biting time. Not only was I very busy with my work at the factory on top of heavy practice schedule, also my wife was not very encouraging. To avoid marital strife I was obliged to cease kicking practice in my home and instead focused all my energies on overall strength training and prolonged bouts of meditation. Only when she was not in the vicinity I would ask one of my friends to kick me in the groin to confirm that resistance still remained there and training regime had paid off. Then the big day came calling. One last appeal to my wife to come and support me went unheard, she remained at home with the child. Despite this snub I left for the venue in frame of great confidence and peacefulness. It was a beautiful sunny day and the almighty was walking alongside me, positive outcome was decided.

Large section of my friends, students and colleagues were gathered at the home of Rajesh Battacharjee to greet my arrival with warmest words of encouragement. Amrit Battacharjee, brother of Ramesh, manager on his behalf of Everest Audio-Video Retail, acted as official video cameraman despite troublesome cataracts and set up in courtyard for capturing the all-important footage for means of official recognition. My student Vijay Two took charge of the stills camera (I had at this time four students called Vijay and it was a joke of ours that I would refer to them by number to avoid confusion). Official count taken by my oldest student Gopal Dutta, who has trained under me since my first karate class attended in Navi Mumbai Sports Association, my local facility, and who at seventy-five years was most trustworthy occupant for this role. He was downtrodden that I did not include him in band of kickers – my observation told me while power was no problem he did not possess necessary speed in legs – but when I conveyed to him the vital importance of timekeeper's job he jumped in with both feet. He joined the practice group in lead-up to the big event to perfect counting method – everyone agreed the best action was to mark each kick with clear downward movement of his hand as well as verbal confirmation so the camera would pick everything up for purpose of verification – and together the six of us formed a tight bond.

By the day of the attempt we were well-drilled squad. No more mishaps of one kicker getting in the way of another and all kicks delivered with matching tension – we had the routine in total control and the smiles on our faces after each practice session were proof of this.

Back to the big day. Myself and four kickers prepared with stretching, period of meditation and intake of water. Final messages of support were conveyed by the crowd, who filled the small space and also watched from inside Rajesh Battacharjee's home where his wife had prepared mango and sweet lime for all-comers. Feeling of love was evident from every side. I stripped to my briefs to confirm to the world and camera that no protective garment had been secretly installed on my person. Also made a short statement that no numbing agents had been used and my conduct was at all times that of honest dedicated sportsman. Then I cleared my mind of all external things. Took ready position. Four kickers made a circle around me as we had determined, all maintaining ideal distance from me and each other to make a smooth action. Gopal Dutta stood in prime spot to carry his duty. Every element was in its correct place.

Needless to say I was very relaxed by now. I could feel the almighty sitting on my shoulder – he spoke very quietly to me: 'You will do it, BB, you will do it. No need to worry.' Everything would click according to his pleasure. I made one final breath and gave Gopal Dutta the nod.

'One. Two. Three. Start kicking!' and we jumped into action. Rajesh Battacharjee delivered the first kick. It was straight and hard exactly as rehearsed. It made its target imperfectly, however, and I widened my stance slightly to take account of this. Next one, delivered by Nihal Prasad, the youngest and most eager of the four, was a real beauty. I sensed the impact of his foot most sublimely and exhaled in a trice to protect myself against the force. His example gave us all a boost and kicks three and four connected on schedule – I felt a small tightness on number four but I quickly erased it from my mind. At this point my concentration was so complete that I was not aware of the world around me. I was focused only on my breathing and counting the kicks as they landed. It was great feeling like floating on a wave of love and positive energy.

My supporters were working wonders, aiming their kicks with great precision and speed. Only Rajesh Battacharjee, who was untrained in martial arts and also unfit due to poor diet and general laziness was finding pace difficult to keep up.

'I cannot carry on,' he whispered, his eyes wearing look of panic and legs beginning to wobble like overladen donkey. I tried to urge him on with reassuring expression but he slipped in trying to connect his next kick and landed in a pile on the ground.

'Twenty!' counted Gopal Dutta.

'I am sorry, BB!' panted Rajesh Battacharjee from his prone position.

Grim looks exchanged between the remaining group but we quickly recovered our senses. The three kickers moved in to close the gap Rajesh Battacharjee's fall had created. We pressed on in seamless style, we would not let any goofup derail us from our pursuit of glory.

'Go on, BB!' shouted a well-wisher from the crowd.

I was comfortable to press ahead for a high total. The kicks kept on coming at steady pace.

'Thirty! Thirty-one!'

'Keep going!'

The kicking was making a tremendous pattern now, sum of the best possibilities in the world was centred in my groin. Each impact was lovely demonstration of the power of the almighty to reward toughest measures – I did not wish to stop. I started to hum along to the sound of each kick, counting each figure in my mind with joy of inner voice.

'Thirty-six! Thirty-seven!' called Gopal Dutta, his voice now distant like waves from the sea.

I knew I was already a record breaker, but still I kept on pushing to furthest edge of mind and bodily limits. Time was like a small bird perched on my hand, his wings brushing against my fingers but no desire to fly off, he was very comfortable there.

'Forty! Forty-one!'

Then the world let out its breath. All the noises from outside rushed into my ears and the light of the day filled my eyes. The pain hit me like lightning, rendering me quite vulnerable from my groin into my stomach and down the complete span of my legs. I freely admit to you that I let out a cry, but it was cry of jubilation as well as agony.

'Do not stop!' I instructed my students. I accepted another kick from Nihal Prasad who was enthusiastic as ever before. The pain was tremendous by now. One final kick was all I could manage before I gave the nod to signal the end of my endurance.

'Forty-three!' Gopal Dutta shouted, and I collapsed on the ground in state of shock and wonder. 'New record! Congratulations! Most kicks to the unprotected groin, World Record breaker, Bibhuti Bhushan Nayak of Navi Mumbai!'

There were loud cheers all round. I remained on my back with my eyes closed, absorbing the news of my achievement. When the pain had grown less I was able to stand and accept the hands of my friends, who were all noticeably proud.

'Well done!' came the felicitation from all corners.

'Lovely, lovely!' said Rajesh Battacharjee. 'My friend BB Nayak, world record man!'

I looked beyond him, searching for my wife in vain hope that she had abandoned her anger and come to witness the pivotal moment. To my great delight I spied her behind the window, standing in Rajesh Battacharjee's kitchen alongside his wife, my son in her arms. I stepped carefully to the house to greet her and the child, my heart bending with affection for them like the branch of a tree in heavy winds. I asked her if she had seen my success. She said she had. I asked was she happy for me and although she did not reply with words her eyes gave the required answer, because they were filled with tears.

There followed a moment of slight unrest while Amrit Battacharjee and Vijay Two reviewed their equipment to ensure the vital footage was captured. Then Rajesh Battacharjee gave a secret indication and before I could protest I was lifted into the air and carried on shoulders into the street. In the excitement I forgot my state of undress as they carried me up and down the road like a statue in Durga puja. The passing cars greeting me with honks from their horns. What a feeling!

It was tense time in the days ahead. My wife became worried when I witnessed bleeding in my urine, and she instructed me to hold off from such dangerous acts for the future. Luckily bleeding did not persist past the first night, and I sensed no further injury or danger.

I was more concerned that the record be correctly administrated, and was in state of high anxiety as I prepared the documentary evidence which Limca required. One requirement was a newspaper cutting of the event and I had to approach several media houses to get my attempt published. My advances received many rejections but finally I found a local newspaper that was willing to support me. I got my news published which helped me get registered in the Limca Book. I celebrated on my own with a day of quiet reflection and silent praises to the almighty for his assistance in bringing my success.

Destiny had come calling and I freely accepted its challenge. I had romped into the limelight from nowhere to announce myself as pathfinder and positive example to the world.

Thank you.

3

India smelt of diesel and ripe fruit and it was too hot for me to think straight. Its voice was shrill and unreserved, too many superstitions spilling from too many radios. I'm only telling it the way I remember it. Just to keep myself busy until Bibhuti wakes up. I'm telling you, God, because you seem to want to know. That's why you're here, isn't it, to get the story in my own words. We haven't really talked before. That would be because I never believed in you, but I suppose that's all changed now. I'm not sure how I feel about that. But since you're asking. There's nothing to do but wait and remember.

I remember I crossed my fingers to make it through the airport. I wasn't sure if the machine guns were just for show or if the skinny men holding them were chosen for some mystical gift they all had for sniffing out my secrets. I didn't know how to walk without stopping every few steps to let Ellen catch up. In the blinding sunlight I was nobody's husband. Every man had a moustache except me.

The taxi driver said I'd picked the wrong time to visit.

'People are falling down dead with the heat and the monsoon is two weeks late this year. Everybody is suffering. You must buy a good hat and drink plenty of water. Only the bottled is safe.'

I had the feeling the weather would enjoy stripping me down to the vulnerable parts I could cover up with clothes back home. I thought it might expose a madness I'd been carefully hiding all these years.

'You are here on business?' the taxi driver asked me.

'No, just a holiday. Just gonna have a look around and see what's what.'

I didn't tell him the truth. Not because the truth was shameful but because I knew he wouldn't understand it and I didn't want to have to explain.

Diesel and ripe fruit. Shit too, there's no getting around it. I took a whiff of it to show that I was fearless and then I wound the window up again. The streets were dust and there were no signposts. The children had no need of modesty. Smudgy cheeks and bare arses and skin that ate the sun. We crossed a bridge over a slow river. At the side of the road a mother was bathing two little ones in a pothole the size of a meteor crater. There was a fruit truck parked up next to them and the driver was filling the pothole from his hose. The children were laughing and flapping around like little birds, their faces open wide and hungry. I envied them their lack of mystery and made them a promise to shed my own. Whatever mystery I had left.

Google said Bibhuti lived in Airoli so that's where I went. The hotel was painted like Miami, a rhubarb-and-custard daydream pasted to the main strip between a plywood merchant's and a mobile phone kiosk. An old man was sitting on the pavement outside. His beard was burnt orange and his bare feet were cracked and grained with years of dirt. His milky blue eyes looked like they'd drip out of his head if he didn't hold his back straight.

He was selling little painted clay gods from a ratty scrap of tarpaulin. They all had the head of an elephant. He offered me one.

It was playing a saxophone. When he looked up at me I saw sorrow in those milky eyes, the wise and unpitying kind that comes when a man gets struck by lightning. I turned him down without thinking of the pain it might cause him. I had my heart set on bigger fish.

The lobby was full of the smell of new paint. A girl was colouring in a snake on the wall, a big daft-looking cobra with fangs dripping blobs of venom. She looked to be in her early twenties and she was dressed in western clothes. There was an outline of a man standing over the snake with a sword raised above his head. I could tell it wouldn't be very good when it was finished. The girl dabbed intently at the snake's belly as if she were making a masterpiece.

'That's a big snake,' I told the man behind the reception desk.

'Yes, very big. Of course I have expanded the size for the sake of drama but only by a small degree.' This was Harshad, the owner of the hotel. He had a comb-over and a drink problem. He rubbed his belly when he talked like he was making a wish. I supposed none of his wishes had ever come true.

He set the box of Officer's Choice down on the counter and lifted up his right hand for my inspection. The first two fingers were missing, chewed down to stumps.

'He found me here,' he said, showing me the fleshy part between the thumb and the forefinger, burnt black where the venom had killed the tissue. 'I was moving some bottles to be recycled when I disturbed him, he was hunting in the grass behind my home. He struck without warning and I was not able to defend myself. In this picture I am taking my revenge. I am not an artist so my daughter is making the image. She is very gifted. This picture will be the talking point of my hotel. I had the option of installing vending machine for soda, but you will find vending machines in every hotel lobby. I thought to myself I must have something more interesting.'

I lied and told him I liked it. I thought it was dramatic. This pleased him. His small black eyes shone briefly and he poured himself a drink. He told me his wife had been expired for five years, squashed by a juggernaut. He was looking after his daughter Amrita until she made a match. She was too picky, none of the boys he'd found had been good enough for her. She wanted an educated heart-throb with soft hands and ambition and she wasn't prepared to settle for anything less.

Amrita was silent. The green she was using for the snake gave it a cartoonish quality and it made me feel momentarily younger than I had any right to feel.

Harshad caught me looking at the box of whisky and offered me a bottle for three hundred rupees. It sounded reasonable so I took it. He led me up the stairs, past the peeling plaster and the burnt-out bulbs to a room that looked as though it was made for the world's forgotten to peacefully die in. The air under the sleeping ceiling fan smelt like the pineapple chunks they put in urinals. A handmade sign said 'No Spitting' where there should have been a fire-escape plan. Harshad started to show me how the TV worked and I had to stop him. I wouldn't have time for TV while I was here. It felt good to say that and mean it.

I went to the window and looked out at the screaming road below and the train tracks behind it. A place of biblical dust, its saving grace a crumbling train station to leave by for the sort of places where shoeshiners are born and everyday dirt gets recycled into nosebags for the poorer horses of the West.

'Do you know a man called Bibhuti Nayak?' I asked. 'He breaks records.'

Harshad's eyes shone again. Yes, he knew him. He put down my case to free his arms and give himself the room to express his pride at being in the man's circle.

'He is my friend. He is famous man, the Bruce Lee of Navi Mumbai. He lives very close to here. You are knowing him?'

'Sort of. I've come to help him with his next record.'

Harshad rubbed his belly thoughtfully. 'Ah yes, the new one. Everybody is hearing about this. I think it cannot be done.'

I was hurt. 'Course it can be done. You know about his other records then?'

'I have seen them all. BB is very strong man. This one I am not so sure. I am hoping for the best.'

'He can do it. Anything's possible. If that French bloke can eat a plane.'

Harshad was confused. I explained. There's this Frenchman who ate a plane.

'A jet?'

'No, just a single-engine thing, you know, one with propellers. But he ate it. He dismantled it and then he ate it one piece at a time. He eats anything made out of metal, that's his thing.'

Harshad grinned. It was the most brilliant thing he'd ever heard and I felt a twinge of pleasure at having been the one to tell him. 'He must have a very strong stomach. And teeth also. I do not believe this. He would surely die.'

'No, he did it. It's on the internet, you can look it up.'

Harshad reflected on the news. He watched me unscrew the whisky bottle and brought two tumblers from the bedside table. He cleaned them on his shirt and left the pouring to me.

'You will help him?' he said.

'That's the plan. If he'll let me.'

'He knows you are coming?'

'Not really.'

'How will you convince him?'

'I'll tell him it's my dying wish.'

'You are dying?'

'Probably.'

Harshad took a belt of the whisky and sucked it through his teeth. The booze seemed to spark a generosity he wasn't used to feeling.

'I will take you to him,' he decided.

I didn't know what else to do so I clinked glasses with him. We drank in silence. When he left I fell onto the clean white sheets and cried. It felt strange not hearing the sound of Ellen breathing beside me. I'd never left the country without her before. I was alone for the first time since I could remember and it felt like being born again into a body I'd already worn out.

4

The first time I saw Ellen she was doing the twist at the Royal and I was trying not to look jealous of the air that held her up. Sipping on my pint all cocksure in the corner, as scared of dancing as I was of dying, a young man lost in the back-end of the Sixties with no real idea of what I'd end up doing with my life or what kind of fears I'd end up losing my appetite to. I'd wanted to hold someone up, I knew that. To be the solid ground for someone, and maybe the air they lived on if I could make myself gentle enough to be breathed in.

Mum always told me to be gentle, it's what girls wanted and there was enough trouble in the world as it was.

So I came to the dancehall every Saturday night with the hope of being the gentle one, the one who stood out from all the lacquered warriors in their rollaway collars, the one without the flick-knife wit and the violent moves. And I looked for a girl who didn't take to violence and who wouldn't mind that I read books, turning the pages with fingers soft from grammar school and high ideals that belonged behind a desk. I tried to be standout by sticking to the walls, thinking it might draw in a quiet girl from the Tottenham crowd with as much need of a slow unwrapping as me.

But Ellen didn't need looking after, I could see that straight away. Whatever man danced with her had to give her some room, she was all over the place and her eyes were shut tight in defiance of the four known dimensions. Unafraid of sheer drops and sharp edges she twisted away whatever sadness she'd woken up to, the rum and the music tricking her into weightlessness.

I was hooked and aware of myself. I wanted to be as light as she was.

In between songs she came to me where I was sitting and asked me why I wasn't getting up. I told her I was happy just to watch. My friends made suggestive noises. I've got a drink, I said. I'm not really one for making a show of myself.

Her blue eyes were bolder than mine, she saw all my secrets before I had a chance to hide them with another careful swig from the glass. She saw a stillness that needed shaking up, that's what she'd say later. She'd call me her snowglobe and I wouldn't protest.

'Come on,' she said, and she held out her hand for me to take. 'You're not stuck to that chair, are you? Get up and show me what you've got.'

I ended up showing her everything. I promised there was more to come and she was happy to wait for it. If she asked for it now I don't know what excuse I'd give. All my excuses went up in flames the moment I first saw Bibhuti in the flesh.

He was standing in the middle of the room dripping sweat and smiling saintlike and there were thirty kids lining up to kick him in the balls. They waited patiently for their turns. There was no talking or messing about. Some of the children were very young and they looked comical wearing their concentrating faces, barefoot and disciplined and stiff with training. Bibhuti would wave each one in and they'd bow to him with their little hands curled into a reverent fist. Then they'd arrange themselves into the right stance and step back and plant a kick between their sensei's legs, true and hard and with meaning attached. Bibhuti would take the blow gratefully and nod his appreciation. Another bow for godspeed and the child would peel away to join their friends in warmdown and Bibhuti would wave the next one in.

Clockwork.

He had a conveyor belt going, smooth and faultless. A thing of hypnotic beauty. It felt like art was being made or history and if I breathed too hard I'd ruin it. I kept my distance. I watched with Harshad from the back of the hall by the badminton nets. There were holes in them I could have put my head through if the mood had taken me.

Bibhuti looked just like I remembered him from the footage I'd seen. Tall and strong, not as bulky as you'd think. Graceful. The full moustache and the dune of thick black hair on his head placed him somewhere in the Seventies, a leftover from the days of strict codes of honour and bad fabrics that gave off extravagant static shocks. In his white karate suit he looked like he should be flying.

The children in his charge kept going and he kept on taking their finest shots without a flinch or a tremble, a strange smile fixed to his face, as if he'd swallowed magic. A little girl was next up. She could only have been six or seven. She didn't have a costume. She wore a Dora the Explorer T-shirt a size too small and she had a ferocity about her that can only come from a precocious awareness of how close death walks alongside the living.

She let out a blood-curdling cry and went arrowing at Bibhuti, her whole weight directed into a spiteful kick that landed with gruesome precision. Bibhuti absorbed it willingly. He waited for her to meet the ground again before giving her a bow that bristled with good humour. He was a tiger scratching at a spot where a fly had just been.

When the kids had all taken their turn at assaulting him Bibhuti clapped his hands and they fell into a semicircle around him. He bowed to them all, slow and ceremonial, and as one they returned the gesture, their little fists clasped in a warrior pose, little brown toes digging shyly in the parquet. He said something encouraging to them in his language and class was dismissed.

My heart was beating fast. All I wanted to do was take a run at him and give him the hardest kick I could. All I wanted was to be one of those children, to enjoy the immunity they enjoyed, so I could do something bold and unwarranted and not have to answer for it.

'It is a shame we missed the beginning,' Harshad said, putting himself in front of me so he could get the first shot at Bibhuti's attention. 'The best part is the sparring. The younger ones are very fearless, they will fight until the last and BB is encouraging full contact.' He nodded to the girl in the Dora the Explorer T-shirt. 'This one is Kavita. She is defeating all comers. Once she made the other child unconscious. He failed to keep up his guard. He may be damaged in the brain.'

The girl and Bibhuti were deep in conversation. They were probably discussing the best techniques for killing a man without leaving a mark. Having received his advice she strode out of the hall spoiling for another fight, her delicate steps emboldened by her sensei's approval.

Bibhuti spotted us. He gave me a cagey look and wandered over. Immediately I felt as if I were in the presence of a man for whom the laws of nature had been tweaked. He was made of something different, I could tell. Harshad lowered his gaze, starstruck. While they spoke in their language the hall emptied of all except one boy, who hadn't taken part in the class but had been watching from the tiered seats. He thumbed lethargically at the mobile phone in his hand.

Bibhuti turned to me beaming, his hand held out for me to shake. My heart beat faster, infatuated.

'Hello, sir, I am BB. Welcome to my country. You want to help me with my record.'

'Yes I do,' I said. 'My name's John. John Lock. I saw you on TV and I read about you, I think you're brilliant. I came here from England, I just got here today. I want to help you if you'll let me.'

I realised how strange and foolish I must have looked to him, tripping over myself trying to get my words out, peeling and tired from the heat and the jetlag and stretching for credibility in holiday clothes. When he looked at me he saw sloping shoulders and pigeon toes and uninvited errands he didn't have the time to run. I did my best to look convincing.

'You have seen me before? Was it the AXN special?'

'Maybe. It was on a programme about world records. The one you did with the sledgehammers.'

'Right,' Bibhuti smiled. I'd loosened up a fond memory for him and he drifted to it. He swam around in it for a moment or two. 'This record is very old. There have been others since then. You have seen them?'

'Yeah, I saw all the clips on YouTube. Then I read the interview you gave, the one where you mentioned the next record you want to go for and how you needed backing.'

'And you decided you are the man for the job,' Bibhuti said.

'I am. I did. Definitely.'

We smiled at each other. A game of chicken. We both tried not to be the first to break and admit the profound stupidity of my coming here. Bibhuti eyed me up, checking for cracks and defects of character. Under his scrutiny I felt weak and unfortunate, an exhibit in once-firm flesh gone softly to seed.

The silence crept in, punctured only by the Space Invaders sound effects that fizzed from the boy's phone.

'I'm not taking the piss,' I said after a while. 'I've got money. I can show it to you whenever you want.'

The boy saw me then and left his seat to join his father in assessing me. His cautious eyes flickered with amusement.

Bibhuti tousled the boy's hair and draped an elaborately muscled arm over his shoulder. 'This is my son, Shubham.'

The boy mumbled a hello. Bibhuti whispered something at him and with a petulant shiver he sent his phone to sleep and slipped it into his pocket.

'He is a good boy. He must study harder and watch less television.'

'We all should,' I said, because it sounded conciliatory.

I'll tell you later how Shubham became Jolly Boy. It's not important to the story. All I'll say for now about the boy is that he wore well the privilege and shame of being his father's son.

He wears it well today, leaning in gently to swab Bibhuti's lips, unqueasily parting the lifelines that trail from his father to rest an appraising hand on his forehead. He tells me it's hot. I say that's a good sign. I don't know if that's true or not.

'He will be very proud of his father when I achieve my big success. Come,' Bibhuti said, and he led us out of the hall and down the corridor, passing walls studded with newspaper clippings of his past successes, and bringing us out into the car park where the children gathered to be collected by their parents in a stuttering tide of Toyotas and country-made SUVs whose wing mirrors still bore the protective film stickers of the showroom.

25

I waited while he returned their greetings, baking in the heat of the Indian dusk as he answered every enquiry into a child's progress in warfare or the best dietary weapon against gout. They all asked to be introduced to the white man who'd fallen from the sky. I was a curiosity brought to them by a generous god to give a glimpse into foreign fashions and a lucky chance to practise their conversational English.

Bibhuti told them I was his friend from England. That was all the explanation they needed.

Kavita's father asked me if I knew Lincolnshire. I said I'd heard of it but I'd never been.

'I have a brother who is a doctor there,' he said, ignoring his daughter as she squeezed in some last-minute roundhouse practice, aiming her kicks in a relentless procession at Bibhuti's groin. He parried each one patiently. 'I have not spoken to him for many years. He accused me of poisoning his dog when we were children. I did not. If I remembered this I would admit to it and apologise but I have no recollection. My brother is a good man, I am very proud of him.'

'Lincolnshire's very flat,' I said. 'They grow a lot of vegetables there.'

'This is so?' the man said dreamily, painting himself a picture of his brother's place of exile.

When all the cars had gone and Harshad had left us to take a drink in privacy from the leather-clad hip flask he'd brought with him, Bibhuti took me for a walk around the grounds. We skimmed the jogging track that ran beside the Navi Mumbai Sports Association like a dry river. The cricket pitch the track bordered was parched and brown and at the boundary two brown dogs lay sleeping, curled in each other like an indecent pretzel. The evening perched over us, a fat bird laughing at me from the treetops as I clumsily tried to convince Bibhuti with my bearing and my listening that I was the man he'd been waiting for all his life.

We sat down on the grass behind the dogs as one started gnawing on the leg of the other, and I was asked if I believed in God and destiny.

I said I'd never believed in either, but that I was willing to be surprised. I didn't mean that. I'd made it through sixty years of living without once hearing your footsteps behind me and I had no expectation of ever hearing them. But Bibhuti needed the lie. He needed to feel a closeness to me so my plea would stick. I told him when I'd seen him on TV a light had gone on inside me and I relied on him to presume it was divinity's hand working the switch.

'I believe in them entirely,' Bibhuti said. 'Everything I do is decided by these factors. If it is God's will to put you here then I must listen to what he is telling me.' He closed his eyes as if listening for your voice in the branches. He stroked his moustache in meditation, something I'd learn to be a habit of his in times of inner turmoil.

I waited. The warm breeze felt good on my bare arms. The light dripping down from the sky was different to any light I'd seen before. I caught a whiff of whisky on me and remembered all the miles that were between me and the things I knew. I remembered the feeling of putting on school plimsolls and I saw the cherries on the dress Ellen wore when we rode the *Maid of the Mist*. There'd been a rainbow behind her, hovering there out of jealousy. She was so bright then that nature had to put on a show to keep up with her.

Ellen sits beside me now, betrayed and asleep with her face pressed into my shoulder. I'm stroking her hair with fingers gone numb from repetition, quietly raging at her capacity for forgiveness and wondering what kindness I should repay her with while I've still got the time. So far I've got nothing.

Bibhuti tapped me on the shoulder to wake me up. 'You understand the thing I am planning?' he asked.

'You want to break fifty baseball bats over yourself. You need someone to do the hitting. I can swing the bats, it won't be a problem.'

'It is not as easy as it sounds. The bats must all be broken. It is not enough just to hit me with them, there is no achievement in that. It will require much strength. Do you think you can withstand the physical side? You are not in good shape, you will need some training.'

'I'll do whatever you need me to do. I'm stronger than I look.'

'I am not a wealthy man. There is no money in my sport, I receive no payment. I do what I do for the love only. There are expenses associated to breaking records, these must be met somehow.'

'I've got all the money you need. It's back at the hotel. Just under nine hundred thousand rupees, it's all yours.'

Bibhuti's eyes widened. Jolly Boy whistled the way he'd seen cartoon wolves whistle. I had them.

'You must be dedicated and do as I say,' Bibhuti warned. 'I will be relying on you for a successful outcome. This is very special to me, my sports career is reaching its peak with this record and I am expecting it to go smoothly. This is very important.'

It was important to me too. More important than I could fully understand at the time. 'I used to work in a lettings agency – renting out houses. I never had a gimmick like you've got, I never had something I could do better than anyone else. Not gimmick. You know what I mean. This is my last chance to do something

28

big, something good, to be useful to someone. I won't let you down, I promise.'

Bibhuti was looking into my eyes now. I felt every tame and uninspired moment of my life replaying in them. I was ashamed of them all.

'We will discuss our strategy tomorrow,' he said. 'I will meet you at your hotel. You must also stop drinking.'

I told him I would.

Harshad rode a scooter that lacked the glamour touches of my old Lambretta. I had to cuddle him to keep from falling off on the ride back to the hotel. I could feel his bones grinding through his shirt, see the flaky bits on his scalp between the strands of hair that flew loose in the breeze. I held on through the hairpins and kicked out at the streetdogs when they got in the way.

5

Amrita was happily colouring in her father's hair, her brush splayed imprecise by the eager application of too much pressure. She had no reason to suppose she should be doing something more important and I had no bones to pick now that I'd slept off the jetlag and won Bibhuti's confidence. I stood and watched her slap the paint on. The figure looked nothing like Harshad. It was strong and heroic and its hair flowed thick like a river of oil. It brought to mind a matinee idol from the time when pictures came in double bills with a newsreel starter and a torch to find your seat by.

Harshad was blinded to its lies by that strange kind of vanity that overcomes a man when he lets himself go. He pretended not to notice the parody growing like a mould on the wall as he set about patiently molesting a portable radio that lay breached on the countertop. A half-empty glass of whisky sat at his elbow. He dug a screwdriver round the radio's guts, humming a gritted-teeth lament to himself. A barbed reminder of the songs the radio used to play in brighter days before its voice had given out. A glance up from his work to check the painting's progress, a single hummed note of satisfaction at the shape his alter ego was taking. A pull from the glass and then another stab with the screwdriver, its blade sharking in between the luckless wires. His song escaped from him as a gruff vapour that caught in the fins of the ceiling fan as they sliced through the sluggish air.

'Noisy in the mornings,' I said. 'Lots of building work going on.'

I'd woken up to a million hammers and horns. I'd reached out to feel the empty sheet beside me, cold from the fan and no other body. I'd been having a dream about Oscar, the budgie I had when I was a young man on my own, before Ellen. He'd perch on my shoulder while I read my books in the eaves room I rented from old Mrs March. Listening to me daydreaming about a life of enquiry and mild adventure and not having the heart to tell me he'd seen my future and it wasn't pretty. He flew away one day when I left the window open. Maybe I left it open on purpose to test his instinct for freedom, I'm not sure. In the dream he was on my shoulder again, pulling at a thread on my jumper so it was slowly coming undone. I liked having him there, feeling the sparse weight of his feet on me, his tiny breath in my ear. When I'd woken up my stomach was killing me and I'd cried when I couldn't feel him anymore.

'Always it is like this,' Harshad said. 'Navi Mumbai is only forty years old and it is still growing. They are building all these office towers, making a nice room for the computers to live. My building has no working elevator after many weeks now but the computers are very comfortable, this is all that matters. There. Let us see what I have done.'

He patted the wire down snug against the chassis, twisted the battery tight and turned the dial. The radio burst into life. A blare of strings and a woman's shrill voice filled the air with sparks of lost love and deceit. Harshad gave a satisfied nod.

'You fixed it,' I said.

'Of course. I am a bringer of life to all dead things.' A look of sadness washed over him and he took a drink. He smoothed his mangled hand over his scalp and started screwing the cover back on the radio.

'I like the hair,' I told Amrita. My words startled her and she swayed as she turned to see me, groping out a hand to steady herself.

'I have modelled the hair on Amitabh Bachchan in *Deewaar*,' Amrita said, as if I knew who she was talking about. 'My father loves this film a lot.'

'I like it,' I said. And with that I ran out of things to say. I tightened my fingers round the handle of my carrier bag, felt for the weight of the money in it. I swung the bag against my thigh to remind myself that I was holding a man's life in my hands.

'BB is pleased with you?' Harshad asked. 'He will let you help him?'

'I think so.'

'You told him about your dying wish?'

'I left out the dying part. I didn't need it in the end.'

'It is lucky that I am a friend of BB, or maybe you would not have found him.' Eyeing up the bag like a cat stalking a bird.

I thanked him and decided I'd leave him a little something when the time came. For cleaning up whatever mess I was bound to make.

The old man sat there surrounded by his little army of elephant gods. A plastic watering can rested at his side. I looked for the flowers it gave life to and saw none. He offered me another figurine. This one was playing a guitar. I refused it and he took the snub on the chin, turned away and carried on staring at the spot he'd been looking at before I'd disturbed him, somewhere past the streaking traffic, a patch of sky above the train tracks that meant something special to him. He waited with a tirelessness that made me envy him.

I had an urge to tickle the old man's feet and I was seriously thinking about it when Bibhuti's car pulled up.

Jolly Boy waved at me from the passenger seat. School was out for the big vacation and the boy had decided to make me the story of his summer. I was the first white man he'd known and I fascinated him. Sometimes I'd catch him peering intently at me as if I were a strange fish behind aquarium glass.

Sometimes I still do, but now his curiosity is a haunted thing, blunted by a sadness inappropriate to his age by the walk we took together on the trail of a tiger.

Bibhuti got out of the car to greet me. The sun bounced off him in his white T-shirt and stonewashed jeans. He looked like he could repel any danger that might come our way. He was the stuff they clad the space shuttle in to stop it burning up in re-entry. I felt safe with him and afraid of my deficiencies. He took a comb out of his pocket and ran it through his hair and then he smoothed his moustache just so.

He froze when he saw the old man. The confidence drained from him. He stared down in disbelief. The old man smiled up at him, toothless and defiant. He chuckled softly, his orange beard blazing in the sunlight.

Bibhuti swayed where he stood, a burning question on his lips. It was as if he'd seen the face of death.

The old man's chuckle broke into gentle laughter. The light crashed back into Bibhuti's eyes and he bent down to shake the old man's hand. They spoke warmly, like friends reunited after a long time apart. Then Bibhuti said his farewells and led me to his car where it was idling at the kerb.

He gave the bonnet a gentle pat. 'Only two months old,' he murmured. 'I wanted a mid-segment for a very long time and finally my wife consented. It is not so much a luxury, I need it for my work. I must be always moving around. We had a choice between a new car and moving to a larger apartment with two bedrooms. In the end I made the right decision.'

He ran his fingertip tenderly down the wing, scared up some dust. He bunched his T-shirt over his fist and wiped the dust away, cooing softly to himself.

'It runs very well. I love to drive. In the summer we visit the hill stations that are close to here, and also to Goa. One day I will drive the whole span of my country from top to bottom. I will drive to my native place in Orissa and I will drive to Darjeeling, up in the mountains. You must come.'

'I don't know if I'll still be here,' I said.

'You will stay. I am sure of this. My country will give you every-thing you need, there is no reason to go back.'

I think he was joking. He couldn't have loved me then. We were still strangers.

He lowered himself carefully onto the plank of wood that had been placed on the driver's seat. He told me it was a measure against a hamstring injury sustained in his previous record attempt. The injury had persisted for longer than he'd hoped, and he'd come to accept that it might never leave him. Such was the way of things for the dedicated sportsman, he said. To bear the scars of past achieve-ments was to always carry a reminder of one's destiny, to be read in times of doubt like a passage from a holy book.

I got in the passenger side. I opened my bag and let Bibhuti see the money. He gave a solemn nod, as if confirming the identity of ancestral bones. Jolly Boy leaned in from the back seat and wolf-whistled again. I stuffed the bag between my feet. On the dashboard a Ganesh unlike the old man's bore witness to the deal. This one was made of smooth stone, like a chess piece. Peering out from inside its Perspex cube, its multiple arms wrapped round itself in meditation, it warned me against exploiting my new friend's hospitality.

Bibhuti didn't know the old man. Their conversation had taken the form of a mutual blessing.

'He reminded me of someone I once knew, many years ago. He looks very much like him. He too had the orange beard and the smell of fire was on him. For a moment I thought he had returned to me but it was a mistake. Nevertheless this is a clear sign that I must accept your offer. I am very happy for your help.'

My heart skipped. Bibhuti turned the key and as the engine hacked into life I congratulated myself on having made it this far, under my own steam and with no recourse to prayer. The old man stood to watch us pull away, happily pissing in the watering can.

The sun struck its killer blows as we walked unprotected to the valley's lowest point. I asked Jolly Boy if he knew what a robot was. He said he did. I told him about the game me and Ellen used to play when I was driving somewhere far. How we pretended the electricity pylons were robots that were shut down or sleeping on the grass banks that bordered the roads and, later, the motorways we hummed down on the way to seaside holidays.

'You had to hold your breath as you went past so you didn't wake them up. If you woke them up they'd go berserk and eat your car. Eat you as well.'

Ellen was always the first to break, her breath never big enough to contain the laughter that leaked from her in habitual swells, the tip of her tongue always sugared with an amusement that hinted at things known that couldn't be captured by looking straight ahead with your eyes on the road. I pretended to go blue when the traffic slowed, and she reached across and poked my cheek to let the air out so I could take another breath. We'd stop by the side of the road to pick blackberries, plump and sweet, to be eaten in the shade of the flyover. The dying sun would chase us to the sea and Ellen would run to the beach to look for shells while I got the stove working, in a caravan small enough to go mad in if the weather closed in and our humour ran out. It didn't run out for a long time. We had the hills to run down and grass to lie in when running got too hard. Even on a pebble beach there were heart-shaped stones to be harvested. Things would only fall apart when I stopped finding them.

'Better hold your breath just in case.'

'They are still far. They will not hear us,' Jolly Boy said.

'I wouldn't be so sure. They've got super hearing.'

The boy looked across to the two rusting pylons kneeling together as if in prayer on the valley floor. No cables trailed from them. The bleached bones of livestock animals were scattered round their feet, maybe offered as sacrifices by superstitious farmers or having wandered to their shadows for shade and fallen there, victims of famine or some native blight. The boy played along. He took a deep breath and held it. We lifted our feet and crept past the pylons. When we'd put them behind us we let out our breaths to show how close our shave had been.

'We are safe,' Jolly Boy declared. 'They will not eat us.'

He quickened his pace to make sure. I followed him. We stalked Bibhuti and his Sikh photographer through the scrub towards the tree-flocked hills that rose above the valley, using his bobbing pink turban as a landmark so we wouldn't get left behind.

Bibhuti wanted to begin our preparations straight away, and later he'd take me to his home and have me meet his wife, but first he had an assignment to complete. We'd joined up with the photographer on the way to the wasteland. He'd appeared on his motorbike when we stopped at the lights and then he flanked us through the streets as they grew wider and older where the suburbs frayed to vine and shadow and the earth took over. I followed Jolly Boy's lead and waved to the big Sikh on his red Hero Honda, gliding alongside us like a summer-drunk swallow, his beard catching a frosting from the blossoms that sailed down from the trees that fringed the road.

We'd stopped off at a minimart along the way and Bibhuti had bought an armful of disposable razors and cans of shaving foam and deodorant, little soaps sealed in plastic. He made me pay but didn't tell me what they were for. I was too hot to ask and feared the answer in case some kind of weird initiation was on the cards. Perhaps he planned to shave and fragrance me, a sterilisation rite before the gutting could begin.

The TV on the counter played breaking news footage of a plane crash in Mangalore. It sounded like a mystical place but the falling to its earth of a planeload of doomed humans sucked all its romance dry. A green hillside churned up and strewn with charred metal, a slice of tail stuck in the mud like a coin.

I pictured the lunatic Frenchman taking a bite out of it, gorging himself with the survivors staggering around him, shaking on some salt and pepper while the fires spat rivets and milk teeth.

We observed a moment of grim silence and then we left clutching our purchases close to our chests, as if they were the charms that would see us through a national mourning.

The hills swept up in front of us and we came to rest where the tarmac ran out, at the edge of a tract of creeping villas that looked like they'd been dredged from the bottom of a swamp. An unfinished storm drain dripped abandoned diesel onto the weeds below.

I realised if they were going to steal my money and slit my throat this would be the perfect place to do it. They could leave me here to quietly spoil and the world wouldn't bat an eyelid.

I thought I might have made the biggest mistake of my life.

'Is it that colour for a special reason?' I asked the Sikh photographer, pointing to his turban. 'I used to work with a Sikh. He always wore a black one. I always wondered whether the different colours had different points, like in snooker. Or like the belts in karate, you start off with a white one and work your way up.'

I wasn't trying to be funny, I really wanted to know. I'd decided that while I was in India I'd be more curious and forthright. Better late than never.

'No, it is whatever colour we prefer,' he smiled. 'I am always choosing this.'

'Right. I like it, it's nice and bright.'

'Thank you.'

The photographer's name was Jagatdeep but Bibhuti called him the Turbanator. He was happy from the moment of our introduction for me to call him that too. He hitched his camera bag over his shoulder and Bibhuti got the toiletries out of the boot. I took my bag of money and off we marched towards the valley, the sun beating down from between high dirty clouds.

6

Jolly Boy was my guide on the climb up the hill. He found a stick and cleared the path of prickles and hypothetical snakes. He went more slowly than he wanted to, looking over his shoulder for me falling behind. His father and the Turbanator pushed on ahead, entrusting our lives to whatever kind spirit watched over us from the canopy. The thorns cut into my neck and I went slapstick, stumbling over myself. I dug in and pushed on. I had to prove to everyone that I was strong enough to keep my promises.

We must have climbed for half an hour. My legs started to shake. The trees hid the sky and I panicked that I'd never see a car again. Jolly Boy talked me through my fear with fresh robot noises and told me about the time he saw a tiger, when his Baba took him to a place where they roamed around uncaged. He told me how he reached out through the window of their four-wheel drive and stroked the tiger's tail.

'It was very soft,' he said. 'He let me hold it for a long time.'

I knew it was a lie but it was such a sweet one that I took it to heart. I chewed on it like it was waterbearing. Its succulence got me to the top of the hill and I fell to the ground and heaved.

I shuffled over to a tree and sat up feeling the bark against my back. Jolly Boy threw some water over me. I drained the rest of the bottle. I forgot how precious water was in a hot place.

I told Bibhuti I'd be alright. I just had to get used to the conditions.

He agreed that there were adjustments to be made. He stood over me, not a hair out of place, his breathing slow and sure. For him, weather and gradient were things that could be overcome simply by thinking yourself above them.

That's when we heard the ping-pong.

It was coming from somewhere round the bend in the dirt path. Thock-thock. Thock-thock. That beautiful funny sound of a plastic ball on a paddle. We all stopped to listen. We laughed at each other. The sound sailed to us through the trees and we followed it.

Bibhuti led us past the orange flags hanging from their bamboo masts and down the track where it turned towards the edge of the hillside. There was the monastery with its little temple attached, a crumbling wedding cake perched over a sheer drop into the waste-land below. Peeling under the sun and cracked where the pious gripes of the monks built up behind its walls until they found release in official prayer. That's what I imagined anyway, like prick-ing a needle hole in a dam. That's what I thought a prayer was then.

There was a courtyard beyond the main gate and the sound was coming from behind the pillars. Louder now and unmistakable. I could hear the shuffling feet of the players as they moved round the table, the soles of their shoes scuffing the flagstones.

I wanted to play, we all did. I wanted it so intensely that I forgot all about heat and hunger and the mechanics of dying.

A white man with shoulder-length hair was waiting at the gate to greet us. He looked young and unsuited to the terrain or to holy vocation. He introduced himself as Thomas, said he was the steward of the monastery. He spoke in a soft German accent. I felt cheated out of my station as the only white man in the country and I let the solemn look I'd been holding go slack.

Thomas walked us through the gate, explaining his role to us. As steward he was the link between the monks and the lay community on whose generosity they relied. I decided he was probably on the run from the law. I couldn't see him killing anyone, he was too slight and weaselly-looking, so I made him some kind of internet fraudster. I hesitated at the perimeter of the courtyard, always wary of places of devotion. They were guarded by invisible forcefields that you could only pass through if your intentions were honourable. I stepped carefully. The dust held my weight and I walked through the forcefield without being fried.

Between the pillars four skinheaded monks in holy robes were playing a game of doubles. They danced round the table as if on springs, their faces intense in competition. An unbroken stream of unerring power shots flowed from their paddles. They looked magnificent. The thock-thock of paddle on ball was the repeated punchline to a joke they were playing on the unenlightened.

The matchwinner was a forehand rocket that went through a wormhole and came out the other side covered in slime from the birth of the universe. The winning team accepted their victory without emotion. The defeated team greeted their loss in the same manner. It was all very diplomatic, as though the intensity of the battle already belonged to a different time and in its ending they'd found release from the torment of human rivalry. They laid down their paddles and greeted Bibhuti with handshakes and smiles. He got down to the business of charming their sporting and spiritual philosophies from them, scratching away at his notepad while the Turbanator lined up his shots, crouching himself into a predicament to capture the monks' timeless weirdness from all angles.

Thomas interpreted for me. He told me how these monks out of all other orders had come to believe in table tennis as the ideal way to practise their religion. They found a peace of mind through ping-pong that couldn't be achieved by any other means. They were in training right now for a big tournament coming up in Singapore, where they'd pit their skills against other ping-pong orders from around the world and through their contests amplify the peace and love that flowed from them, creating a surplus that would circle the earth, healing manmade ills and setting lame animals back on their feet. They were seeking donations to make the trip possible. They weren't allowed to handle money directly, so any contribution had to come through the steward.

I tightened my grip on my bag of money and watched the monks as they posed for their close-ups. One of them was older than the rest and I took him to be the chief. I caught his eye and raised my eyebrows, pointed to the table and wiggled an imaginary paddle. He smiled his consent.

I gave Jolly Boy the nod. His face lit up mischievously and he followed me to the table. I let him serve. I chased the feeling the monks had already captured, of being expert and unbeatable. It didn't work out that way. The boy beat me mercilessly. I lacked the skill and the audacity to wipe the smile off his face. My body creaked and wobbled. Every shot of his flew past me unquestioned. By the time I gave up I wanted to kill someone.

'Good game,' the boy offered, buzzing with the glory of an easy victory. I didn't respond. I walked back to the others without looking at him. Bibhuti had finished his interview and was steadying himself for a kicking. The youngest of the monks planted a beauty between his legs and his righteous companions applauded the endeavour, all of them bonded over a shared devotion to the sporting principle.

The Turbanator rounded up the monks for their action shots, switched lenses to catch them in play. The thock-thock of the ball rang out like a fearful pulse between the flagstones, and the clouds went sticky again, teasing us with the suggestion of rain to come.

When Bibhuti said we were going to be blessed I felt my blood go cold. I told him I didn't believe in that sort of thing. But he said it was safe and would offer us protection in the trials to come. I went along with it to avoid offending anyone. We had to take our shoes off before entering the temple. I had a hole in my sock and seeing my toe made me feel acutely godless and fond of myself.

We followed the monks inside. There was a strange smell, something ritualistic and sweet. My head filled up with all the small and stupid things I'd done, and with the biggest stupidest thing of all. Something was waiting for me in the dark heart of the place. It would come dressed in the splendour of religion but it would be vicious and there'd be no way around it. I'd be told what my life's definitive failure was and I'd have to stand there and hear it read back at me in front of everyone. I got ready to run away from it.

Then there was every colour all at once and too many gods hanging from the walls. A woman in a spiky hat dancing with elephants. An altar with a Buddha looking sleepy and self-satisfied with his bowls of fruit arranged around him, and flowers that masked the stink of human sacrifice. The monks bowed to the Buddha and we did the same. They went to the far side of the room where a new monk sat cross-legged, wearing robes of a different colour to the rest. The chief snake-charmer. He was a pearl and his minions were the grit that stuck to him. He saw me and his fat face split into a warm smile.

Bibhuti bowed to the chief. I copied him. We were told to sit down on the floor. I folded myself up as best I could. My heart was beating so loud I was sure the monks could hear it and from its pattern tell how salt-rich my diet had been.

The youngest monk approached the altar and lit candles and incense sticks. Smoke whispered up and more of that sweet smell filled the air. He picked up a ball of orange string from the altar and started winding it out. He threaded it round the Buddha then he walked the ball over to us and wrapped the string round our shoulders so we were loosely bound together. Then he gave the ball of string to the chief, who held it softly and started mumbling a prayer to himself.

The younger one sat down next to him, all of them lined up in a row. The chief unwound the string and passed it down the line. Each monk wrapped it around his hands before he passed it on. When they were all joined together they raised their hands in prayer and the chief closed his eyes and started chanting. The rest joined in. The chant built up in layers until it was a wave they were all riding. The wave rose and fell and repeated and with every repetition the swell became stronger. The noise grew louder and expanded like a feeding fire and the walls seemed to stretch out to contain it. The noise carried the monks off in its arms to some other place I didn't know about.

I glanced at Bibhuti and saw that he was being carried too. A look of blank serenity had come over him, the look of someone who believed with ease in man's aptitude for self-cleaning.

They kept on chanting. The noise made the thread around me vibrate. I plucked it like a guitar string but it didn't stop them. I was the only one left awake. I sat there waiting for them to come back from where they'd gone. The thread was cutting in to me and I was just about to slip out of it when the chief monk opened his eyes and stirred slowly, as if coming round from anaesthetic. He stopped chanting. The others stopped a heartbeat later and the silence that fell was shocking and wonderful.

The chief monk let go of the string. He looked extravagantly gratified, as if his sing-along with the unknown had unpicked a knot in his belly that had been bothering him since the day he was born. His minions came round and dropped their portions of the string and all together they let out a communal breath. The string fell away from our shoulders and the chief monk gathered it in. With the scissors the younger one passed him he cut a length off. He cupped the loose thread in his hands and mumbled another prayer to himself and then he blew into his hands. He leaned towards me and gestured for me to reach out my arm. I gave him both my arms, wrists up as though ready for handcuffs. He swatted my left arm aside and turned the right arm fist-up and he tied the string round my wrist.

I said thank you. He said nothing in return.

He cut another length of string and repeated the process with Bibhuti, who received his gift routinely. He'd been blessed more times than he could put a number to.

When it was over I looked at the piece of orange string around my wrist. The skin there felt different but my heart hadn't changed as far as I could tell.

We handed out the razors and the deodorants, customary gifts for the monks in return for our blessing. None of them said thank you. Bibhuti said they weren't allowed to, it was against their code.

'If you receive thanks for your charitable deed it is like a reward. The best charity is given without expecting a reward, then it is meaning more for the giver.'

He asked me if I felt better. He didn't wait for my answer.

'This is the prayers infused by the string. Wearing it will block all negative energy. We will be protected from all harm, our success is walking in spontaneously.'

'Are you a Buddhist then?'

'I have no religion, I have only faith. I do not believe that God is one thing. He is everything all around us, the names we give him and the shapes we make for him are just inventions. But it is good to accept their offer, we are drawing from the same energy and all blessings are welcome.'

'That's sensible,' I said.

'Yes. And my paper will give them good coverage for their donations appeal.'

'Everyone's a winner,' I said, and immediately regretted my witlessness.

The monks escorted us to the boundary, a pair of them peeling off for the table as we passed. They took up their paddles and began at once to tear holes in the air. I imagined they were immortal and would still be playing their game on this hilltop when the rest of the world had crumbled to ash around them. We passed through the ring of holiness with our sins intact and stumbled back down the hill. On the valley floor the robots were still sleeping.

7

Bibhuti's wife hasn't said more than a handful of words since her husband fell asleep. She's barely looked at anyone else in case she misses the moment of his waking up. Her vigil is quiet and spiteful. She wills her husband to come back to her with a force that shakes the birds from the trees. Her hands have been balled into fists that hold hope like a bleeding stone. I remember how I told her with confidence that her husband would go global thanks to me. If I catch her eye I'll be turned to stone myself, I'm sure of it.

She looks at her husband, waiting. She counts the bruises she can see under his plaster casts and imagines soldering his cuts back together again. Her name is still a mystery to me and now there'll never be a right time to ask it.

I smell the solder in the air, from the summer job Ellen had making piecemeal circuit-board connections at the kitchen table, back when we were saving up for a nursery and all the things a child might need to make it strong and happy. The radio on and the window open to the sounds of the street, kids playing football on the new patch of grass and her fingers glossy and black from an assortment of painless burns. I remember how ashamed I'd been that she'd had to take a second job because I couldn't bring her golden eggs, and I remember telling her we'd try again and get it perfect when the first life we made fell short of the sunlight.

Promises. I used to make a lot of them back then. Now I know how stupid it is to say something that can't be taken back.

The two women sit next to each other now, Ellen having woken up with a start and felt the need to remove herself from me before word gets around that she's on my side. The nurse has just been in to change Bibhuti's piss bag. We were all drawn to the colour. Brown isn't good. It's a powerful feeling to know that you can change the colour of a man's water. It's not a feeling I'm enjoying.

His wife's first inclination was to feed me. She gave me her food without reservation and it revived me. The flavours brought me pleasure while I thought about the possibility of killing her husband. When I coughed at the initial heat of it she passed me water and a tissue to dab my nose. When I asked for more she filled my bowl again.

Bibhuti's apartment was in a low-rise concrete box on stilts a couple of minutes' drive from the hotel. Japanese cars slept under its belly in various states of undress, shedding their superficial parts like a dog shaking loose its fleas. The little courtyard was bare except for a badminton net Bibhuti had put up so he and Jolly Boy could play in the evenings when the temperature drops and the boy needs a dose of the ennobling power of competitive sport.

An elbow-high wall divided his building from the bungalow next door and where it was broken I could see the neighbours as we pulled up, sitting on plastic chairs in their front yard. A young couple with eyes that shone brazen with contentment, as if they knew the steps to all the world's dances and would happily teach them to me if I showed the first sign of wanting to learn them. The wife was peeling almonds, her skilful hands a blur. The husband watched the sky for thieves and kept the bucket centred between her feet to catch the stream of kernels as they fell. Bibhuti waved to him and pointed me out. They spoke briefly in their language and the husband gave me a thumbs-up. He welcomed me to his country and wished me good luck. I thanked him and fled to the shade of the stairwell that led up to the apartments.

To reach Bibhuti's door we had to tiptoe past a prosthetic leg that someone had left on the stairs. The little moulded toes were so poignant that I felt like crying.

A swastika was painted on the wall next to Bibhuti's door in a small meticulous hand. I knew it meant something different here than in the West and I wasn't afraid to look at it.

I copied Bibhuti by taking off my shoes and leaving them outside. He opened the door and Jolly Boy slipped past him into the apartment and flopped down on the zebra-print sofa that dominated the small living room. He clicked the TV on and in a moment he was lost to the events onscreen.

The plane-crash site had become a feeding ground for ghouls. The reporters were fighting over the walking wounded. The interviewee couldn't hear their questions and her hair was smoking.

I felt nervous and alone. The absence of familiar TV programming reminded me that I was now nationless and spun free of all my comforts.

One side of the room was a shrine to Bibhuti's madness. His Guinness and Limca certificates hung from the wall in an irregular flock. The newspaper cuttings of all his records were propped in tortoiseshell frames on the sideboard. Every one was real and in each he looked lifeless, the shock of strange victory draining the history from his eyes. Sitting on a disciple's shoulders for a sweat-soaked fool's parade. Straddling the slab at the instant the sledge-hammer struck.

I saw a picture of him topless punching a fish and I had to bite off a smile.

'This is not from a record,' Bibhuti explained, 'this is from a long time ago, when I was thinking of becoming a model. The stream I am standing in is feeding Thane Creek, which divides Navi Mumbai from the mainland. I did not want these photographs to be taken but I was persuaded when my fame started to grow. They did not reach wide distribution. I am keeping this one here because my wife likes it.'

I looked in his eyes for the light of sincerity that was missing in the photographs. Finding it, my fears for his mental rigidity were dispelled.

'Welcome to my home,' he said. 'Now it is your home also. We usually are only eating two meals a day, one in the morning and one in the evening, but we make a special lunch for you. You are my visitor from across the seven seas, this is a big blessing for all of us.'

Bibhuti's wife came in then, quiet and expressionless, trailed by a jealous fog of cooking smells. Sweat from the kitchen trickled from the folds of her neck. She said a shy hello to me and put three glasses of orange squash down on the coffee table. I could see her handprints in the steam on the sides of the glasses. I could smell the work she put in to making her world seem fresh and new at the start of every day. She wouldn't look at me and I couldn't blame her. As far as she knew I was the angel of death come to herd her husband to the next world before she could redeem the promises he'd made her in their private moments.

We ate in the bedroom, a brightly coloured shawl draped over the bed they all shared to make a tablecloth. My quick acceptance into their intimate arrangements made me feel uncomfortable. When Bibhuti asked me if I had a wife I told him she was dead. It came out before I could stop it. Shame whispered over me and stood my hairs on end. I hated myself for always being too weak to tell the truth.

They were very sorry for my loss. They knew how difficult it must be for me without her.

'I would not wish to be the one left behind,' his wife said, and shot Bibhuti a quick ferocious look. He didn't catch it.

'This will not happen,' he said to me, charging his bread with something I'd soon come to know as aloo gobi.

I copied his technique, my fingers recoiling at the first touch of the food and then relaxing into their new expectations.

'I am under the protection of the almighty and no harm can occur. I could go into the road now and a car could strike me and I would walk away without one scratch. This is the strength that God has given me.'

'You said you will not try this again,' his wife said.

Bibhuti waved away her complaint. 'I began an attempt to stop one car travelling at forty kilometres per hour,' he explained. 'In practice it was not successful so I aborted the plan. This was long time ago. I escaped with small injury, a fracture to my pelvis only. I think perhaps I should lower the speed to thirty kilometres. Perhaps I will try again one day. God tells me when the record is not meant to be. I am only going where he puts me.'

His wife bit off more than she could chew, and there was a tense wait while she safely swallowed what she needed to. Everyone ate their food with renewed determination. Our eating noises made it feel like we were all the same. I was glad Ellen wasn't there to see the mess I was making.

Before I could hold a bat I had to prepare my body and my mind. No more meat. Bibhuti had followed a strict vegetarian diet for many years and it was to this that he attributed his mental fortitude and immunity to all illnesses. His wife would cook all my meals. I was not to accept anything from outside.

No alcohol, no tobacco, no caffeine. Sugar only in moderation. I was permitted sexual release but not to excess. I could keep hold of my money and distribute it when the need arose.

Bibhuti was an early riser and he expected me to conform to his schedule. Every day would start at 5 a.m. with fitness training. I'd need loose clothing and a good pair of sneakers with adequate cushioning around the ankles. The ankles were prone to sprains if not properly supported.

I'd be required to do what he said without hesitation or challenge. He was the expert after many years of training and competition. He knew what was best. It would be hard. It would demand every drop of blood and sweat I had to give. It would be the making of me. When we reached the end I'd be changed for ever. I'd know what it felt like to defy death and all the fears that make the lives of others so small. I'd know the face of God.

I told him I was in.

First of all I had to learn how to breathe. I told Bibhuti I already knew how, but he was having none of it.

'Your breathing is all wrong, I noticed this when first we met.'

'What's wrong with it? It's breathing.'

'It is all wrong. Very bad. You are lucky to be alive for so long if this is the way you have always been.'

He took me to the courtyard underneath his apartment and made me sit on the concrete with my legs crossed. Everything was done outside, in full view of the world. Shame wasn't in the national character and if I wanted to fit in here I'd have to get comfortable with eyes and hands on me.

Bibhuti knelt on the concrete behind me so that his thighs rubbed against my back. He took hold of my shoulders and set my back straight. At my resistance he placed a hand on my chest and pulled me up to my full stretch, then plied me into a shape that pleased him.

Jolly Boy lounged on the floor in front of me, propped up on a puppy-fat arm, staring at me in a kind of prurient trance. He wore a shirt embroidered with a silver dragon for warding off death, and a plastic stopwatch slung round his neck, ready on his father's cue to assist us in counting down the seconds to our date with destiny.

Bibhuti's neighbour rested his elbows on the dividing wall and followed my manipulations. Behind him his wife hung banana skins from the washing line. They were black and dripping. Some murky invocation to charm the gods into blessing me and the attempt.

Breathe in through the nose to the count of seven.

Hold to the count of five.

Breathe out through the mouth to the count of seven.

Rest to five and repeat.

Repeat.

Repeat.

This is the way to breathe. This is how dragons are slain.

'It feels hard,' I said. My chest felt like it had been stuffed with thorns. Every inhale and exhale, when asked to comply with this ideal new formula, came tight and panicked. My body wasn't used to paying such close attention to itself. I was built for living with my eyes closed.

'It is very natural,' Bibhuti insisted. 'You will pick it up easily. A little time only and then it will become automatic. You will feel the benefit immediately. It will save you much trouble and add many years to your span.'

I tried. I tired. With Jolly Boy timing the movements I chased the rebirth Bibhuti promised when the breaths clicked like locks into their prefabricated places. Nothing happened. The sun beat down and I crabbed to the shade of the car port to deny the neighbour the spectacle of my failure. I realised I'd always been doing everything wrong.

I drank the rest of the bottle down when I got back to the hotel. The humiliation of improper breathing had cast a weight over me that only drunkenness could lift. Once I'd loosened up I took an account of my second day as a castaway and a mythmaker and I called it a qualified success. Nobody had died and the various bugs I'd been worried about hadn't shown themselves yet.

8

World Record Number 2: 1,448
stomach sit-ups in one hour (1999)

In the days after my maiden World Record of groin-kicking feat I made a solemn promise to my wife that my thirst for extreme activity was satisfied and I would return to everyday life with no regret. She was worried for my health and it is every husband's primary duty to respect the concerns of his wife and conduct himself accordingly. However I found myself gripped by a powerful determination to follow up my first achievement with even greater success. Despite much introspecting I could find no competing argument strong enough to topple this wish from central role in my imagination. I was hooked.

This is inevitable consequence of becoming a World Record breaker: when you beat the odds like I did and reach the top of the mountain you do not want to climb down again. You have the taste of the rarest kind of air in your lungs and it does not seem practical to suck on the dusty air of lower regions again. Also there was some frustration biting at the back of my mind:

while kind people at Limca had been gracious in certifying my groin-kicking record, I could not call myself a true topper until I had gained recognition in the *Guinness Book of World Records*. This book enjoys renown second to none around the globe, and it is every extreme sportsman's goal to be included in their family. Therefore immediately after blood had passed from my urine and swelling went down around genital region I set about to find a record they would support.

My wife was quite shocked by my decision. She asked who would fill the family's bellies if a disaster fell and I was snatched from her.

Shubham's small fingers were resting on his mother's shoulder, with fingernails in place and wrinkled knuckles, and a deep sadness burrowed in my heart that my wife should not believe my ability to make all good things come true for us. I took the child from her and held him tight. He had the weight of a feather only and I told him that I was the stone wall that stood before all winds that came to carry him away.

'Not to worry,' I assured my wife. 'No harm will occur. I breathe the air of mountains now and my protection is assured. I will do this to honour you and the child. A Guinness World Record will put us on the map. It will secure our future in bright sunshine. It is the path the almighty has picked for me and I must walk it with high head.'

My wife was convinced by my decisive manner and by my pledge to purchase new country-made A/C unit for our home when success was in the bag (you may see the proof of this on the wall in my bedroom, still running smoothly to this day some ten years later. I owe its long life to use sparingly only when heat is at its fiercest height – this is better all round, for pockets and for bodily function).

I declared my intentions to the Guinness people soon after. I chose for my next attempt stomach sit-ups because a Guinness record already existed in this area, therefore my effort was certain to be ratified. Also I was already in the habit of performing one thousand sit-ups per day as part of my usual fitness regime so I knew it would prove no problem for me to overtake the previous number. Actually, it was a match made in heaven. Nothing could go wrong.

The event took place in the main hall of the Navi Mumbai Sports Association, which is my local training facility being only a short drive from my home in Airoli. I come to practise gymnastics in surrounding gardens and I am still holding my regular karate classes here having built up my enterprise from scratch. I have many students who have stuck with me through thick and thin, of all ages and abilities but with same common goal of excellence and improvement through dedicated training. The place was full to capacity with my loyal students, co-workers and other well-wishers who had been alerted to the event by the word of mouth Rajesh Battacharjee had flung far and wide. Despite my giving up my job with his company to take on full-time journalist role he remained a true supporter, informing his important friends in the Corporation of Navi Mumbai that I possessed untapped skills which merited wider appreciation. Several new faces were mingled among the crowd and it was lovely to feel such generous backing from the big brass of my city as well as the common man to whom all my successes are dedicated.

My wife also was there from the start, having chosen the A/C unit she preferred and also bearing no unwieldy concerns for my safety since I hit on the idea of sit-ups. She had witnessed me performing them in countless number and was satisfied that no dangers lay ahead. This attempt was a simple matter, no special considerations or additional helpers required. Just me and my stomach against the clock. Training had gone smoothly with last timed rehearsal producing number of 1,389 which was only six shy of the existing record. Only slight tenderness in upper abdominal region throughout later stages of training period but this did not cause alarm.

This time Vijay Five captured the footage as Amrit Battacharjee, brother of Ramesh, was by now completely blind. I met Vijay Five when I began working for the *Times of India*, which is the biggest circulation English-language newspaper in the world. He is a fellow reporter there covering political beat. He quickly became the fifth Vijay to join my karate class after I recommended the martial arts to him as best source of health and fitness and inner calm.

The story of my introduction to the journalism profession is a great example of God's bounty falling into the arms when they are outstretched and ready to receive. Really it was a wonderful thing to happen unexpectedly and I will briefly tell you how it came about. You will remember that I was required to give Limca a newspaper cutting before they would recognise my first record: the fellow from local newspaper who helped me opened the door to the journalism profession for me. He asked me to write what I wanted to be printed and seeing my write-up he offered me to contribute for his paper. That prompted me to take up the cause to help others with my involvement in the social activities as a journalist. Soon after I was offered the job from *Times of India*. I became a full-time journalist due to the apathetic approach of media which dumped many sportspersons like me. I took the cudgel to promote sporting talents through my write-ups. This mission is still ongoing to the present day.

Back to the attempt. After my usual period of meditation I was ready to begin in spirit of great optimism. My oldest student Gopal Dutta was again my counter. He wore his best linen bandhgala for the occasion, and no evidence of the tumour which would soon begin to pester him.

Before I took my position I cast an eye to the watching masses. Around sixty souls arranged on the pitched seating, already wilting under the heat which could not escape the room (I had instructed Valmik, the custodian, to leave the windows closed to aid the efficient performance of my muscles). All come to witness the next stage in my trajectory to extreme sports pioneer. I spied my wife in the front row holding Shubham, and her smile convinced me that all marital strife was behind us. I felt the expectations of the spectators and found them to be reasonable: I would not let them leave that place bearing disappointment. Instead I would send them back to their lives carrying treasured memories of a unique event in the history of our humble community.

I lay down in the starting position, flat on my back, and awaited with a clear mind the commencement of my allotted hour. Then at Gopal Dutta's command I began the attempt.

Everything passed off without a hitch-up for first portion of the attempt as I romped to 1,000 sit-ups in just thirty minutes. I attacked each movement with high energy level: body up, body down, body up, body down, body up, body down like the rolling of a great locomotive down the track. I settled into a satisfying rhythm, listening to Gopal Dutta's voice counting out my repetitions, breathing in each time my nose touched my knees and breathing out each time my head hit the floor again. Time passed very quickly. On every occasion that my head hit the concrete I knew I was one step closer to achieving my cherished goal of a Guinness World Record.

Then I felt losing strength at neck area after crossing 1,000 line. Something unplanned for had happened but at this moment I could not identify and I did not hold back from completing the attempt. I pushed forward but with slowdown in speed, owning to frequent bang of back of head on the concrete hard floor which was now causing some concern.

'One minute!' Gopal Dutta announced, and at this the crowd began to applaud my every repetitions. Their clapping gave the boost I needed to see out the final seconds. At the very moment that pain began to grow too big and fill my vision with blackness, Gopal Dutta called time and the audience raised the roof.

'One thousand four hundred and forty-eight!' Gopal Dutta declared, and I lay down in complete exhaustion. It was a very emotional response. I gave silent thanks to the almighty for allowing me this moment. Then my wife and son rushed to join me and I looked up at them through eyes swimming with tears of joy.

'I did it!' I said. 'I am a Guinness man now!' I pulled myself to a seated position so that I could accept their embraces. It was then that my wife's eyes widened in alarm and all colour fell from her face. She dropped the child into Gopal Dutta's arm like a hot stone.

'Your head!' she cried. 'What have you done?'

I touched my fingers to the back of my head and removed hair and pool of blood from outer portion. I looked in turn at the faces of my friends and each one was marked with fearful panic.

'It is okay, BB,' Rajesh Battacharjee told me, his eyes fixed on the part of my person that I could not see. 'I am sure it is nothing to worry about. Congratulations! You have done it!' He lifted me to my feet and faced me to the onrushing crowd. 'BB Nayak, Guinness World Record breaker! Son of Navi Mumbai, former employee of Everest Engineering, friend to the common man! Come!'

The crowd swallowed me and once again I was lifted onto their shoulders. They did not seem to notice my blood smearing their clothes as they carried me around the hall and out into the gardens. I reached out for my wife's hand but she was too distant to take it.

I should tell you here that I do not believe in doctors. I have always known my own body better than any doctor: he will only take an X-ray of the broken bone but you must still wait in pain for the picture to come back. It is the inner energy of the person that will finally mend it. Speaking from the age of forty-one years, I have never in my life visited a doctor except for this one exceptional time. I have broken every part of myself in pursuit of my sport and on each occasion no lasting harm has followed – I have healed myself with complete satisfaction, using my own expertise to aid the physical recovery. Injury has become a routine now after so many years of training. My medicine is turmeric powder and milk as painkiller and great healer and if the fracture is serious then I do plastering/bandage on my own with conventional method. I have graduated with the experience how to handle trauma, agony and pain without bothering anyone here.

Therefore when next day I made the dash to hospital it was only to save my wife further worry. The continuous vibration in my head that had kept me awake throughout the night was just a temporary blockage before the solemn celebrations could begin presently.

The doctor at the hospital expressed grave concern when first he saw me. His expression prompted my wife to resume her weeping, which did little to restore my balance. At this stage I realised I could not walk unaided and I was compelled to be seated. 'It is not as bad as it looks,' I told her. 'I have a small headache only.' In truthfulness I was in some agony but I knew that in my new office of Guinness World Record holder I must keep at check my suffering to encourage those aspiring sportsmen who aim to follow in my footsteps. I was therefore quite ashamed when one moment later I was unable to stop myself from falling into small coma.

When I woke again I was fully on fire. The entire span of my body felt like it was ablaze. I opened my eyes to discover that I was confined to a strange bed. Upon feeling my head I noted a heavy bandage wrapped there. I tried to lift my head but it was very uncomfortable position. When I moved even in a small degree a great wave of pain broke over me and I let out a cry. My wife came into my vision and I saw that her face was wet with tears. My son asleep in her arms was not aware of the anguish that infects the lives of the adults. Doctor stood beside my wife, and Rajesh Battacharjee, all wearing looks on their faces as if they too had woken from long slumber.

The doctor told me that I had received surgery to my brain: I had no recollection of this. The knowledge was quite surprising but I accepted it with steady nerves. He then conveyed to me that I had slept for three days. I was shocked by this because I did not feel suitably refreshed. Heaviness and pain only.

'Do I still have the record?' was my burning question. My own voice sounding many miles distant. This was of course my primary anxiety. Curse my luck if while I was sleeping the deep sleep a misfortune or technicality had stripped me of the record I won by rights. I did not wish all my hard work to slip by unnoticed.

'Yes, BB, the record is yours,' Rajesh Battacharjee assured me. 'I have sent the documentation myself. We wait only for the Guinness people to ratify. This will come in a few weeks. You did it, my friend.'

I heaved a sigh of relief, and the pain subsided significantly. Then I had to listen to the doctor explaining to me my injuries. Not only had I sustained deep wounds to the entire back of my body from head to toe due to the friction performing such an unprecedented number of sit-ups had created, but the repeated striking of my head on the concrete floor had caused haemorrhage to my brain. These injuries could be easily explained by the lack of precautionary measure we had taken, as the event was new for everybody present on the occasion. It had not become obvious to us to install any sort of padding on the ground or that I should wear any kind of protective gear on my head: I prefer the natural way of doing things, and this is a principle that I must adhere to through thick and thin. Therefore I accepted my misfortune with a mild heart.

'When can I leave?' I asked the doctor.

'You will require a long period of recovery,' he told me. 'We operated to alleviate the swelling to your brain but we must be on the lookout for further bleeding and complications. The wounds on your back are quite severe and there is a risk of infection. They will require rest and possibly skin grafts. It is a tricky road ahead for you but we will do our best to get you back to your previous level.'

Having no confidence in the treatment I might receive in the hospital, I promptly removed myself from there to complete my healing at home.

I remained bedridden for three months to recover from the pain and damaged skin. The complications that the doctor mentioned did not come calling but boredom and frustration was sorely felt. No certificate was arriving from Guinness due to unforeseen delay and not only was I unable to perform my usual duties and regular training but also was distracted by my wife's constant requests to end extreme sports ambitions for ever. Once out of bed I did yoga, meditation and breathing routines to get it recovered. I lost 30-40 per cent memory power since that day. Even now if I do intense training related to the head I feel the pinch quite prominently. I spent some hard-earned money during the recovery, which was a tough time to handle with entire family depending on me. I had to face hurdle of losing quality time to earn wages which went blank.

It was during this testing time that Rajesh Battacharjee was on hand to keep my spirits high. I could not attend my work at the newspaper but he generously gave from his pocket to fill my family's bellies and keep the roof over their heads. Also he visited my bedside on many occasions to remind me of the bond of obligation I had made between myself and my well-wishers.

'I sense a great appetite for your message among the people,' Rajesh Battacharjee conveyed to me. 'They might not yet know it but I will introduce them. We can show them that simple spirit of hard work and humility can take anyone from the lowest depths of anonymity to national esteem and even worldwide fame. You could be a symbol for them. One day they might buy their dreams from you. I have the power to put you on the platform, BB. Just say the word and I will do this. This is only the beginning, you cannot give up yet. You will recover and then we will begin the next phase of our journey.'

I was impressed by his speech but I kept my thoughts to myself to preserve good feeling between myself and my wife. However she made no such effort to keep her feelings hidden.

'I do not want him to be a symbol,' she told Rajesh Battacharjee plainly. 'I just want him to be alive. I want him to be a good husband to me and a good father to his son. That is all I pray for night and day.'

'Your prayers will be answered, Bhabhi. But a good husband and father is one who provides an example for his dear ones to follow. BB's example is more persuasive than most common men can give. He can inspire the world if only you allow him to follow his path. A good wife will not stand in the way of her husband's destiny.'

She did not answer this with further words, but with lowered gaze which indicated that she was preparing to submit to the undeniable strength of Rajesh Battacharjee's argument.

At the same moment I was trying to assemble in my mind ideas for my next record attempt. I knew that the next record must be something equally special or more so if I were to confirm for all time my place in long history of my country. I said these words to myself in forceful tone of determination: I am Bibhuti Bhushan Nayak of Cuttack, proud resident of Navi Mumbai, Limca World Record holder, Guinness World Record holder. I will share with the people my message of love through discipline, sports and vegetarian diet, and my achievements will be an inspiration to the common man and young generation alike.

Thank you.

9

I look out of the window and see a circus closing in. The road is blocked by some disciple's car and an ambulance mounts the grass to get past. When it meets the slope its doors swing open and a woman on a trolley comes soaping out and freewheels across the lawn. She hits a lamp-post and rests there. Breaking orderlies toss their cigarettes and rush to her aid. They carry the trolley into the emergency department. The woman doesn't stir throughout. She's old and she's lived through indignities more damning than this one. She sleeps peacefully.

In the car park familiar faces are raised to the sky, looking for the window where their fallen idol is niched. Everyone who saw me strike Bibhuti down is there. There are the Vijays and Harshad. There's Amrita and the ping-pong monks. The Turbanator is zipping up his camera bag against the prying fingers of the beggar children. Kavita is ferocious in her Dora the Explorer T-shirt, sparring with her father, unloading all her little sorrows on him in a blur of arms and legs. She thinks her sensei's already dead. She thinks the world has ended.

Someone needs to put her somewhere high up where she can't cause any damage, sit her in a tree until the thunderstorm passes. But no one wants to risk their hands. She's a wolverine. I broke her heart.

They came in a pilgrim's trail, following the cavalcade that brought us here after Bibhuti stopped moving. His friends first and then the AXN cameraman and the beggar kids who'd stopped by the temple to see what was happening and to catch the spectators in distracted generous mood. They came in trickles, pulled by the prospect of a glamorous death. Now their mouths are open and their eyes are searchlighting the building for a glimpse of their villain. Pitchforks are hidden behind their backs. I'm their monster and I don't know how it happened.

I hide behind the curtain.

'They must know it wasn't my fault,' I say.

'Whose fault was it?' Ellen says, her voice cracked and scolding, standing at the door waiting for Bibhuti's wife and Jolly Boy to come back from their meeting with the doctors. She didn't want me there. Ellen leans on her stick and the stick wobbles. The victim of a disability, she's stronger than I remember her.

'I only gave him what he wanted. I didn't know it'd turn out like this.'

'How could you not know?'

'I thought he could take it. He told me it'd be alright. I was only doing what was best for him.'

Bibhuti's piss bag is full again and I should change it but I don't know how. I tell Ellen to call a nurse and I swab his lips, wipe the crust off. I tell him to wake up. His eyes are swimming in their sockets. He's dreaming. He's dreaming so he must still be a man. A vegetable doesn't dream. He's still a man and everything will be alright. Wake up.

Wake up.

I whisper it in his ear. I get close enough to smell his breath. Rotten eggs. I close his lips again. I was never a father but I know how it feels to have a child. Right now I'd give anything to die in his place.

I might still get my wish. It's a race to the death between the two of us and there's no telling which one of us is the closest. Only you know that.

The pain is getting worse.

It went away for a bit when I thought Bibhuti might save me. Then it came back and it's growing into something I can't shake off with fresh perspectives or new breathing. It's a scorching sand that's filling me up, getting into everything. Every grain a wrong turn or a harsh word or a compliment left unsaid, and I can't breathe for them. Regret is burning through my bones. Now I know what that pheasant must have felt as I watched him die, the first time I killed something. He must have been reliving every moment of flight and cursing his stubby wings for the taste they gave him of a sky too big to let go of.

I'd been on my way to work, taking the country roads to avoid the motorway traffic. It was winter and the sun was just coming up. The road sparkled. There was still frost on the windscreen. Sometimes I'd go this way just to try and spot some nature before the day got started and human toil took over. I used to see pheasants quite a bit. I saw a deer once, nibbling at the bushes by the side of the road. I could get quite close and if there was nothing behind me I'd slow down for a good look. There was quiet on these roads and the trees hid the industrial parks and let me forget what was going on in the world, what-ever wars were still stretching out and Ellen at home singing baby names to herself. Something scared him up and he came flapping out of the hedges and I hit him full on. The noise pulled the wind out of me and I braked hard. I sat there for a while watching him twitching on the road. Then I pulled over to the side and got out to be with him.

I went to him slowly, watched over him as he waited for the pain to stop. There was nothing I could do for him. He was broken all over and leaking into the dawn. I thought about reaching out to try and reshape him but I didn't want to hurt him any more than he was already. He looked at me, his little eye blinking. I looked for understanding or forgiveness, a soul maybe, but there was just dumb waiting. Tears came. I wiped them away and shrugged aside the cold to wait with him. The air tasted fresher than I'd ever known it. The quiet was beautiful, and I saw the true colour of the trees. I saw cruelty and wonderful disorder. I didn't see you. I thought everything was an accident, everything good and everything bad.

I told him I was sorry. I asked him to forgive me if he could. He shivered. Important pieces of him dripped on to the road and shimmered in the early light. He blinked three more times, quickly, and then he died. The world contracted a tiny amount and I felt something in me drop away. I went and pissed in the bushes and then I got a blanket from the boot to wrap him up in. I couldn't bring myself to touch him. Feeling his body through the blanket as I picked him up I cried again. I thought of myself as a sickness. I laid him down in the boot and let him sleep while I lumbered through a working day. His face kept coming back to me and I left early, having heard none of what had been said to me and having felt none of the things I'd picked up, pens and dockets and a coffee cup stained brown on the inside.

Ellen watched me dig the hole and she didn't say a word about the state of the garden. She knew I had to do right by him. She knew as well as I did. I picked a good spot up at the back under the crab apple tree. He'd like it there. There'd be shade in the hotter months and the songs of other birds perched in the branches above him. While I shovelled in the dark she fussed over the bird, cleaned as much of the blood up as she could and made him look comfortable. She replaced the rough blanket with something softer, a woollen crocheted thing Mum had given us for the baby that never was. Lemon yellow and still creased where it had been folded and left at the bottom of the drawer where cufflinks and premium bonds lived. She stroked his dead face and plied the grit from his feathers.

I found an old satchel to make a barrier against the worms and she cried too when the zip went up. I lowered him in gently so I didn't disturb him. We both said sorry, as much to each other as to the bird. I patted the earth down neat and tidy and stepped away to make room for a ritual. Ellen just held my arm as the stars blinked down and looked away into a future she was seeing for the first time. A future that would never mould to the shape of a new life, where our own lives with their hangnails and heartburn had to be enough to clothe us. Whatever had dropped away in me had dropped away in her and I knew we'd never get it back. When we got indoors she cut a slice of cake for herself and she turned the light off before she got undressed.

There's a bang from outside. I go to the window. A van from a TV channel has crashed into the car that was blocking the road. A reporter stumbles out of the passenger side and smooths her hair, strides through the crowd to claim her spot at the hospital entrance. Her cameraman jogs behind her, carrying one of her shoes. It's a red slipper.

It's Vijay Five's car. He tears at his hair as he inspects the damage to the nearside wing. He goes to remonstrate with the reporter. Two media dogs snarling at each other over a prime patch of story.

But Vijay Five doesn't have his notebook. Bibhuti isn't a story to him. Behind his back naked children climb onto the roof of the car and start dancing. It'll rain again soon.

The flooding has been minimal in this part of the city. The gutters have been sucking the water up and the roads incline towards the sea. I only saw one dog swimming on the way over, making frantic circles in search of dry land. That was miles back and a day ago. He would have found a safe place by now. We're safer here than on the mainland where the worst of it has hit. We're the charmed ones.

Every time I close my eyes I see myself hitting Bibhuti with the bat. I see him bent and crumpling with a look of joy on his face. He loved me then. He'll love me still when he wakes up. We're brothers, no questions asked. Yesterday was the greatest day of my life. I need him to wake up so I can thank him for it. I need to say sorry for lighting my fire with him.

Jolly Boy was sitting next to the old man, hugging his knees on the tarpaulin outside the hotel. The old man had been talking to him and now he was staring again at his favourite patch of sky. Clouds were forming there, as if by his will, stitching themselves together as he watched through his malfunctioning eyes. I asked Jolly Boy what the man had said.

'He is waiting for the monsoon to come. When the rain is here he will be rain and he will go up to heaven like that. He has been waiting for this for twelve years. Every year he thinks it will happen but the rain is never strong enough to lift him. This time he thinks it will happen.'

'What do you think? Do you think it'll happen?'

'Yes. He is very sure. He has been praying for a long time. I think this year he will make it.'

'Why does he want to turn into rain?'

Jolly Boy asked the old man and interpreted his answer. 'He says it was always promised to him that he would die this way. He thinks it is the best way. He doesn't want to be here anymore, he is too heavy. When he is rain he will be light and he will go to heaven very fast. His family is there waiting for him and his goats are there. He misses the goats very bad. God made the promise to him a long time ago and he cannot wait anymore.'

'Tell him I hope it happens this year.'

Jolly Boy passed on my message. The old man gave me a tooth-less smile. He offered me another trinket god and I refused it gently. It was the same one he'd already tried to sell me. We left him stewing on the promise he'd been made, his rain dutifully making itself in the clouds above our heads.

The dashboard Ganesh kept his own counsel in his little Perspex prison. Bibhuti sat on his plank and ground his gears, turned the A/C on with a harried cluck of his tongue when Jolly Boy's pleas started to grate. The bridge was jammed with the rush-hour commute. Every car had the same slogan painted on its back, 'Horn OK Please', and everyone took the request to heart.

I saw a man throw a dog in the creek, its lifeless body splay grue-somely as it hit the water. The man gave no salute, just got back on his motorbike and merged into the traffic. He passed us expression-less as we inched towards the mainland.

Old Bombay. Where death spills songlike from every doorway and untapped dreams rise like smoke from the rubbish fires and rat holes. Even through the air conditioning I could smell the place as it got nearer, fertile and teeming with tradition and mundane terrors. A place to get lost in and to be startled by into revisions of previous wisdoms. Bibhuti turned the radio on and he and Jolly Boy sang along to the first song they found. I didn't understand the words and I was an outsider again.

Bibhuti could barely contain his excitement. He vibrated in time to the music as we lurched between the bumpers, took both his hands off the wheel to clap impatiently.

'I found this man after much searching,' he said. 'My friend Santosh, he is also my student, he told me about him. As luck would have it he has a large amount of bats which he has no use for. I was unable to pay but I made him promise to keep them for me until a time when the money arrived. He accepted my request in return for one small favour only which I must grant him when we complete the transaction. He is an honourable man. The bats are unused and there are many. I am very happy today.'

He carried on singing. The early start had drained me and I dozed off. Then the traffic eased and the new speed brought me round again.

The streets had peeled and blistered while I'd been out and the buildings had grown grander, colonial mansions with book-lined drawing rooms where syphilitic viceroys and mutton-chopped tea merchants had once wrestled naked for diamonds the size of ostrich eggs. That's how I imagined it, anyway. The thriving trees hung with lanterns that became fruits when I looked closer. The children who strayed near the roadside were lighter, their faces unsmudged by the trials of their namesakes who prowled the poorer parts. Their hair was neatly combed and their eyes were violent with the restrictions of family wealth. They were lazily occupied in a game of leverage, trying to prise open a manhole cover with a tree branch. They didn't try and stop the car or hold their hands out for our money.

We passed out of the old ways, turned a corner and we were back in the modern world again. A heaving road buffed smooth by the tyre rubber from every car and bus and tanker truck in the city all visiting at once on some kind of pilgrimage for the petrol age. A storm of horns beat against the car, and we were slowed down again to crawling. I saw my first holy cow emptying itself on the roadside, tethered to a scrap-iron kiosk that sold SIM cards and sweet lime. The cow's sharp shoulders looked mythical and nobody seemed to notice the waterfall of shit streaming from its back end. They just stepped instinctively around it, not looking up, as if making eye contact with the animal in its time of public indelicacy would break some ancient code of ethics.

Bibhuti parked up on the fringe of the puddle the cow had made. I had to stretch to clear the mess and Jolly Boy pulled me up to the kerb. I turned my nose up at the smell and he wrinkled his nose in solidarity. We went in the Cafe Coffee Day and sat down at a red plastic table. The girl who took our order wore a baseball cap. The tea came in a paper cup. For some reason I was expecting a proper china teacup. I was disillusioned at how easily India had surrendered its traditions to the dogma of convenience. It wasn't my place to say it, but I thought it should have fought harder.

B Pattni brought the smell of the street in with him, of commercial agitations and milky coffee drunk in a hurry between the marking of cards. The little bell tinkled when he came through the door. He greeted me with a handshake that was designed to test me for structural weaknesses. His hands felt like they were less used to dispensing pleasantries to out-of-towners than to driving telegraph poles or throttling intruding leopards.

He asked me if I had the money and I lifted the carrier bag.

'They're not for baseball,' I said. 'They're for a special thing. We need them to be pukka.'

'I know what they are for, sir. Trust me, they are top-notch. Come.'

We followed him outside. He took us down a dank alleyway that led to the back of the shops. Industrial bins and rubbish bags overflowed with the stinking leftovers of fast food joints. At the far end of the alleyway there was a row of lock-up garages. B Pattni walked on tiptoes, trying to save his patent-leather shoes from the shit. He unlocked the furthest garage, hauled the door open and disappeared inside.

Bibhuti and his boy had gone quiet. The air around us crackled with flies and anticipation. We approached slowly, pyramid breakers sniffing for a dead king's gold.

A rat ran past my feet and squirmed into a hole in a rubbish bag. It was wearing a diamanté collar and its little black eyes were intent on thievery.

B Pattni emerged and handed Bibhuti his first offering. Bibhuti's eyes went wide when he saw it. He accepted the bat greedily. He stroked the length of it from the business end to the grip, smoothing his palm over the lacquered wood. He felt for faults in the grain. He read the bat like a sacred text.

'Lovely, lovely,' he murmured. He slapped the bat from hand to hand, felt its weight and breathed in the prophecy it carried. A shiver of something lustful went through him when he struck the bat against the air. Maybe he was thinking of the first strike against his own flesh and bones, the unsticking that would come with it.

'It is good?' B Pattni asked, dragging a shipping crate out and loosing another bat that he passed to me for inspection.

'Lovely,' Bibhuti repeated. He turned to me grinning, eyes vivid. 'It has the perfect feel. We could not ask for better. Feel.'

I took a token swing at the air. 'Feels good,' I said.

Jolly Boy grabbed a bat for himself and imitated our ritual, weighed it up against the slim resistance of the air. Soon the three of us were waving our bats around in a solemn display, swinging at the ghosts of our former disappointments, planting our feet in the diabolical future. The same goal had taken hold of us all and we were lost in its grip like boys at play. Father and son hit synchronised home runs and then me and Jolly Boy were swordfighting.

A mood for clowning fell over us and the alleyway rang with our make-believe war cries.

Jolly Boy took a swing at Bibhuti's head. He ducked to evade it.

'Break one now, Baba,' he pleaded. 'I will make the hit.'

'Not yet,' Bibhuti said. 'Uncle has the job. We must let him have the first hit, he has come a long way.'

The boy pouted. He took a consolation swing at the air while his father freed another bat from the crate and stroked it, spellbound.

There was something printed on the shaft of my bat. In English: 'B Pattni Fine Leather Goods, Import and Export, Wholesale and Retail'. An address and phone and fax numbers. I saw that Bibhuti's bat had the same branding. They all did.

'There was mishap,' B Pattni said. 'They are all useless to me. My son plays baseball, his team is the Malad Maroons. Last year was their inaugural season in Mumbai junior A league. I spent small fortune to supply the team with bats, and I paid extra to have them printed with the particulars of my business. I thought this would be great advertising opportunity.'

He pointed out the message on my bat. 'B Pattni Fine Leather Goods, this is my business. I have just opened my second retail outlet in Evershine Mall next to Cell-bug cellphone showroom. You must come in, I have everything you will need: wallets, purses, iPhone case, briefcase, attaché, everything of finest quality.'

His mood darkened. 'The bats are arriving tainted. The entire batch permanently disfigured. Look here, you see the telephone number? It is the wrong number. That should not be a two, it should be a seven. I clearly expressed my requirements when I made the order, the mistake was theirs but they would not accept responsibility.'

Raw emotion frayed his voice and danger had draped itself over him like a mist. I stepped back, putting some room between us in case he lashed out.

'I am always doing these things by hand, you see, I do not trust the online forms. You will see there is no website on the bat. I do not conduct my business this way. The internet is not safe, this is how Pakistan is spying on us. I made the order by fax and they misread my instructions. Clearly my seven does not look like a two, my handwriting has always been very clean. It is the fault of the reader. If I had my pen with me I would show you.'

'That's okay, I believe you.'

'I tried to reason with them but they would not amend their mistake. I had to place fresh order for the correct printing, I could not let my son down with pre-season practice around the corner. Now I have one hundred and twenty bats which I cannot use. They are collecting dust for the past year. Then BB is coming along and all is saved.'

There was a crash. Jolly Boy was pounding his bat against the door of a garage, caught in a whirlwind of sweet violence. Bibhuti snapped out of his trance and bounded over to take the bat from him, scolding the boy for disrespecting the equipment. He checked the bat's snub end for damage.

The noise had nudged B Pattni off his stride. He licked a blob of spit from his lip.

'I ask only that you cover the printing,' he said. 'I do not wish for further embarrassment.' He looked anxiously to Bibhuti. 'Did you discuss my price?'

'It is decided,' Bibhuti said.

Bibhuti steered me towards a neutral corner and shook me down for thirty thousand rupees. It sounded like a fair price to pay for two souls and all the highest hopes they had between them. I counted out the notes and handed them over. He thanked me ferociously. I was his benefactor now. Handshakes all round. But Bibhuti and B Pattni still had some unfinished business.

B Pattni hitched up his shirtsleeves, took a handkerchief from his back pocket and mopped the sweat from his face. His legs were parted and he was trying to bounce on the balls of his feet like a shadowboxer. It only made him look heavier.

'I will take off my shoes if you prefer it.'

'Let your shoes be there, it is no problem,' Bibhuti assured him. 'After you will help us transport the bats to my home, yes?'

B Pattni tilted his head, done deal. With no further ceremony he drew his foot back and gave Bibhuti a tentative kick in the balls. He paused to make sure there was no ill feeling, then gave him another one. All was well. He asked for one more, and he made it a showstopper. Bibhuti rocked on his heels and called time. Another handshake to seal the new friendship, and then they each took an end of the first crate and walked it to B Pattni's pick-up.

Jolly Boy still held his bat jealously. He took a lazy swipe at a passing rat. The rat disappeared into the same hole the one in the diamanté collar had found. I imagined the first rat was an escaped pet. That it had found life on the streets hard at first, but had risen to the challenge of freedom. No longer was it the butt of the other rats' jokes. It had earned respect through fighting and repeated displays of ingenuity.

The drive back to Bibhuti's apartment took us past a tiny clapperboard church, wedged between more colonial relics. The sign outside said 'People are so often lonely because they build walls instead of bridges'. I thought of Ellen and how lonely I must have made her, and my heart missed a beat. I wondered if they'd found the car yet and what she'd fill my coffin with. Sawdust to preserve my dignity in my absence or pebbles so the rattling would drive home my betrayal.

Bibhuti's wife was waiting for us when we got back with the bats, dripping down the stairs in her dress of golden threads. A regal petulance flared in her eyes. She looked like she'd been waiting a lifetime to tell a home truth. Bibhuti was cornered as soon as he got out of the car. Me and Jolly Boy stayed out of the firing line, busied ourselves unloading the crates from B Pattni's pick-up.

Bibhuti's neighbour offered his help. I manfully refused it. Behind him a constellation of butterflies had formed in our absence, lured there by the banana peels hanging from the washing line. Their wings beat slowly as they fed on the rotting pulp. Others flew in from the surrounding trees to wait their turn, dancing colours in the still air. They studded the neighbour's wife like jewellery.

'My wife's favourite is the gaudy baron. She likes the shade of green on the base of the wing, do you see?'

He pointed out one of the feeders, the jade fringe at its tail end.

'Beautiful,' I said. The word felt silly coming from me but I stood by it. I went over to get a closer look.

'This is good time for butterflies,' the neighbour said. 'The monsoon is coming and they like the humid condition. The banana is very attractive to them. We have gaudy baron, great eggfly, common Jezebel, blue oakleaf – this one here.'

'Oh yeah, it looks just like a leaf.'

'Of course. And here is a striped tiger.' There it was feeding out of his wife's palm, living up to its name with its orange and black markings. Jolly Boy drew up beside me to watch, leaving his parents to bicker uninhibited.

He reached out a tentative finger to stroke it. A fear came over him, of breaking spells, and he pulled back. 'I stroked a tiger's tail. It was at Tadoba. He walked past our Gypsy and I put out my hand and he stopped and let me do it. It was very lovely.'

The neighbour smelt a lie and the generosity drained from him. The boy waited for him to acknowledge the brilliance of what he'd just told him. I stepped in when it looked like he might crumble.

'It's true,' I said. 'He told me.'

'Wow,' the man grinned. 'Imagine stroking a tiger. You are very lucky.'

Jolly Boy bristled with pride, a mirror of the butterfly's wings unfolding to snare the sun's warming rays.

Meanwhile Bibhuti had accepted defeat. Heartbreak showed in the sag of his moustache. His wife was climbing the stairs, a vindicated streak of gold.

'We cannot bring the bats into the house,' Bibhuti said. 'It is tempting to fate. We must keep them in the yard.'

Me and Jolly Boy were called back into action as B Pattni sped away in a cloud of diesel, gone to investigate an opportunity in shark skin.

The three of us shifted the crates to the patch of wasteland at the back of the apartment building. Bibhuti lifted a lid and cast a final look over the bats inside. He freed one and indulged himself in another caress, a sculptor falling in love with the block of stone that would yield his masterpiece. He eased the lid shut again.

'My wife is very grateful that you have come to help me,' he said. 'Before you came I had no hope of achieving this record. Nobody wanted to help, they were all too afraid of hurting me. Now the record is in my grasp again and she sees the light returning to my eyes. It is a big relief for her. She prays for your safety also.'

'She doesn't have to do that.'

'It is not a problem for her, always she is praying. You are our friend now and she is pleased for this.'

I skipped back onto the concrete before the snakes could sniff me out.

I fell asleep to the restful tapping of computer keys. Bibhuti had to write up his interview with the ping-pong monks, ready to file for tomorrow's edition. I'd let him lead me to his bed and pull the blanket over me with the tenderness of a mother nursing a feverish child. Jolly Boy had sat with me for a while, watching over me while I curled myself into the imprint Bibhuti had left in the sheet before me. He'd slipped out of the room when I feigned sleep, leaving me to agitate in privacy on the liberties I'd taken to insinuate myself into his father's clothes.

The Thums Up T-shirt stretched tight round my grumbling belly. The sweatpants biting in where the waistband hugged my hips. White socks with threadbare heels, a gift given so carelessly that I'd felt obliged to weep when I was putting them on and cursed my ingratitude when no tears came. It was an outfit apt for testing the limits of my old body, and for disappearing into the grain of a new family.

Maybe in these clothes, in the dark or in a rush, Bibhuti's wife would mistake me for her man and show me the same patience she reserved for him. Maybe she'd be fooled long enough to accept me curled up like a cat on her lap, to stroke my cheek and tell me everything was going to be alright.

I woke up to the sound of her flip-flops flapping obscenely on the floor tiles as she moved around the kitchen. I had to sneak past her to the bathroom. Their toilet was a hole in the floor to perch over and ceramic footholds for stability. The house held its breath to listen for my mistakes.

Jolly Boy was waiting outside for me. He'd been assigned the task of checking my aim. He made a quick assessment of the state of the room. He was happy to see that I'd taken to their ways like a duck to water.

The next days were for slipping under the waves of the routine Bibhuti prescribed and for making complaints that he nobly ignored until the fight fell out of me. Harshad showed me how to let myself out. I'd lock the door behind me and post the key back through the letterbox. Bibhuti's place was just a few minutes' walk away and I'd pad the empty streets with the sleepless dogs, a ghost in the blue half-light until I arrived at Bibhuti's courtyard and the disgraces began.

First there was a salute to the sun, then a chair and a downward-facing dog. The yoga was to make me supple and to rid my mind of any thoughts of recrimination for the abuses my new master would inflict. Then there were sit-ups and push-ups to strengthen my core, and squats to enlarge my thigh muscles where the power to drive my swings would be generated. I'd crawl to the apartment's underbelly to stretch and shake, suck up my humiliation while the sun cast its first splinters, heaving with Bibhuti's hands around my ankles, holding me down and holding me to my word. My stomach straining and my shoulders grinding as he shared with me his passion for life and its many opportunities for self-mutilation.

The smell of his deodorant and breakfast sprouts. Breathe in through the nose to the count of seven.

His wife's wary eyes on me from the top of the stairs as she wrung out the washing. The soapy water slapping down on to the courtyard in noisy lascivious streams.

Hold to the count of five.

Jolly Boy bedheaded and smelling of sleep in his dragon-embroidered shirt, skipping past his mother to mark time on my creaking repetitions, the stopwatch his translator between childhood arithmetic and the strange numberless world of men and their obsessions. Hanging from his father like a tree, riding him while I rested. His small hands slipping over the scars that crossed Bibhuti's back like ancient migration routes.

Breathe out through the mouth to the count of seven. Hold to the count of five and repeat.

The daily hanging of banana skins and later the catch, after the startled rise of the sun and the slowburning delay, watching the horizon for the incoming storm. Black clouds boiling and the wild descent of wings. The butterflies' colours my consolation for the pain of ageing with too few stories to tell.

The neighbour watching me the way someone might watch a flower of blood forming under a freshly killed man. I'd never understood exactly what morbid curiosity meant until then. I mumbled sand-mouthed profanities to a country that had the measure of me and a sky that wanted to squash me into steam.

And repeat.

I'd fold my arms to cover my spare tyres, stripped to the waist while Bibhuti rubbed sun cream into my blistering shoulders, his breath warm and shocking on the back of my neck. I kept my eyes open so it wouldn't look like I was enjoying myself. I missed Ellen's hands on me. I missed having no gods to hide my ugliness from.

Then there were the games. Special tasks Bibhuti cobbled together to test my resolve and sharpen my instincts for desecration. To teach me patience he spilled a bowl of rice and made me pick it up one grain at a time. This after he'd smelled booze on me despite the promise I'd made to stop drinking. The sack bore a cartoon of a young boy wearing a baseball cap. The brand name was Tolly Boy. I misread it as Jolly Boy and before I'd realised my error I'd given Shubham his new name. He was delighted with it and so it stuck.

In return Jolly Boy helped me scratch up handfuls of rice when his father ducked inside to answer nature's call. With half the rice returned to the bowl I'd learned all I needed to know about patience and respect. I'd learned that the god Bibhuti set his clock by was disinclined to both.

After the morning indignities Bibhuti would go out into the field, notebook in hand, to capture the unsung lives of his scrap of the country – a woodland sports retreat for blind kids, a powerlifting trial in the lobby of a Thane primary school closed down for the summer   and me and Jolly Boy would kick our heels on the outskirts of the action while he got his interviews. The Turbanator would always arrive at the last minute to immortalise the encounters in pictures that half the time wouldn't make it to print for a lack of column space between the Monsoon Madness Sales adverts and the sex advice.

I remember watching the sightless children dangle from the trees like broken windchimes, their stiff flailing limbs trembling the anchor lines, lashed two feet off the ground between the trunks. A clumsy suspension of disbelief. They laughed. They jerked fearlessly and laughed without remorse because they couldn't see how unbeautiful they looked. They'd looked for the ground with dead eyes and they'd found only sky. A groping for sensation, spirits twisting momentarily free from the deadweight of their orphaned bodies.

One girl's leading foot slipped off the anchor line. In the instant of treading air her miracle was undone. She lost the grip of one hand and was tangled in her harness, spun there like a turning fruit. Her face contorted in panic, her useless eyes swimming in their sunken cavities. I thought about running to her rescue but I decided it wasn't my place. Soon enough a chaperone came to steady her, coiled her fingers gently back round the rope above her head. With a few words of encouragement she completed her crossing, to be met with well-meaning plaudits and wandering hands.

In the evenings I'd ply Bibhuti for his secrets between my trials at the badminton net. Jolly Boy didn't live up to his promise to go easy on me.

I asked Bibhuti how he beat pain.

'I have trained myself. Pain is a choice. I have chosen not to accept it.'

'That's handy.'

'Yes, it is very useful.'

'How though?'

'Come,' Bibhuti said, and he got up and planted himself by the badminton net. He parted his legs just so. 'You will kick me and you will see.'

I couldn't do it. He tried to convince me but I was frozen, some righteous portion of my brain wouldn't let me cross the line. I told him I had a tight hamstring. I'd wait until it was better.

'Very well,' Bibhuti said and waved Jolly Boy in. Still holding his badminton racquet he took a casual swipe at his father's groin, the action so familiar to him that it seemed almost involuntary. No emotion played on his face. His father accepted the kick in a similar fashion. I imagined countless mornings of stiff routine, father goading son to harder and faster, teasing from him by attrition the bravery that would see him carry on the family name.

'You see?' Bibhuti asked.

'I saw it, yeah. But what I want to know is how.'

I hadn't swung a bat in anger. I had a taste for his blood.

'It is a switch. Like light switch. I press the switch and the light goes off. Then it is darkness and the pain cannot be seen. I know it is there but if I cannot see it then it cannot grab me.'

'But how?'

'Breathing. Meditation. Training. Diet. The grace of the almighty. All of these things.'

I nodded my head to show that I believed him. I asked him if he'd heard about the Frenchman who ate a plane.

He hadn't. I told him the story. He was appalled.

'This is not a serious man,' Bibhuti said. 'He does not value the true meaning of the extreme sportsman's ethic. It is same with my fellow Indians, many silly records. The fellow who balances candles on his moustache. Another who is just sitting still on a wall for eleven hours. What good is this doing? How does this provide positive example for common man and next generation?'

He became agitated, paced the courtyard stroking his moustache. His eyes blazed with the perversity of a world where the sacrifices of simple men go uncelebrated.

'What I am doing is telling the people that if they endure the pain they will reach happiness that comes after. My country is very difficult place. A lot of people very poor and hungry. Life is constant struggle against all the odds and natural disasters. I am from a family of four brothers and two sisters in my native place. It was challenging to upbring six children in competitive world. The food grains produced from our land had never been sufficient to find ends meet. We used to go to bed with empty stomach every alternate day.

'I am leaving home at twelve and handled myself all alone living in slum pocket and footpaths. I did odd jobs like taking tuition, working in hotels as waiter and grocery shop as supply boy, selling cow dung cake, taking care of cows, all for just one hundred rupees a day. I changed many schools and colleges due to lack of finance to finally complete postgraduation on my own. When I first came to Mumbai after my degree I spent many months in the streets.'

He squeezed his eyes shut, as if to banish the ghosts of his dissatisfied past. I reached up to pat him on the shoulder but he roused himself before I could touch him.

'But this does not matter now. I found my intended path through many struggles. This is the message I convey to the people when I am breaking my records. The happiness is coming after the pain. Forget these emotional moments. I am very sorry.'

Bibhuti took a comb from his back pocket and went to the step to scrape thoughtfully at his hair. Silence fell. India got hotter. My past trickled away like rain into pavement cracks.

More sprouts and spices for the last meal of the day, and Bibhuti's wife asked no questions of us. All she cared about was that we wash our hands and empty our bowls. The less she said the more I wanted to know what went on inside her, just like I'd wanted to with Ellen, so that I could reassure myself with something beautiful and ageless. I wanted to see the place where she was born. I imagined she'd grown up among fawns and chemical smog and that the river had brought her here to be a testament to the unknowable, to give comfort to the lost and to incite the jealousies of men like me.

Jolly Boy would walk me back to the hotel to make sure I didn't get lost and to scare the prying dogs back into their shadows. We'd talk about sports cars and our differing names for chocolate. He'd turn and run when he saw Harshad at the door, his goodbye echoing between the billboards and the sleeping windows. Harshad would always greet me with a haunted look in his eyes, as if I'd caught him weighing up the rights and wrongs of staying alive for another day. I'd hide the money and count my bruises, and then I'd lie awake for an hour fretting over the next morning's inconveniences and wondering about the friends I'd had at school. What they might have done with their lives and what they might have believed in.

If they could see me now how sick with envy they'd be. I'd be the first of us to go viral and the last to give in to religion.

World Record Numbers 3 and 4: 133 backhand push-ups in one minute; smashed 3 concrete slabs of 18kg each in the groin by a sledgehammer (2001)

As you will recall from the previous chapter, I was confined to my bed for three months after my success with sit-up record. My only comfort during this inactive spell was the thought of embarking on another great sporting journey as soon as my body had recovered its full power. I freely admit to you that I had become hooked on the special feeling record breaking provided. I could no longer imagine my life the way it had ticked over before I committed to this adventurous path.

This is what you must understand: in my country the common man is many but his chances to shine are few. Either he is Sachin Tendulkar or he is Salman Khan or he is nothing at all. The people labour in darkness only to fill their bellies while their dreams are forgotten in the dust. They do not complain because they believe this is God's plan for them. I am here to tell them that God has another plan, and if only they will lift their eyes from the ground they will see it clearly. The almighty has given me one life on earth of one hundred years or less and he has conveyed to me his instructions for what I must do with it: to show the common man what can be done with dedication and positive spirit.

There is actually no limit. This is the remarkable thing I have discovered.

When he sees me on the record stage or romping into limelight of media coverage I want him to say, 'There is a man who has achieved his dream with no help from rich father or corporate sponsorship. He has beaten the pain alone through strength of mind and body. Look how happy he is. If he can do it then so can I.' I would like to be the example to awaken the fate which lies sleeping in his heart.

When I told you that I awoke from my coma on fire, this is not so far from the truth. Because while I was sleeping I received a powerful vision from my past which ignited the flame of desire that my injuries had snuffed out hitherto.

The vision was a memory of the time when a fire-eater visited my native place. It is the most important event to occur in my childhood and it is from this root that every branch of my life has grown to provide rich fruit. I was only seven years old and I had not yet discovered the purpose of my life. The fire-eater was a large man with wild orange beard who came out of the forest while I was tending my father's goats. He had been travelling for many days and was in need of food and water. I took him to my home and my mother fed him. He accepted my father's offer to stay with us one night, wanting only to rest his feet and recover his strength before he continued on his journey to Puri in time for Bahara Chandana, which is important festival taking place at the Jagannath temple there.

During his short stay the fire-eater would not tell anybody his name. He said it was not important. He did not need a name in any case, for the children of my village had already crowned him Ram because he came from the forest. Ram is the seventh incarnation of Vishnu who was born to free the earth from the cruelty of the demon king Ravana and killed many demons in the forest. This is what we believed as children.

The man we called Ram became a god for the one day that he was among us, because he was so large and had such a fine physical presence and also because we had not seen a man eat fire before. It was very exciting for us as youngsters to watch Ram take the torch, lit before our eyes from the fire of my mother's tandoor, and swallow it without any sign of pain. The first time was quite a shock and we all gasped in surprise. Then we asked him to do it again to prove that what we had seen was not a trick or a strange dream we were all having. Surely enough he repeated the feat and we were convinced he was indeed a divine incarnation. He did not speak because words were unnecessary to him in this moment.

Then to further entertain us he covered the torch with paraffin and this time when it was lit the flame it produced was awesome in scale. He blew the flame to make it leap like claws of a wild beast. Again he swallowed with no ill effects but great feeling of calm and happiness. Also he ate a coal from the fire.

This day was magical in my childhood. The time passed very slowly and when the sun went down my native place had been changed into a land where the wildest dreams of our lives were coming true. Ram slept in my bed with me beside him on the floor. He snored heavily all through the night. In my childish mind I imagined the snores to contain secrets to his art that I might learn if I swallowed them. So I kept my mouth open to receive his wisdom. When I awoke the next morning he was gone.

Through the days and months I kept wishing for his return but he never came back. However he left behind a clear indication that God's power existed in the world. From thenceforth onwards I tried to harness it the way Ram had done. I now believe this was my first inspiration for the extreme sports path I would later follow. God was talking to me but I was too young to hear his unaltered voice so he spoke through Ram the fire-eater.

Therefore it was no surprise that in my coma Ram came back to inspire me again. He told me I must not step off my path at the first setback. I must bounce back from injury to continue on my journey to the same place he had come from. So this is what I did.

My wife was troubled by my decision to go on after walking so close to expiry. She can be very stubborn but fully devoted to me, she has always praised the strength of my body and although we were not a love marriage we fit together quite comfortably.

'Not to worry,' I told her. 'I will make provisions for my safety henceforward. The first records were just a stepping stone, now I am a Guinness man I will approach things with a professional attitude. I will not repeat the mistakes of the past.'

And so I approached the job of selecting my next record with great vigour. I was in high spirits having finally received the certificate from Guinness after a nail-biting wait of nine months. Guinness World Record, 1,448 stomach sit-ups in one hour, Bibhuti Bhushan Nayak of Airoli, Navi Mumbai, India. After small celebration with nearest and dearest for unveiling of the certificate in pride of place on the wall of my home, I retired back to privacy to plan the next phase in my sports career.

You may be asking why there was such a large gap of two years between my previous record and the next. Unfortunately this is not an unusual sequence. It is with much regret that I convey to you the difficulties the dedicated sportsman of my country must endure: India may be booming in certain aspects but in less high-profile areas such as individual and extreme sports it remains poor. The government does not make adequate provision for people like me. We are not considered important despite the great works we do for our communities, and there is lack of facilities all round. This is reason why Indian athletes fare so poorly at the Olympics despite the huge numbers of children and young people across the length and breadth of the land who could make great strides if right encouragement was given. (I personally trained two of my students for Beijing 2008 in floor exercises, they made it to the nationals but failed to qualify for the big show. What I have observed over the years of training is there's lack of zeal and interest among the youngsters nowadays in the changing scenario, thanks to care-less government and distractions of cellphone and couch potato lifestyle.) Plus the sponsors do not recognise us. They give all their attention to the IPL and even to the inter-state cricket leagues which often display to empty stadiums.

Painful result is I must fund and organise my own events. It is always an uphill climb. In addition to raising the funds to stage an event – to hire a venue if one cannot be obtained by favour, to provide equipment necessary in the practice period as well as the event itself – there is also the cost of administrating any record attempt. An official record must be made of the event and sent along with any supporting materials to be ratified. This is a cheaper method than having an official adjudicator attending in person, as their presence attracts a hefty fee for travel and accom-modations expenses, etc. Really it is very expensive and time-consuming process which must be achieved around the demands of the daily life.

Many changes were arriving in my life during the two years between the last record and this day. Firstly I had missed my regular income during recovery period and it took many months to replenish my savings to their former level. I took on more responsibility at the newspaper, adding the culture beat to my sports coverage and freelancing for the *Hindustan Times* as well. Working night and day to recover lost earnings. Then God showed his kindness by presenting me with a new opportunity in the shape of no less a man than the managing director of Konkan Railway.

He had heard of my record feats from Rajesh Battacharjee, who at this time knew everybody of pull in my city and beyond. Being the first and only multiple World Record holder in Mumbai and state of Maharashtra it attracted him as he then called me up and offered me the job of technical director of fitness on contract basis to train their employees in martial arts, yoga and fitness. This was a plum role as Konkan Railway is very important project for my country, an 800km coastal rail system linking Mumbai to Mangalore, completed with great speed due to skills, courage and team spirit of best Indian engineers and fittingly redeemed in the fiftieth year of Independence.

However such a monumental development attracted many unfortunate problems. The innovation and beauty of the system and its connection to major cities made it a target for terrorist threat and liquor smugglers from Goa and adjoining area. Thus a need for professionals of the highest order to keep security of the line, ensure passengers' safety, keep a tab on train ticket examiners and antisocial elements on train duty.

'It will be my honour to take the job,' I conveyed to the managing director. 'I will whip your men into tip-top shape for the national interest.'

First batch of trainees lined up one week later in stockyard of Thane train station and very keen to be put through their paces. Many different skill levels but united in their desire to serve their country with life-giving dedication. What a proud moment for me to be overlooking their meeting with destiny. In following months and years I would take weekly sessions here and at various stations between Mumbai and Mangalore such as Goa, Karwar, Ratnagiri, Chiplun, under bright sun and pouring rain, listening with joy to the combined sound of one hundred-plus men honing the techniques which would protect them and make the railway a beautiful experience for every citizen. It was also here that I hit upon the idea of pulling a locomotive with my hair but this proved to be impossible despite many full-blooded attempts.

I was responsible for training over one thousand employees in martial arts from 2002 to 2008, till my last date of job. Out of these, twelve were given black belts after five years of vigorous training. They were inducted in a newly constituted wing in Konkan Railway on the lines of national security guards who provide security to Prime Minister, President and other VVIPs in India. Konkan Railway was immensely benefited from their service as honest officers. It fills me with tremendous feeling of satisfaction when I introspect on the role I played in keeping my area of the country free from assassins and other bandits.

During this period Rajesh Battacharjee was working tirelessly to publicise my name to all corners of my city. With help of Vijay Five he arranged interviews with *Mumbai Mirror*, *Twin City Times* and my prestigious employers at *Times of India*, covering my meteoric rise from unknown status to multiple World Record holder. All this hard work paid off when the invitation arrived from

Australian-based AXN channel, who are the world's finest extreme sports specialist, to take part in unique upcoming event.

In fact the conditions were unusual as it was mass event with 7,500 fitness freaks from all over the world all taking part at the same time but in different locations globally. Competitive and entertainment element across many different disciplines for enjoyment of the worldwide audience, with only one dozen events titled to be World Record attempts. Mumbai segment to be held at the Grant Medical Hall on Marine Drive, a venue with great history, where many fine scholars have studied and a large number of weddings are held for the top members of Mumbai society. The scale of the opportunity could not be underestimated and the need to make up for lost time was keenly felt. Boldness came calling and I decided to go for two records on same occasion.

In keeping with the extreme nature of my speciality I chose two records of particular challenge. Both had remained unbroken for many years. The backhand push-up is an unpopular technique because it is very difficult to perform and the possibility of sustaining injury is very high due to the fragility of the area in question when put under stress. It is not usual to bear the full weight of the body on the wrists, and I broke the wrist of my left hand a fortnight prior to the event in the process of preparation (in fact I am yet to recover from the injury since 2001 as the bone has come out from its original place, but this does not cause me any undue impediment to daily functions). The Guinness people were very accommodating to my unfortunate setback and gave me special permission to use a wristband for the event – the question of my failing to go through with the attempt did not emerge even for one moment, and any pain I felt from the affected area in the build-up became extra fuel to spur me on to a success.

The grand venue was a full house and a special stage was erected for the event. The television cameras all around plus large contingent of local and national press to capture the drama. Students, friends and colleagues squeezed into the hall and swelling the grounds outside for my first test under spotlight of television broadcast. As this was mass event under global banner an AXN representative was on hand to adjudicate and announce my success in timely manner. Evidence would be submitted to Guinness for ratification after the filming. 'One hundred and thirty-three! New world record, Bibhuti Bhushan Nayak of Navi Mumbai!' This was fine as I had shattered the previous record of only one hundred and sixteen. My fellow fitness freaks interrupted their own preparations to greet the announcement with generous applause. This was an inspiring moment which gave me an extra boost to press on to my next attempt.

The record-breaking life is a solitary existence and the chance to mingle with like-minded fanatics is very uncommon: it is in triumphant times such as this that our connection is felt most strongly, and we may use the positive energy we share to stretch higher towards our individual goals. I am firm believer that the goodwill of others when blended with the desire of the almighty makes the most potent mix. When a person drinks from this source he truly becomes unbreakable. I am the living proof of this.

My wife however has no understanding of such things. Unfortunately she is unable to enjoy my achievements fully due to narrowness of mind and persistent worries for my safety. I believe it is this fear which took her over in run-up to the double record event and almost ended my career in unfortunate circumstances. Just a few days before I took a tumble in the kitchen which could have produced show-stopping injury. My wife had washed the floor but forgotten to tell me. Entering the kitchen unaware I slipped on the wet tiles and in the mishap wrenched my shoulder and hit my head on cupboard. This on top of injury already sustained to wrist. My wife was horrified when she saw me getting up from the floor. Only grace of God and my supreme reflexes prevented more serious accident. Her worrying had made her forget to convey important detail and this is a timely reminder of the damage that may follow. This is why I do not allow undue worry to enter my mind and build a trap there.

With time only for brief meditation period it was on to the second record attempt of the day. I performed a final stretching, removed my trousers and climbed back onto the stage where a seat had been constructed for me from iceblocks covered with a towel to prevent any numbing effect from entering my groin area. My student Vijay Four accompanied me to deliver the fateful blow (Gopal Dutta was disappointed that I had not given him the nod due to his ongoing battle with enlarged tumour, but he swallowed his pride to attend at front of stage, dressed in his customary bandhgala for appearance in spotlight).

We had practised for many hours the correct speed and trajectory for a perfect swing and were confident that the slabs would be broken in the single action required to satisfy the record limits.

I took my seat and maintained a steady breathing while Vijay Four placed the three concrete slabs, each weighing 18kg, in a layered formation between my legs.

Here you may be asking why the Guinness people would allow such a dangerous event when they had refused to recognise my similar achievement of being kicked in the groin repeatedly. Really there is nothing to it: a record of two slabs already existed, and when I enquired of their support for this activity they were happy to confirm that as the concrete slabs would absorb most of the energy from the hammer's impact before it reached my groin the risk was considered acceptable.

As luck would have it I was able to secure a supply of slabs of the right dimensions on which to perfect my technique. My student Mehtab was construction foreman and he provided me with quantity of used slabs for my heart's content. Only expense incurred was the sledgehammer, and he advised on the right selection. Vijay Four made himself available to my needs and over many happy evenings in the yard below my apartment we hit upon the ideal method. The attraction proved so popular that I had to decline several kind offers from neighbours keen to lend a hand. Therefore I was quite comfortable when the moment came to put my practice into full effect. Needless to say, the outcome was as expected. The three slabs were broken with no difficulty, Vijay Four making a perfect swing on first attempt. Storm of praise greeting me when I lifted the broken pieces to confirm my success.

The enjoyment was felt across the world. I must say that this is a Guinness history, as I broke these two records within a span of ten minutes, a feat that had never been achieved before or since. But the main thing was this: I had proved that I could overcome major injury and return stronger than ever. This was all the confirmation I needed to march on with extra confidence through every obstacle which may lie ahead.

It is here that my story reaches a strange turning point. The attention I received nationwide after the AXN event introduced many shocking elements into my life for the first time. Think about it: one day you are a freelancer in Navi Mumbai, living a simple life with your wife and young son, doing your work so that you may have your two square meals per day and a roof over your head.

You practise your martial arts and teach others the skills you have learned for their wellbeing and successful spirit. You follow your record-breaking journey alongside your daily trials because the almighty has planted the dream in you. It is a dream which you share with the common man and for no selfish motive. You do not seek money or fame, only to inspire the world through simple actions of duty and suffering. Your only reward is to know that you walked the path laid down for you from beginning to end.

But no man can be sure enough of his path until temptation blocks his way, and my temptations came all together like troop of monkeys to my door. If I welcome them or turn them away, this will decide the ending of my journey in darkness or light.

Thank you.

Having fixed the radio Harshad had turned his attention to the portable TV that had sat silent on the counter since my arrival. He wanted all lines of communication open before the rains came. His clumsy-looking hands were calmed into surgical precision by the importance of the task. He snapped a part into place on the circuit board and the LCD screen jumped to bold black. He took a blind sip from his glass in celebration.

'Now we are back in business,' he purred. 'A new inverter is all it needed.'

He replaced the TV's cover and found a channel. More on the Mangalore plane crash. The news anchors' suits were shiny and out of date and their producers had added Hollywood strings to the location footage and pressed the slo-mo button to keep the viewers interested. Wailing survivors tore their hair out and banged their fists on the ground, trying to dig themselves down to the centre of the earth where their lost ones were waiting for them.

I checked on the mural in passing. The snake was finished and the figure of Harshad wore slip-on shoes. Laces were too fiddly to paint.

The old man was sleeping soundly, curled up on his tarpaulin. His army of gods stood guard over him, watchful for whatever dreams might leak out from the many holes in his head. I stepped round him and carried on walking towards the spot he always looked for when he was awake.

Bibhuti had given me a day off to heal. He had reports to type up and I was craving a rest from voices that demanded answers of me. India for the unassimilated was too many people and no time alone.

Airoli's main strip was all falling-down food places and spilling-out tat shops, once bright colours faded from the sun and savaged by the dust kicked up from the dirt pavement. Men in shirtsleeves lined up at the tap on the corner to wet their handkerchiefs and wipe the sweat from their necks. I went into a bazaar that sold cartwheels and moulded plastic tricycles hung from the ceiling by wires. I bought a beginner's football for Jolly Boy that I hoped would entice him away from racquet sports.

The shopkeeper asked me if I was here on vacation. I told him no, I was here to help someone break a world record. I was going to hit him with a baseball bat until it broke. I was going to keep doing that until we ran out of bats.

He knew all about Bibhuti and he suspected it couldn't be done. He wished us good luck all the same.

I crossed the road frogways between the buzzing scooters and the auto rickshaws dangling legs and trails of headscarves and bright flowing skirts. I went to the station to be quiet and to watch the trains coming in. I sat on the platform floor, hugging the football to my chest and revelling in my loneliness.

The trains weren't steam-powered like I'd imagined them to be. Still they spoke of a time when things were simple and built to a looser standard. They came in slowly with people hanging out of the open doors, jumping off before they'd stopped with a careless heave, as if they'd been pushed from behind by something big and invisible. Their god of the day was an impatient one who wanted them all out in the open where they could be counted and assigned their latest portions of luck. Behind each arriving train a gang of stealthy vagrants would creep in, crawling out from the plywood foxholes at the side of the tracks. Men my age, sometimes a young boy or two in tow, dust still in their hair from the last inbound trip. All crouching and bent with their bags of turning fruit. When they got up close they'd spray out like wings and ease on board just as the train was pulling out again, swarming the carriages in the hope of unloading their bananas on the drowsy general bogies.

It was cool and dark under the terminal roof. I could be anyone and I didn't need a reason to be there. I could just sit and watch the trains come and go and the people they carried, brown faces all poised and shiny with the places they had to be. The waiting men shuffled in cocky circles round the edge of the platform, spitting on the tracks with unhurried finesse. I dozed off. The new weight of my obligation pulling me comfortably down, I felt myself spread out like a burn and I was gone.

I woke up to a hand tugging at my sleeve. The football slipped out of my hands and I reached out and grabbed it before it could roll away. A boy's hairless genitals were hovering in my eyeline, close enough that I could have lifted my hand and jingled them like bells. He had Tom and Jerry colouring books to sell. His friend was naked too and she held out her hand to me. In her palm was a chick, newly hatched and chirping for its mother.

I could have either of these things for one dollar.

They looked at me with meagre hope.

'Please, sir,' the boy said. 'Only one dollar. You buy.'

I tucked the football under my arm and dug some rupees out of my pocket. I handed them to the boy, keeping my arm straight so he had to step away to accept them, relieving me of my proximity to his trembling bits and pieces. He gave me a colouring book. It came with a packet of felt-tip pens in a small rainbow of colours.

The girl lunged at me with the chick. I told her gently that I couldn't take him. I had nowhere to keep him. Her face fell. I gave her some money.

'For his food,' I said. 'You have to look after him. What's his name?'

A blank stare. She didn't understand. I longed to tell them all about Neil Armstrong and how he'd sprinkled stardust over my impressionable years. But it would have meant nothing to them.

'Call him Oscar. That's a good name. I had a bird called Oscar once. He was a good bird.'

The girl squeezed the chick and it let out a screech. I gave her an instructive look and she loosened her grip.

'That's settled, then. Oscar. Make sure you give him plenty of worms.'

They tilted their heads in a show of comprehension.

One of the spitting men came and kicked out at the children. Maybe he thought he was doing me a favour. They ran away, tumbling like spilled matches down the stairs into the darkness of the terminal. I wanted to have a go at the man for his unkindness but I couldn't get the words out. Having children of my own would have made me braver, I thought, and my spinelessness came to me all at once like a visitation from a world beyond my reach. I went back to the hotel to sleep it off.

Ellen grew heavy before I did and I just watched it happen. I should have said something but I didn't want to make her feel bad. She went from being as light as air to slow and grudging. She stopped dancing and took up bingo instead, so she wouldn't have to think about the body that had failed her, she could hide behind a table and concentrate on the numbers. She filled herself with small complaints to close the hole the hysterectomy had left. Everything became a trial and a mockery, life was too high-stakes to laugh it off and the only compensations came in low-denomination wins and short-haul getaways on the Provident book. I think she wanted to stay stuck to a moment of loss. I think she preferred being there to being with me. Staying hopeful took too much out of her and I just reminded her of the son she'd promised me over nights of careless wish-making. I kept out of the way as much as I could, took to working longer and driving further down the back roads to see where they led and what might be going on in the fields before all the horses disappeared and the scrapyards took over.

It's the weight that age puts on that made us indifferent to our blessings the way a failing eye becomes indifferent to the changing colour of the day as it passes. It's the weight of unsurprising years that killed us. She gave away the small clothes and found new uses for the baby milk cupboard, put a record player where the rocking horse would have gone and buried herself in Johnny Kidd and Eddie Cochran. I tried to make up for every missing thing with softness and undaunted desire, but you can't draw blood from an arm made of stone. I grew heavy too, by the sky pressing down on me. If I'd believed in you then I would have said it was your hand pressing down. With you to blame I could have been defiant. Instead I accepted the fate of people in trouble. I told Ellen when she needed to hear it that I was happy to be hers and I did my breathing outside. I went out into the world and made myself reliable. The days were to be slipped through like ink through paper and we had each other to come home to. We were swans on a lake, moving alongside each other undemanding and courteous, never turning our heads from the slow approaching storm.

One time I saw her in town. I was on my way to a job, to walk someone through a house they couldn't afford to buy and tell them all the things about it that were a perfect fit for them. The space and the light and the features. Always play up the features. Ceiling roses and mixer taps, bare floorboards and wall tiles that had survived the wars and the purges that razed the pie and mash shops and re-zoned them into nail bars. I was stopped at the lights and there she was, across the road looking in the window of a toy shop. I could tell it was her from the stoop of her back and a sadness came over me, a sense that I'd never known her and could never make her happy again. With the windscreen glass between us and the traffic streaming past we were very separate and each of us very alone. All I could feel for her was pity, that the world she walked through when she was without me should be so full of hurts and that I could do nothing to protect her from them. How lost she looked, out on the street surrounded by strangers, her shopping bag hung on the crook of her arm and her head still and tilted to the window display where wind-up carousels and snowglobes were ranged in so many varieties that each one seemed like a thoughtless reproduction of the last and the next.

When the lights changed I made a sharp left and parked up on the kerb opposite to watch her. I could see her face from there and my heart stopped when I realised that it wasn't sad at all. She was smiling to herself and her eyes were girlish and dancing. Her movements were slow and unlaboured like the slide of water over smooth stones as she leaned towards the window, and I saw that her slowness now was a different thing to the slowness she trod through the house, it was something willed, meant to capture time and make it useful to her for reliving a moment of wonder. She stopped, drew herself in and was still. She'd found a favourite. I saw the wonder on her face and knew that it didn't come from me. I couldn't share it or take credit for it and this hurt deep in the part of me that still believed she was mine to hold or to lose or that my privilege lay in choosing the things she found pleasure in.

I drove off before she could spot me, my mind racing with anger and longing. It felt as though I'd caught her in the act of cheating on me. I wanted to ask her what she'd found that could make her smile when she'd used up all her smiles for me. I wanted to know how I'd come to be so unimportant.

At home that night we were the same people we'd always been. Nothing had changed. No mention was made of where she'd gone or what I'd seen. It became just another thing that went unsaid, a spiteless secret to add to the pile that grew around our feet. I took a perverse comfort in being right. Her life and mine were two separate things and we'd chosen quite reasonably to ask no further questions of them.

14

Bibhuti sleeps and Ellen snaps at me when she asks for my help. I take her to the staff bathroom to shower and wash her hair, her stick clicking resentfully down the bright corridors and her arm in mine just one more measure against gravity. She lets me in with her to lift her clothes off over shoulders too stiff to obey her commands. I wipe the sweat from her back with polite imprecision. Revealing her body to me is a necessity she performs without relish. Her body has taunted her ever since illness slumped and slackened it and my remarks on its residual beauty have always fallen on deaf ears. She's the thing you made for me and I want nothing more than to disappear into her, to be held and sucked in and finally absorbed, but the water runs cold and she cringes and stumbles backwards and it takes all my strength to keep her upright. The feel of her soft against my stomach brings on a nudging that stops her breath. I wait a moment for an invitation that doesn't come and I pull away. I whisper sorry and wrap the towel round her.

I want to ask her why we stopped trying to impress each other but it sounds like such a childish question. It means the world and it wouldn't change a thing.

I look down at her feet all misshapen from the diabetes and ashamed of the baby steps they have to take to keep her from falling and I remember how once the world was new to her and so was I. I want her to have what I had in India, a taste of something larger than life. I want her to have always stayed the same as the first time I saw her.

I kneel down and dry her feet where she stands holding on to the sink. I'm very careful. I don't look up. When I spread her toes and ply the towel between them it should tickle but she's numb in her extremities. That she feels so little of the world around her strikes me as the saddest thing, and I tell her my crying is in reaction to the ammonia in the floor cleaner they use here.

A nurse follows us back to the room with a needle for Bibhuti and a pot of kheer for Jolly Boy, stolen in kindness from the lunchtime trays. He picks out the pistachios and gives them to me. He knows I like them. We all hold our breaths while the nurse refreshes Bibhuti's drugs. The old line when she removes it weeps bright red blood and we've all agreed to take this as a strong sign of life. We should only start to worry if the blood dries up.

Bibhuti breathes loud and steady, unhurting in sleep. The nurse stabs at his hand in lining up the new needle and beads of fresh blood rise on his skin. I feel it as an outrage. No one else will say it so I do.

'Can you be careful, you're hurting him.'

I hear anger in my voice and I'm not surprised by it. If anyone hurts him they'll answer for it.

No one mentioned the blood. I went through the whole day stained by it and no one had had the decency to tell me. In the office they grumbled and clicked their mice like nothing was different. I stalled at another red light, no one sounded their horn or flashed me to clue me in. I showed a couple round a house and the man's eyes skimmed over me like I was a body misplaced and found again in the wrong shoes, the woman whispered something to him on the way out that I'd taken for horseplay and made no move to enlighten me. The birds didn't change their tune.

I came home from work and Ellen jumped out of her skin. She took me to the mirror so I could see for myself. My neck was covered in blood. A thick vivid band of it spread from my ear to my collar.

I couldn't tell her how it had gotten there. I wasn't even sure it was mine until I felt it. Then I found the gash. I retraced my steps and decided I must have cut myself shaving in the morning and not noticed. The blood had leaked, unchecked, and dried over the day. I'd been walking around with it, defaced, and no one had said anything. No one had asked if I was alright, everyone too wrapped up in themselves. And I hadn't had much reason lately to look at myself in the mirror.

Ellen cleaned me up. Her fingers on me drew out goosebumps. I held her to me as she dabbed at the wound, pulled myself in to the softness around her middle. I felt an intoxicating pity for her and her for me.

'What did you do to yourself?'

'I know,' I said. 'I'm silly.'

We were sexless and hypothetical. Children playing war wounds, finding intimacy in skinned knees and bee stings.

Later on I sat in front of the TV and pushed some meat around my plate. I was shaken and fired up for a killing. I watched a crocodile eat an ox because the ox was too slow crossing the river. There was no urgency there. I sided with the predators.

I changed channels and there was Bibhuti.

He was stripped down to his underpants and straddling three slabs of concrete. He was sleek and fearless and he didn't flinch when the sledgehammer came down. I watched him take the hit. I heard the crack of concrete and felt the release when the fragments fell away. Someone lifted up the pieces to show that they were broken.

The studio audience applauded the footage. They were shown it again in slow motion and they applauded even harder. There was laughing too but it was the nervous laughter of people who'd just witnessed a miracle and didn't know how to greet it.

'Look at this guy, he's brilliant,' I said to Ellen when she came in from the kitchen. 'Look how calm he is. He doesn't give a shit.'

'He's mental. They're laughing at him.'

'They're idiots, they don't understand.' I was lost in admiration. I couldn't put my finger on it but there was something about him that triggered the same nerve in me that fired when I first saw George Best cut a shaky defence to ribbons. It left me bewildered and short of breath. It plucked at my manhood and incited my sense of the magnificent. Ellen didn't get it. She dunked a biscuit in her tea, swore when the biscuit broke in half and fell in.

Bibhuti's face was unmoved, his body unmarked. He'd bargained with death and come out on top. He acknowledged this without surprise or ceremony. That's what impressed me the most. He'd known all along that he was the stronger one. He'd always believed in it as firmly as the ground beneath his feet.

I wanted what he had. He shimmered and crackled and the world bent to his will.

They lifted him up on their shoulders and offered him to their gods but their gods felt unqualified to take him. He looked into the camera. He was looking right at me.

He made a dare.

That's what it was, pure and simple. He dared me to forget the blood on my neck and my oxen caution and find in myself something unassailable. I sat up in my chair, a strange electricity running through me of decisions made that would change the way my life would turn out. I resolved to find out as much about him as I could, to steal his secrets and make armour out of them.

15

I woke up under floodlights and a sky of unholy noise. Someone hit a four and a celebration jingle thundered around the near-empty stadium. The small pocket of diehards in the terrace below us blew their plastic trumpets and banged their drums. They prodded their giant foam fingers skyward. They weren't fooling anybody. There were more people on the pitch than in the stands.

'It should not be like this,' Bibhuti grumbled, brushing his moustache with restless fingers. 'Nobody is interested in the state league. It costs more to run the generator to light the stadium than the teams can repay from ticket sales. If there was not a sponsorship agreement in place the entire league would shut down.'

'Are those real cheerleaders?' I asked.

The girls standing pitchside were glittered up to the nines, shimmering semi-precious behind the boundary line. I could tell from up here that they were as bored as me. Their pompoms were heaped on the grass like sleeping emus.

'There is a halftime show, with dancing and music. The league introduced these measures to attract the audience. It has received a mixed response.'

A man with a clipboard wandered over from the pavilion and gave the girls a motivational talking-to. The girls shook themselves into formation and ran through a game rehearsal of their routine. The pot-bellied cameraman resolutely ignored their bouncing, kept his lens pointed at the players.

Bibhuti took a reading of the score from the Jumbotron and jotted it down in his notebook.

Behind us Jolly Boy pretended to be imprisoned in the corporate box. He made a panicked face against the window, pasted a ghostly wet kiss onto the glass. It magically evaporated in the conditioned air.

The phone had woken me up from another dream about Oscar. This time I was chasing him through our old house, room by room. He was always just too far ahead of me to see. I could still hear his wings beating when I picked up the phone. Bibhuti had an assignment, a report for a cricket match at the new stadium in Navi Mumbai. He had open access, having set a record there a couple of years ago. A mile of cartwheels on the knuckles of one hand. He wanted to show me the scene of his triumph. He thought it would inspire me. I'd reached for the fresh bottle by the bed and taken a drink to steady myself. I'd bought mints to mask the smell of booze on my breath.

The players went through the motions, made lethargic by the world's inattention. Their paltry tactical chatter echoed eerily around the bowl of the stadium. The bowler threw the ball. The batsman hit it back to him and stayed where he was. Everybody had decided to embrace self-loathing in the arc of the clean white light.

The diehards' drums tapped out a fading heartbeat. They raised their foam fingers in stubborn salute to the men slowly dying down on the pitch below.

I was dying more slowly than I'd bargained for. Bibhuti was still untouched by my bat and my time was running out. You weren't with me then, to encourage me to forbearance and to console me with the memories of other spectacles I'd witnessed. I was on my own with my pain.

It was happening. A pain I hadn't felt before. A slowing down and a growing sense of burden, a breath now aware of its own importance. The world was closing in on me. I was being hunted. Anger itched through my veins, scratched my eyes like the branches of every tree I'd never climbed. The hurt pinned me to the plastic seat, I couldn't get away from it. I was going to die and it wasn't ten years away, it was close enough to be now. Close enough that I could see myself crying out and falling.

Something needless had to be done while I could still feel it.

I climbed over Bibhuti and onto the steps. The whisky swilled around my belly and made me clumsy as I started walking. The fans on the terrace below opened their arms to welcome me. When I wobbled, big soft hands came out to break my fall. I was righted and an expectation rippled through them that I might join in their dance. I swatted them away. My eyes were on the pitch and the travesty unfolding there, of men too lazy and content to run when death was chasing them.

There was a deafening blast from the speakers. Another four and the ball was good. The batsman scratched himself and waited to be adored.

I felt a rush of cold air and turned to see the door to the corporate box slide shut. Jolly Boy was scurrying down to join me. We found in each other's eyes confirmation of our wildness, and we took the steps two at a time. We streamed down the terraces to pitchside. I took off my shirt as I made level ground.

The cheerleaders halted their practice to clear a path for us. They were all very beautiful and they scowled piously as I trampled through their sacred ground. The man with the clipboard lifted his walkie-talkie to his mouth, poised to call a posse.

'You cannot be here,' he said.

'I'm with Bibhuti,' I said. 'I'm gonna be a record breaker.'

Bibhuti came to face me down. There was panic in his eyes. He tried to hand me my shirt. I wouldn't take it. There was petulant music in me and it wouldn't be doused. I tap-danced around the cheerleaders and inched to the boundary line. I bent to take off my shoes and socks. I rolled up my trousers to make shorts. My pale shins glowed like milk bottles in the night. I tickled my toes on the pristine grass.

The deep purple of Ellen's nail polish made a pleasing contrast against the green. I remembered the night before, painting my toenails in a drunken moment of abandonment. It had been harder than I'd predicted and I'd gone over the lines. There was no shame in it. Trendspotting, the colour was called. I felt a sharp pang of love for Ellen, she who'd briefly stolen me from loneliness.

'I'm gonna be a record breaker,' I told the cameraman in passing.

He tilted his head in a gesture of understanding and carried on with his work.

I jumped on to the outfield and tested the spring in the turf. Reckless blood chimed in my ears, drowning out Bibhuti's protests against my sudden lunacy.

'We're running out of time,' I told him by way of explanation.

The night fell like hair over my bare skin. To be close to naked under floodlights was to be dancing bashfully with my younger self.

Jolly Boy drifted to my side. He looked up at me, his eyes fearful with questions.

'Are you coming?' I asked him.

He shook his head.

A wicket fell with a crack and the speakers erupted. The cricketers were awoken and in the mess of high-fiving I grabbed my chance and ran. I picked out an advertising board on the far side of the pitch and sprinted for it. I tore through the outfield, the hot air chasing me down.

Within moments I was out of breath and everything hurt and I slowed to a trot.

I heard footfall gaining on me and Jolly Boy was at my shoulder. His face was split by a mad grin. Behind us Bibhuti was quicksanded at the boundary line. Clipboard tripped over a pompom and went flying.

We skimmed the wicket, worming between the startled fielders. They stepped graciously out of our way.

Ourselves as giants flashed up on the big screen and we stopped to take it in. The spectacle of it left us breathless and broken free of time. I used the image on the screen to locate the camera and waved to it. I did a little jig for the cable subscribers. I was brave and unreachable, I'd crossed over like the ping-pong monks to a place of serenity. A place where no one could touch me.

'Uncle, over there.' Jolly Boy pointed at the trio of security guards who were running for us. I felt all my holes clamp shut.

One of the batsmen sauntered over and asked what I was doing.

'It's all a waste of time,' I told him tenderly. 'No one's even watching.'

'You are a waste of time,' he said, and he kicked my legs from under me. I fell to the ground. He spat on the grass near my feet. He smirked at my painted toenails. Security arrived in a murderous clatter of limbs and I curled myself into a ball and waited for the sky to shatter.

I watched my replay while Bibhuti bartered for my freedom. I looked quite persuasive blown up out of all proportion.

'We look very good,' Jolly Boy said.

'We do. You're famous now.'

Bibhuti traded my life for his access all areas pass. He made a grim ceremony of handing it over. His eyes when they turned on me were desolate. My heart flooded with regret.

'This is very unfortunate,' he pouted. 'I had hoped perhaps to stage our record attempt here but that is not possible now. I am very disappointed.'

I told him I was sorry. But I hadn't even picked up a bat yet, he wouldn't let me do what I'd come here for. I didn't have for ever.

'All in good time. We must prepare in the right way to ensure success.'

My frustration spilled out in a feeble croon. 'You don't get it. There is no time.'

I made a quick estimate of the effect a confession might have on him and the agreement we'd made. Whether it would be the fire that would hurry us on to our shared destiny, or the foam that would suffocate the plans we'd made. He had to believe I was strong enough to break him. He had to share responsibility for the condition of my soul when I gave it to the darkness for inspection.

I told him I had cancer. The word tasted like toffee in my mouth, thick and childish.

Bibhuti stroked his moustache for a minute or two. Then he promised to cure me. There was no doubt in his mind that he could.

16

The bellyaches came a couple of months after I first saw Bibhuti on TV. They started to bother me and they didn't go away. Movements were getting harder and my energy was gone. I knew what it was before I was told. I'd been feeling like the end of something was coming for years but it had been coming so slowly that I could call it my imagination if I wanted to. The scans made it all real. They gave me a reason to be feeling the way I'd been feeling that wasn't just grumbling at life's failing to live up to expectations. My expectations didn't come into it. It was a real thing, a disease. It was something I'd done to myself.

The consultant showed me a picture of the tumour. It looked like an alien being, something out of science fiction. She used a technical name, I can't remember what it was. It reminded me of the word they'd used when Ellen wouldn't stop bleeding: ectopic. I wondered if it had hurt her like this hurt me, the same kind of way in the same kind of place. Probably everyone's pain feels different, something they alone can feel. Ellen wasn't with me, I'd gone on my own. I didn't want to be responsible for another disappointment. I'd told her nothing, hidden the letter with its hospital stamp. She had enough to worry about.

They wanted to open me up and cut a section of my bowel out, stitch the two new ends back together again.

Wasn't it complicated down there? Would I be walking funny for the rest of my life?

She promised they'd put me back the way I'd always been. Chemo to mop up any traces that were left and more cameras up the bum to check it hadn't come back. Five years of monitoring and optimism. She wanted to give me another twenty years.

I watched the creases round her eyes ripple as she spoke and wondered if all the bad news she carried around with her meant she couldn't enjoy slapstick anymore. I thought about sliding off my chair to test her laughter reflex but I couldn't figure out a way to do it that wouldn't look premeditated.

There was outrage and at first it was directed at fate. Then it turned back in on me. I heard the rotten cells racing around inside. They made a high-pitched whizzing sound and they were hell-bent on killing me. I couldn't blame them. I'd done everything wrong and the payback was a fair one. It was my fault for all the meat I'd eaten and for going too slow. The animals were getting their revenge on me and I was being taught a lesson for my lethargy, for my lack of gumption. Another twenty years sounded like a bad joke. I didn't know what I'd do with them. I was very tired.

I asked the consultant what would happen if I didn't have the op. How much time would I have and when would it start hurting. She gave me her best guess.

It's not that I wanted to die particularly. I just didn't think I had the fight in me. I was too old and it was too big a thing to go through. It would be too hard. Ellen would have to look after me and that wouldn't be fair. I was supposed to look after her. I thanked the consultant for everything and told her I'd take my chances.

The cleaner was blocking the corridor with her bucket. I couldn't wait for her so I took a run up and jumped it. For the split second I was airborne I still hoped a mistake had been made. When I landed again the hope was gone. The mercenary cells were raging. It felt like the years I'd been alive were all in my head. As if I hadn't really lived them, just been watching them on TV. Now the programme was finished I could hardly remember what it was about. All I could see was Bibhuti taking the sledgehammer, choosing not to crumble. Standing up and smiling shyly for the cameras. He knew how to hold himself when death came marching at him. He knew it even if I didn't.

The birds were singing too loudly for the time of day. The light was brighter and I smelled freshly cut grass. I dipped my foot in a puddle and pasted my shoeprint down on the tarmac in front of the car so I could watch it dissolve while I worked out the best way to leave so that Ellen wouldn't blame me.

I stopped off for fish and chips on the way home. The boy who served me was wearing an earring in the shape of a skull. I told him to go to Niagara Falls if he ever got the chance. He said he would but it lacked the substance of a genuine promise. Nobody ever took me seriously.

Ellen was out when I got back, buying things at the market to turn into my dinner. I looked through her drawers and found nothing incriminating. No proof that she'd had an affair, no bundled letters or pictures of strange men. Just the special knickers she used to wear sometimes, balled up at the back under her everyday pairs. I took them out and held them. There were pulls in the satin and the lace was coming away at the trim. I pretended I knew what it meant to be a woman. I felt her hope and her fear and I was in awe of her, of the kindness she showed in reaching for a quiet inelegant man when there must have been other better handholds out there in the world.

Her fish and chips went cold but she ate them anyway, happy not to have to cook. That night in bed when the darkness hid me I brought up the dream she'd had, the one I'd tried to make true. The one that proved I was once as kind and honourable as her.

'Do you remember?' I said. 'The one about the piano?'

She didn't say anything for a while, and the silence was stifling. I lay beside her in the dark and wished I could undo all the moments when she'd felt like a stranger to me.

'I was hoping you'd forgotten.'

'I'll never forget it. I'd rather die first.'

'Don't say that.'

I meant it.

She'd had a dream that she could play the piano. It felt real, more than any other dream she'd had. She'd woken up with the music still in her fingers. The feeling was so strong she'd been convinced something magical had happened, that somehow the capacity to play had been breathed into her while she'd been sleeping.

She'd pawed me awake to tell me. She went through it all while it was still fresh, and her eyes were sparkling. I breathed in early days asbestos and listened to her, enchanted. She could play. She was sure of it. It didn't matter that she'd never played a note before, the dream had changed all that. A miracle. She got up and went to the window and played the windowsill as if it was keys. She played the kitchen table the same way, and she knew she was putting her fingers in the right places, she could hear the music, flawless in her head. It felt true, as true as anything she'd known, and she had to find out for sure before it wore off. She had to see for herself if dreams could come true.

We skipped breakfast and drove to the nearest music shop, a cluttered vault on the high street with ukuleles hanging like fruits in the window. She told me on the way how she'd always wished she could play but she'd been scared of never being good enough, that her hands could never reproduce the sound inside her head. The dream was a gift from herself, a wonder that happens sometimes after a trauma or an injury or just because you want it and it's your turn.

'I know it sounds silly,' she said.

'No it's not,' I said with conviction. I believed in her right to dream the improbable. I felt it was the least anyone owes another person.

She was like a little girl wandering between the scuffed uprights, feeling nicotined horseteeth keys that other people before her had wrung music from without a second thought for their good fortune. She touched every one, thoughtful and slow, feeling for the perfect symmetry between her new gift and the instrument that would bear it out.

She found the one she was looking for, sat down, rested her fingers on the keyboard.

'What if it isn't true?' she said fearfully.

'You'll never know if you don't try. Just give it a go. What's the worst that could happen?'

Her expression answered for me. It said the worst that could happen would be the death of that part of herself that danced with its eyes closed. A loss I'd have to spend the rest of my life atoning for in acts of duty and diversionary bluster.

The sales assistant came over and I told him we were just looking. I shielded her from him while she took a breath, wriggled the wisdom into her fingers. She shaped them into a pattern that felt right. The movement on her lips might have been a prayer. Breathing fast she turned to me, young and hopeful, sweet-smelling of rain, and asked for luck.

'Luck,' I said.

She pressed her first key down with the little finger of her left hand. It made a sound that could easily become music. She pressed the next finger down. My heart was beating so fast I thought I might be dying of hope. One by one she pressed the keys down. The sounds they made individually rang true. She picked up her hands and moved them to a new configuration and with a final surge of fierce belief she brought them down.

'I don't know what I was thinking,' Ellen said, her voice gaunt in the darkness. 'I must have looked like a right idiot. You must have thought I'd lost it.'

'You were beautiful. You believed in something magical. Even if it was just for an hour out of the day, you believed it and so did I. It broke my heart when—'

'Don't. I don't want to think about it.'

It wasn't the music her dream had promised. It was just noise. She'd kept going, looking for the sweet spot, waiting for the moment when everything would click into place, but it didn't come.

It was just a dream like any other dream. It meant nothing.

I told her to keep trying, it might still happen, maybe there was just a delay in the signal between the heart and the hands, but it started to feel like a cruelty and I had to reach down and peel her fingers from the keys, as gently as I could.

'Fuck it,' she said.

'I know,' I said.

'It felt so real.'

'Dreams are funny. It's not your fault.'

She slowly closed the lid on the tactless keys, got up and walked out the door. She didn't cry, not on the way to the car when my arm around her was supposed to be a sandbag against her sadness. Not when we got home to a silent house. I filled the kettle with hard water and when I kissed her I could only feel what wasn't there. I had no means of making up for it so I lurched for levity with a clumsy joke.

'There's always the tambourine,' I said, and she laughed in spite of me. It was a Saturday and she went back to bed as if she had the flu. I wandered round the house like a stranger, opening cupboards to see what was inside and planning the best place to put a rocking horse. I heard her crying softly in the night and then it was done. We never talked about it again.

'What made you think of that?' Ellen asked.

I couldn't tell her. I couldn't say it was a parting gift, so when I left she'd know at least that she'd been understood. I couldn't say it was a breadcrumb she could follow, something that would lead directly to a comforting reminder of our common weakness for dreaming.

I said nothing, slid out of bed and went to make a cup of tea. Her aborted music followed me downstairs and Bibhuti danced behind my eyes. I saw him shining faultless and uninhibited on the TV screen, gliding through the pain barrier like a perfect arrow. I knew there was a message in him from a place beyond the idea of God, a message that I alone would see if I could crack him open. I knew it would invalidate death's claim on me and rewrite it a brave end to a life poorly lived.

I read the printout I'd made of his interview where he appealed for witnesses to a miracle he'd thought up in his own head.

Something beautiful, it was, a tragedy in the making that would sweeten the blood of whoever stood beside him for its duration.

I didn't need a dogged wife to feed me from a spoon and hold my hand when it got cold. I wanted to die on my feet in a place that was warm and didn't know my history.

Gopal Dutta was eighty-seven years old and when he did a jump-ing roundhouse kick he put five full feet between himself and the ground. He climbed the air like a ladder and made the world pause in quiet reflection. He landed without a sound.

The other students made nothing of the feat because to them it was expected and had lost its novelty. They paid no attention to him at all. Instead they focused on Bibhuti out front and centre, calling out his instructions with modest persistence. They all jumped and kicked and landed as one, starlings flocking in the shape of a bird. I watched Gopal Dutta. I looked for the springs welded into the soles of his feet. I looked for the breaks in the seams of the old man costume that might reveal the young boy hiding inside.

I couldn't find them. I fell asleep.

Jolly Boy woke me up with a tap on the shoulder. There was worry on his face. I reassured him, said that whenever I fell asleep I'd most likely wake up again. This arrangement would hold for the foreseeable.

Standing behind him were his father and Gopal Dutta, impa-tient to be introduced. The older man's legs were hairless in purple running shorts with gold trim and too much of his thighs was on show. A lurid man and one to be grudgingly admired. Bibhuti had told me on the way to class how he'd cured Gopal Dutta of cancer. I'd dismissed it as well-meaning fancy. But face to face it became immediately obvious that cancer had never stood a chance. Gopal Dutta wasn't prone as other men are to the quirks of disease. His tiny frame, now denied the freedom of the air and tethered ground-ward, stooped under the weight of a century's failed assassination attempts. I wondered how many dynasties he'd sired and if he'd thought about making a fitness video.

'He is my oldest student,' Bibhuti said. 'He received a tumour in his liver in 2001. I cured it with yoga and diet. Doctors declared that he could not survive two months but with my help the tumour disappeared and here he is nine years later in the flesh.'

'Bloody hell,' I said.

'This is not unusual. Before that I had a student with tubercu-losis. He was cured of the ailment in three months under my guid-ance with breathing exercises and positive thinking.'

'Breathing is everything,' Gopal Dutta said, and he shook my hand. His grip was strong and he tilted his head goatlike and peered into my eyes as if he might see the cancer there and by his stare petrify it into surrender.

The fearsome Kavita shrieked past us. Her foot speared for the head of her luckless sparring partner. Frozen, he accepted his fate with dignity.

Gopal Dutta spoke with confidence. 'If you do what Sir instructs you will defeat the cancer,' he said. 'I thought my time was over but he extended my span. This was nine years ago. His knowledge is from God, he has a direct link. Mostly it is the correct breathing. People do not breathe right and that is why they are dying. They think they know the right way but it is not as easy as that.

'I was pilot for Indian Airlines, I flew commercial jets for eight years. The lives of the passengers were in my hands. All this time I was not breathing correctly. It is a miracle that I did not crash. The crash in Mangalore was terrible, the news has stated weather was the factor but I believe it was down to incorrect breathing of the pilot. Everything stems from this. Now that I am breathing the right way I feel many years younger and I cannot make a mistake. I would like to fly again and have written to Air India to offer my services. They have not yet replied. I feel very young. You also will recover lost years under BB's guidance. I thank him every day.'

Gopal Dutta's eyes shone behind the dust motes dancing in the air around us. I looked down at his big toes as he rubbed them childishly against their neighbours. It provoked a strange feeling of loyalty. We were all children no matter how hard we tried to hide it.

'I know I haven't been breathing right,' I admitted. 'I'm doing better now. I'm trying my best.'

'There is no reason to give up hope,' Bibhuti said. 'If I can cure one man I can cure another, you and Gopal Dutta are not so different.'

I was made to stand still while Gopal Dutta demonstrated his vivacity by kicking the air a hair's breadth in front of my left eye. I felt my skin tingle as the air changed and when I chanced a look up he was above me, suspended as if from wires. He might have winked at me, I can't be sure. When he landed I was a believer.

Gopal Dutta wished me good luck and padded away, revealing the lower curve of his left buttock as he went. He picked up where he'd left off, making leaping roundhouse kicks for the pleasure of it, treating his observers to the illusion that the air was more amber than oxygen.

Later Bibhuti took me shopping. We'd decided, since I was going to survive, that I needed workout clothes of my own. Bibhuti wanted to show me the mall in Vashi where he'd broken the last of his records. A bicycle had been ridden over him twenty-three times in one minute to mark the mall's grand opening. He'd shared the bill with a man who threw knives at his infant son.

'The knives were not sharp,' Jolly Boy complained. 'I saw one hit him and there was not much blood. Real knives would make more.'

They carried on singing along to the radio, stopping only when Bibhuti had to swerve to avoid a pedestrian who'd taken on a battle of wills with the traffic at the interchange where Vashi's immodest towers rose from the dust like the ribs of excavated giants.

The commercial heart of Navi Mumbai. Home to the flat-pack call centres and the four-star hotels where the toppers of international business came to discuss in piped-in comfort the most efficient ways of sucking India's marrow from its bones. One of them was right next door to the mall. Hotel security was sweeping a car full of arriving guests. Their hands hovered over holstered sidearms. They checked the car's boot and ran a mirror along its undercarriage in search of explosives. When none were discovered they rolled back the blastproof barrier and waved the car through. Its passengers showed no signs of having been inconvenienced.

On the landscaped lawn outside the mall two holy men stood praying in barrels, submerged to the shoulders in symbolic water. They petitioned the sky to let loose its cooling rain and wake the world from its seasonal indolence.

People were lining up for a bodysearch outside Kentucky Fried Chicken.

Inside, Bibhuti and Jolly Boy stopped to marvel at the central atrium, fringed with common franchises and patrolled by a pair of bumfluff security guards whose main duty was to flutter their truncheons at the resting consumers perched on the lip of the fountain at its northern end until they took the hint and moved on. The fountain like their epaulettes was supposed to be admired from afar.

'This is where I achieved the record,' Bibhuti said. 'I was lying here. Two bicycles came from this side, where you see Costa Coffee, and one bicycle from this side. They rotated in sequence until the minute was up. They rode over my solar plexus area where I am holding most of my strength. Only once did my student Rohan miss the target. He went over my neck just above the collarbone. Luckily he was able to find his way across without falling. The collarbone was broken but Guinness allowed the record to stand. No specific area of the body was declared, the only requirement was that they travel over me individually and remain upright.

'Come, we will find you some nice sporting clothes. You are becoming a sportsman and you must have your own selection.'

He picked out the same clothes he wore and held my bag of money while I tried them on, sucking my belly in for the mirror. This would be me in my last days, abandoning my style to roam unfettered through the land that vanity forgot. The thought made me smile. Maybe I'd come to prize the comfort of sweatpants. Maybe through the routine Bibhuti had devised for me I'd blossom into beauty in time for the mortuary portraits.

We came out again into the sunlight glancing through clouds that were swollen now like malnourished bellies. The wind was rising and a small crowd had formed around the holy men in their barrels. A little girl tiptoed to the rim and stuck a flower in the older one's beard. Her father took a picture on his phone. The holy man resisted the temptation to smile.

The monsoon had just left Chennai, Bibhuti said. It would reach us in a week.

'Is the rain really that heavy? I've never been in a monsoon before.'

'Yes, it is very heavy. Every year many problems. Landslides and floods and people falling down the manholes. Every year the city is in a scramble to cover them before the rain arrives. Many times a drain lid is caving in or missing. People cannot see the dangers when the ground is beneath the water, they are falling in and becoming victimised. My advice is to watch your step very carefully.'

The children came running at us from nowhere. A tide of brown skin flecked with the white of chattering teeth. My wrists were worried by little grabbing hands, my toes trodden on. A rushing of volatile limbs and dancing private parts.

'Hello, sir, hello! You buy, one dollar!'

I recognised the drooping eyelid of the ringleader, the birth-mark smudge on the girl's hip. The kids from the train station. I felt giddy with relief that they'd survived the days since I'd last seen them.

They were still peddling their Tom and Jerry colouring books but there were no chicks to be seen. I asked the ringleader what had happened to Oscar.

'Soli eat,' the girl said. I guessed that Soli was the boy's name.

'You ate him?'

Soli tilted his head bashfully. There was no regret in him.

'But he was a baby,' I said.

'You buy,' he said, shoving the colouring book at me. 'One dollar.'

'I don't need another one,' I told him.

His face fell. He found it hard to accept that all my colouring needs could be so easily satisfied. When it became clear I wasn't buying he turned on his heels and ran, the girl chasing after him. They tested the brakes of the auto rickshaws as they dashed across the road and made the sweet lime seller jump when they spun past his cart.

I felt a dread of the coming rain. I kept it to myself.

The door flies open. Jolly Boy steps aside before I can stop him. I brace myself for violence. There are two policemen and behind them a camera crew tripping over themselves to catch me in repentant close-up. My only surprise is that they didn't come sooner. I've spent the last two days waiting on a lynching. One of the policemen shoves the camera away and the other makes a grab for me. A lathi swings at his hip and fennel seeds nestle in his moustache from a meal eaten in a hurry. No words are spoken. I'm led away. Ellen looks after me. I tell her not to worry.

Outside the crowd claws for me and is beaten back. I search for allies among the smoke of vengeance. The familiar faces I see are soured, mouths that once greeted me with fascination now spit at my feet.

Kavita makes a run for me and her father has to scoop her up before she can land a blow.

The door is slammed and the siren is deployed. We pick our way through a hail of fruit and fire fed from a communal pyre. I'm starving and in fear of my life. I nearly laugh. This is fame. I don't want it anymore.

The police station is a single-storey concrete shed on the outskirts of a residential district, simmering like an unexpired curse across the road from a scrap-metal kiosk where a fat man and his wife offer coconut water to a passing trade that doesn't look like it will ever turn up. The man scalps the coconuts with a blunt-looking machete and lines them up on the table to be forgotten about. His hopeless occupation must be a penance of some kind and I try not to think about the atrocities he must have committed to land himself in such demeaning shackles.

The constables walk me inside and take me to an office with no windows or cameras. Another policeman is waiting for me there, standing with his arms folded. He has the sullen poised demeanour of a weekend psychopath. He wishes me harm. The desire of it drips from him. He introduces himself as an inspector and tells me there have been some complaints. One of the constables closes the door and guards it.

I tell the Inspector I've got my passport and a valid visa. They're somewhere safe and close by, at the home of my friend. I can get them for him. I'm English. I'm above board.

'The friend who you are trying to kill two days ago?' he asks.

'It wasn't like that. I was helping him.'

'This is not the way it appeared to some of the witnesses. They have described it very differently.'

'Then they don't understand what we were doing,' I say. 'They don't know what Bibhuti's all about. I made him happy. He'll tell you the same thing when he wakes up.'

'If he wakes up,' the Inspector corrects.

'I know it looks bad. I was just doing what he asked me to do. We trained for it. It's what he does. Look him up, you'll see. He never ended up like this before.'

'He did not have you to assist him before. I am asking myself what is your desire to kill this man? Why is it so strong that you will come all this way to strike him down? Indians are killing each other every day. The Naxals are killing us. Pakistan is killing us. The rain is killing us. We do not need another method of killing Indians. You could perhaps restrict these habits to your own country. Or did you think nothing would happen here? Did you think my country would allow such a thing? We are all ignorant, yes? We will tolerate this? Is that what you thought?'

I remind him that I haven't killed anyone.

'It is only a matter of time,' he says. His daydreams hang on the air, of all the things he'll do to me when he gets the chance.

I ask for Jolly Boy. He'll speak for me. Someone has to speak for me before things get out of hand.

They make me wait in the corridor while someone fetches him. No one's in much of a hurry to put me out of my misery. An hour crawls by. The sounds of the outside bleed through the cracks in the walls. The crying of unseen living things. Birds mating on the satellite dishes and dogs furiously eating themselves. A crashing somewhere, cars trying to kill each other. Three men are brought in and put in the cell across the room from me. They're scabbed and chattering, bony limbs jangling against the walls. Their eyes dart to me for mediation. I give them a look that says I'm sorry but I can't help them. We're in the same boat.

'They robbed a tourist,' the Inspector tells me. 'Left him broken and tried to set him on fire. Perhaps I will let you join them. I am sure you will have something to talk about.'

The threat passes through me like thin soup. Death by their savage hands would be a leniency, right now. The stomach cramps are back and I'm sitting on razor blades. I listen to my vital organs winding down, the grinding of bare metal when the brake pad wears through. I try to picture Mum's face but I can't settle on it. I can't remember my favourite song. I hug myself around the middle to try and wring the pain out and wait for sleep to come around again.

They bring Jolly Boy in on his own. He rushes to me and grips my arm. The hairs on it shiver in the breeze he makes. I tell him not to be afraid. They take him away.

I warn them not to hurt him. I try and make it sound decisive.

When Jolly Boy comes back his eyes are red from crying and he stands taller. He's walked through fire and become a man. I look him over, searching for their infringements. He tells me he's okay. I take his shoulder but he worms away. He doesn't need my hand anymore. I'm free to go, for now.

We're driven back to the hospital. The constable on the passenger side curses me in the wing mirror, his gaze burning a hole in the place where my third eye would be if I were one of his gods.

The grounds are scarred by scorchmarks from the extinguished torches of Bibhuti's disciples. When they see me they light them again and take up a howling. The fruit comes pelting down on the car. Among the limes and pomegranates are boulders. One of them comes through the back window and showers my neck in glass. I drape myself over Jolly Boy to shield him.

Harshad and Amrita are in the first wave. They beat the car with their fists as it inches past. Amrita screams, her head thrown back and her mouth open wide. She stomps her feet, scaring up an earthquake. Paint scabs still adorn her elbows but they're from a different project, the sign she's given her father to carry reads 'Hang the Killer of Bibhuti Nayak'. It leans over his shoulder like a cross. For the first time he looks sober. I gave him a cause to pin his cleansing outrage on.

'I didn't kill him,' I shout at him. 'He's alive.'

Amrita spits at the window. I'm impressed by the volume. I watch it slip down the glass.

The monks are praying in a circle behind the welcoming party, their ping-pong table standing dormant. Among them is the boy who unravelled the string that blessed me. I move away from the spit so he can see me. Our eyes meet and he smiles. The smile tells me that everything will be alright. I'll meet my judgement honestly and my judgement will be fair. I can't ask for any more than that. My monk picks up a paddle and initiates another game.

We make for the entrance and the constables run us to the door. Other officers have arrived in our absence to keep the protesters from storming the building. We're pushed between them and birthed out into reception where the doctors greet our return with open hostility. They're fussing over stab wounds and furnace burns, rubbing ghee on the raw stumps of grinning amputees. They don't need the disruption my circus is causing. I head for the lift, pulling Jolly Boy with me.

I ask him what he said under interrogation.

'I told them the truth,' he says, as if the answer's an obvious one. 'I told them Baba wants you to hit him. You are his friend and you are helping him.'

'That is the truth.'

'I know.'

'He'll wake up soon. He's probably awake already. He'll be asking for you. He'll be wanting a mirror to check on his hair.'

The boy smiles timidly. Pain rips through my guts again and it's the least he deserves.

The reporter is sitting outside the room, a paper cup of coffee held tight in her hand. Her little knuckles are white and her cameraman's nowhere to be seen. Her eyes flash as we approach and she fumbles with her iPhone, cueing the video recorder for a global exclusive. I give her nothing, steer Jolly Boy into the room.

The women run to us in their individual fashions, Jolly Boy's mother the first out of the blocks. She takes hold of him roughly, pulls him as far away from me as the arrangement of the furniture allows. She checks him for bruises and tears and then she sits down and draws him into her, her arm curled like a rustler's rope around his waist.

Ellen hobbles to my side and asks me the same question with a raised eyebrow. I tell her we're both fine, they didn't touch us.

'I was worried sick,' she says.

'It wasn't that bad. They tried to scare me but they've got nothing on me. I've done nothing wrong. Jolly Boy was brilliant, he straightened the whole thing out. Everything's gonna be alright.'

His mother explodes. She shoves Jolly Boy aside and springs from her chair, takes her flip-flop off and slaps me hard across the cheek with it. It hurts.

'His name is Shubham,' she says quietly. 'I do not like you to call him Jolly Boy anymore.'

She sits down, slips the flip-flop back on and reels the boy in again. She smoothes his shirt down over his hips, looks up into his eyes as if she might find his father there, his spirit transplanted somehow from the body that lies broken in the bed beside her.

My ears are ringing and I want to go home now.

19

My first night in Bibhuti's house I didn't sleep a wink. I couldn't find a comfortable shape to fit his sofa and when I'd looked up and seen Bibhuti's outline hanging over me I'd thought he'd had a change of heart and had come to strangle me and steal my money. It was either very late or very early and my paranoia had been fermenting through the sleepless hours. My breath failed me and I lay there waiting to be mercifully done in.

He was just checking on me on his way outside. Bibhuti only slept two hours a night. He'd had his allowance and now it was time for his first training session of the day. He told me to go back to sleep and slipped past me and out the door. I heard him padding down the concrete steps, spring-loaded and sure in the darkness.

I wondered where I'd found the boldness to put my life in his hands.

Harshad had been sorry to see me go. He thought it was something he'd said or a failing of his to meet my Western needs.

'Would you like another room?' he asked. 'I will put you in the executive suite, no extra charge.'

'I didn't know there was an executive suite.'

'Only one. For special guests. It has a sofa-cum-bed and extra soft linens, you will be very comfortable.'

I told him it was nothing personal. Bibhuti had insisted I move in with him. It was more practical that way. He wanted to keep an eye on me, and besides, I needed to be careful with my money in case I lived any longer than I'd expected to.

The TV Harshad had resurrected showed a graphic of the monsoon's projected path towards us. When it arrived the mercury would dip by a few degrees and the air would feel fresh for the first time since winter. The price to pay for this would be crumbling roads and more blackouts, and a drop in revenue from the foreign businessmen who'd take their conventions to Jaipur and Delhi, chased north by the rain that would settle over Mumbai like the arms of a jealous lover, concealing the city's treasures from the greedy eyes of enemy satellites.

Harshad rubbed his belly thoughtfully. 'You will come back to see me, yes?' he asked. 'I am not far away.'

I realised that he'd formed an attachment to me, the foreign listener to his Indian woes. When I left I'd take with me my well-intentioned credulity and my weakness for legend. He was afraid that in their absence he'd have no filtering curtain between himself and his stories.

I told him I'd pop in whenever I could.

'You must be here for the completion of my painting. Soon it will be done.'

Amrita was painting the grass beneath the snake-killer's feet in a green that reminded me of the South Downs seen from above, passing over in a plane on European flights. Those city breaks we took on the cheap in teeming Prague and rainy Budapest. So much of the world still unseen. It was too big for one measly lifetime.

'When she has finished my painting you will be the first person to see it. You will bless it and it will open the next chapter in my business. Then Amrita will paint a picture of you and BB breaking your record. It will go on the opposite wall, even bigger than mine. People will come from all over to see it. My hotel will be famous as the place you stayed when you first met him. I will arrange a tour of BB's places, everybody will want to see this.'

His eyes were wide with the potential of it. He'd found a money-spinning fantasy to compensate for my leaving.

He remembered himself, took my case to the door and set it down on the pavement.

'You will come back.' He nodded a seal on it. I watched him creak back to his desk, pick up his glass and empty it.

The old man smiled up at me through his blazing beard. He looked at me differently, with a startling and unforeseen joy, as if recognising for the first time that we shared a common ancestry or an affiliation to the same football team. His voice when it came was songlike, a lullaby from the dawn of time.

'You have New Balance!' he trilled.

'Sorry?'

'Your shoes. They are New Balance. I once owned these shoes. Very comfortable. Somebody stole them.'

I looked down at my new trainers. The old man was right. They were very comfortable. He wriggled the toes on his wrinkled brown feet in remembrance of the luxury they'd once enjoyed.

'These are mine,' I said. 'I need them.'

'I do not want them. They are yours. I am happy for you. Where I am going there is no need for shoes. Still I am thankful for the time I had with them, although it was very short. I hope your time with them is longer.'

The old man turned away and stared at his magic spot. Our moment of bonding was passed and I was no longer alive to him. He was gone to fly over the places he'd known, a last visit before the rain came to snatch him up.

In his patch of sky the clouds were towering. I'd left a half-full bottle of Officer's Choice in my room and some nail clippings stained with Ellen's Trendspotting in case anyone wanted to clone me.

The morning came to Bibhuti's house and I was still alive. My money was where I'd left it under the coffee table and the dogs that had barked through the night had failed in their undertaking to drive me out of my mind. Maybe the god of the house had taken pity on me while I squirmed in search of sleep. He hadn't granted sleep to me but he had in the provocations of sleeplessness gifted me the anger I needed to rip Bibhuti's soul from its socket. All I had to do was remember that feeling when we stood up together in front of people.

I came to suspect quite quickly that Bibhuti might save my life, at least for long enough to get the breaking done. The food he gave me and the breaths he made me take muffled the pain to a bearable hum. By his encouragement and my morning repetitions I felt myself grow stronger. I found the courage to start chewing my food. Bibhuti's wife gave me salt water to soothe my loosies. My thanks bounced off her like hailstones off a tin roof.

I would hurry over ablutions in the cramped bathroom, stepping queasily around the hole in the floor. At least the door could be bolted. At least the neighbour's satirical commentary on my sit-up technique could be drowned out if I pressed my elbows to my ears. When I ran out of steam I'd take a nap in their marital bed, slipping under to the flapping of wings somewhere out of reach. Ellen's absence was a dead weight on my chest that pulled me effortlessly down.

My daydreams filled up with the perfect swing and the cracking of obedient bones. I still hadn't hit him and the thirst for it was ever-present, a drunkenness that didn't wear off.

I taught Jolly Boy what a nutmeg was in the footballing sense and Bibhuti got me washing my hair in urad dhal. It would make it strong like his.

'I have been looking for a record I can break with my hair for some time,' he said, running his comb through the black waves. 'I would like to pull a locomotive with my hair but I do not know how to attach myself. I have tried several times with no luck, each time I am removed as soon as I begin walking.'

'That's annoying.'

'It is big frustration to me. Not to worry. Now I am reaching the pinnacle. No other record will compare.' He inspected the comb's teeth for foreign bodies, found none, and slipped it back into his pocket. 'History will not remember you for what you attempted to do, only for what you succeeded in doing.'

I told Bibhuti about the blood on my neck and by the end of it he'd fallen in love with me.

'You saw me this day?' Bibhuti asked. 'When you cut yourself?'

'Funny, isn't it. Just by chance, there you were.'

'This is not chance. Did you know about the cancer at this time?'

'No idea. That was a few months after. But it's funny, as soon as I got here I thought to myself, that wouldn't happen in India. People are kinder here, they wouldn't let someone go around bleeding all day and not tell him. Maybe that's what I was looking for, some kindness. Maybe that's what I was missing all along.'

A now familiar look came over Bibhuti, a light shining suddenly from somewhere inside him. He leoparded to his feet and started stalking the yard, his whole body fizzing with the desire to right the world's most evident wrongs.

'You see? Your old life was killing you and that is why you were brought here. You did not come here just to help me, not entirely. God sent you here to be healed. And he gave this job to me. Together we are helping each other. It is the love in our hearts which is the key, this will unlock both our destinies. I am loving you and you are loving me. This is how the pain of the past is erased. This is God's message to us.'

He was getting loud and the neighbour was amused. He pretended to be hanging the banana skins when I looked his way.

'We must be loving each other,' Bibhuti went on. 'We have both known great struggle. You come to me from across the seven seas and tell me of your pain. I bring you into my home and provide the cure. This is beautiful. Who could predict such a turn-up? I know our friendship has no definition. How it's evolved I'm clueless. It will become stronger with every passing days.'

He told me to kick him. He said I was ready.

My heart was racing. I felt clumsy and teenage, my legs too heavy to move. I took the sort of breath that was going to keep me alive.

He parted his feet. Jolly Boy sat watching from the top of the stairs, in the puddle his mother's washing had left. He didn't know whether to time it or not, and in the end he left his stopwatch to dangle at his chest.

I kicked Bibhuti where he was soft.

I felt something give. Bibhuti grinned at me. His son grinned at me. The afternoon light embraced us all.

'Again,' Bibhuti said. 'You can make it harder.'

I did it again. He was pleased with me and there was no pain.

20

My Bollywood Stint (2002)

I am not an admirer of the Bollywood films as many of my countrymen are. I am too busy in my daily endeavours to know the latest releases. Also the stars of the silver screen are not my favourite role model thanks to their unquenchable thirst for limelight which often leads to immodest behaviours. So it was a great surprise to receive a call from big-time Bollywood producer Kailash Karkera after the news of my four World Record haul had swept through my city. He was very impressed by my achievements and invited me to dinner at the prestigious Taj Hotel to discuss important plans for my future.

I must tell you, walking into that place only a handful of years after arriving like a washed-up coconut on the shore of the Arabian Sea was like a dream coming true for me. This was before sad events of 2008 terror attacks and everything was calm. My wife was very happy to have the door opened for her by the doorkeeper in his red turban and sash and Shubham made us all smile by returning his bow in very respectful manner. Into the lobby and we were surrounded by gold statues and fine fabrics. It was as if we had been invited to the Raja's palace. Mr Karkera was our introduction to the splendid inner secrets of a world beyond the imagination of a common man from humble country background.

Rajesh Battacharjee the snake who slithered at his feet, but at this time I was still gladly unaware of his intentions.

'Your story is of great interest to me,' Mr Karkera said. 'How a simple man from humble beginnings can find his own way to greatness.'

I allowed his praise to tickle my heart only softly. To receive admiration is not the sportsman's primary goal.

Mr Karkera had seen my success with the concrete slabs. He asked me how I was able to control the pain. I told him of my methods and to demonstrate I invited him to deliver a kick to my groin. He participated sans delay, giving me a polite kick which only passed by the target area. After grabbing my advice to kick harder he made several further impressions to my groin. The result of a good hit was most pleasing for both of us.

Mr Karkera asked me if I had thought about bringing my talents to a bigger stage. How would I like a place in the film industry?

The idea nearly bowled me over at first glance. I listened carefully to his proposal while inside my mind was spinning like cyclone.

Mr Karkera was of course the producer of many successful action blockbusters with a reputation for creating the most spectacular fight sequences in the business. The stars of these actioners must be toppers in their field with great martial arts skills and onscreen charisma. Although the fight sequences are actually an illusion, with no real contact received, they are created with much care to trick the audience into believing they are seeing real combat spilling from the screen. Mr Karkera picked me as the golden choice for this role. He said my feats in movie would be a boon in helping the common man to enjoy brief respite from a life of hard toil.

I pondered this conclusively. I thought of the common man and his sore need for enjoyment and positive role model in a dark and dusty world. If he could receive this positive standard from the characters I am bringing to life on the screen, then perhaps this was God informing me that my inspiration was reaching a wider area than I imagined hitherto.

I would be relocated to large new apartment in Lokhandwala Complex, home locality of many Bollywood professionals. My performances up on the screen would reflect directly my principles of accuracy and truthfulness to the skills and beliefs of my trade. And salary would be five times more than I ever held in my hands before. It was a dream in the making.

'This would be a new life for you and your family,' Mr Karkera said. 'No more hand to mouth, every comfort you could ask for, and your work would be there for display to millions of your countrymen. How could you turn your back on such an offer?'

My wife gave me a smile which conveyed all her belief that I should accept the gentleman's offer sans delay. But still I introspected. Each grain of rice I chewed on was a reason either to shun the big-shot lifestyle or to embrace the openings it brought, and my tongue could not sort them apart from each other.

'I believe BB's story itself would make a fine film,' Rajesh Battacharjee declared. 'Perhaps the right people can be found to bring his biography to life.'

'This is my area,' Mr Karkera said. 'We might have to introduce an element of fiction as well for commercial viability, if this does not offend you?'

'It would be fine,' I said. 'You are the expert on these things.' And to prove my trust in Mr Karkera I offered him my hand.

Some fear persisted as I made my first step onto set for maiden day's filming of *Vengeance at Midnight*, the latest actioner in Mr Karkera's stable on which I was given small role. FilmCity was a very strange environment for me unlike anything I had seen before. My mind was unprepared for such a mysterious level.

First glimpse revealed gigantic area comprising lake, campus street, library, prison, temple and beautiful gardens all appearing large as life. It was as if the almighty had dropped every possibility from life into one location. All close to each other with no requirement to travel far between. Plus many large sheds in close arrangement where interior sets were installed to replicate any room from the imagination – Ashok, my guide for feet-finding period, opened the door to one shed to reveal a courtroom complete with every detail such as chairs, desk, judge in official garb and dragooned defendant guarded on both sides by khakis with solemn expression of duty. The only clue that this was not in fact a real scene came from the array of lights hanging from ceiling beams. The judge also having make-up applied to his face by make-up man and when I reached out to test the wooden wall I discovered it was only a plastic imitation with grain painted in.

Then we arrived at our location, the exterior of a prison. Large wooden doors and thick stone walls just like in reality. The director welcomed me and we had a nice chat about our native places while the other actors' safety features were installed. Foam pieces covering groin and major joints to absorb the impact of the blows from a big fight sequence. The actors playing the revolting prisoners would attack the actors playing the prison guards and deadly force would be required to subdue them. Every punch and kick must look real and the audience must believe real danger was in the offing at every turn. This is what the director conveyed to me. The padding a precaution only. No real contact to occur.

I experienced a moment of deep sadness. It had been many weeks since I had shaken hands with Mr Karkera to put the seal on our association. We had left the Taj that night as a family on the brink of an exciting journey to upper ranks of human achievements. Bollywood arm was reaching around us in a welcoming embrace and all wishes for success were hatching. But since then there had been no word from Mr Karkera on my promised move to Lokhandwala Complex and apart from one meeting to sign contract and receive small advance (enough for new zebra-print sofa with real cherry-wood frame from Monsoon Madness Sale at Classic Solutions) no instructions had been conveyed until this morning. My wife had been waiting on tenterhooks for the all-clear to start packing her things and I had made a temporary hiatus in my preparations for upcoming record. Time could not move forward without clear signals from my new employer.

Then out of the blue the call came to say the car was on its way to take me to FilmCity. No briefing or training time, I was put on the spot and given my role as first prison guard. I was to fight the film's main character in deadly duel and come out as the loser in last moments. I conveyed my disappointment in the strongest terms. Why must I be the villain?

The director said it had already been decided. The main character was played by a popular star of the time and he must always win. No matter that my skills and philosophy should give me the hero's role. Other fellow was expected to triumph and his fans would not accept it if the roles were reversed. There would be riots in the picture houses nationwide.

I swallowed the sadness like a bitter herb and said to myself, 'BB, this is what your employer expects of you. It is your duty to listen to him. Think of the opportunity you have been given to create beautiful moment onscreen for the public entertainment. Be the best villain you can be and next time the hero's place will be yours.' So this is what I did.

This was a very lonely day for me. All my suggestions to improve the sequence went unheeded. The director stubbornly maintained his own way of doing things despite absence of expertise in my area. There was no time for the added grace and difficulty level which I wished to weave in. The sun was setting when the director called for a halt in proceedings. Shubham was already asleep when I returned home that night. My wife greeted me with excited response and we discussed all the details of our new life in Lokhandwala Complex once the long-awaited move was made. The best schools for Shubham. The landscaped grounds where we could stroll in the evenings and play badminton. The gelato parlours with full range of flavours (my wife and son love them despite the damage they create to the internal balance). We looked ahead with the same pair of eyes to our final years spent in lap of comfort and success.

This was God's chosen time to remind me that a family man is the luckiest man in the world. He was telling me that my record-breaking path had reached its end and a new path was beginning. After meditating to ensure the message was genuine I accepted his decision with calm outlook.

Next day's filming took place not in sheltered surroundings of FilmCity but out on frantic streets of Colaba Causeway, with constant difficulties from curious tourists and annoying drum sellers. Cameras set up outside famous Cafe Mondegar to catch a long chase sequence between the hero, on the run after his daring prison escape, and a number of the don's henchmen hell-bent on making a pounce before he can clear his name of false Mafia crimes. The hero would be cornered among the bookstands and he would fight his way through the thugs. I would be the main thug. Only different clothing and wig to distinguish me from the role I had played the previous day. They wanted to rearrange my hair but I found this suggestion unacceptable.

This time Mr Karkera was present to help disperse the crowds during important shots. For this he used several khakis with heavy-handed tactics. I was quite shocked by the liberal use of their lathis but my concerns were waved away. Mr Karkera explaining that outdoor filming on real streets was a very dangerous undertaking, with thieves and pickpockets all around ready to steal expensive equipment or kidnap stars for ransom. Khakis were necessary to ensure the safety of the crew.

The cameras started rolling. Such was the hustle and bustle around the location that the cameramen found it impossible to capture a shot which was not in some way obscured by an unwanted body. The khakis did their best to keep the interlopers at arm's length but it was no good, we had to keep stopping to reset the action and try again. This was exhausting for the poor actors who were required to run up and down the street countless times under the beating sun, and proved a real headache for the director and Mr Karkera. Both of them reduced to screaming and tearing of hair. Finally Mr Karkera was about to let go of all composure and he asked me to step in to persuade the crowd.

'Look at this fellow here,' Mr Karkera said, pointing out a small boy who with his friends had been attached to us ever since we had arrived, offering to carry equipment and fetch water from the nearby cafe to save us from our thirst. 'He is just waiting for me to turn my back so he and his chums can strip me of everything I have worked for. One well-timed kick will put such ideas out of his head.'

'I do not believe they want to steal from us,' I protested. 'They are just sadak chaps, they do not mean any harm.'

'You are too trusting, BB,' Mr Karkera told me. 'You do not live on the mainland, there is not such a rat problem on your side of the creek. Here we have to step very carefully around them. Now is time to step on them. You have been waiting to practise your skills in full contact. You can begin by stepping on this rat for me.'

Needless to say his request produced some disgust in me. He was asking that I attack an innocent and unarmed boy. I made my feelings clear. I told him I cannot do this.

Mr Karkera seemed confused. 'Come, BB, it is just one rat. Is your loyalty to him or is it to the production? We must work for each other, this is how the best results end up on screen. I have been very generous to you, have I not?'

The boy appealed to my mercy with tender look. Khakis poised like cobras to make another charge with their lathis should I resist Mr Karkera's argument.

'You have been very generous, sir,' I told Mr Karkera. 'But I cannot strike the boy. It is against my beliefs as martial arts professional and God-fearing citizen.'

'These beliefs are very unfortunate for you,' Mr Karkera declared. 'While they are in your way I fear you will not meet your ambitions.' And with that he gave the nod and a khaki struck the boy sharply on the back. The boy squealed and ran, his friends close behind. My blood boiled up inside me at the injustice I had just witnessed.

At this point I knew my association with Mr Karkera must come to an end. I realised he did not have the interests of the common man at his heart. To accept his money was to smear my hands with the blood of all my country's children. I walked away from this enterprise before my hands became stained.

'You are making a big mistake,' Mr Karkera told me. 'You cannot walk away from me in the middle of a shoot, I have a film to complete.'

'Then you must complete it without me. I am no longer in your employment.'

'Think very carefully, BB. If you walk away you will never work in Bollywood again. The door to fame and riches will be closed for ever. This is my promise and I can make it come true.'

'I do not listen to the promises of men,' I informed him. 'Only the promises of the almighty reach my ears, and he has built a house for me where no lies or dangers are living.'

And with that I left the scene, my head held high and my heart beating again with its original passion for simple life.

Needless to say my wife was shocked by the news of my swift departure from Bollywood life. At first she did not understand the strength of my reasons. There followed another period of stiffness in the house while the news sank in. For one week she refused to talk to me except to bark like a dog whenever I got in her way. Cooking standard reduced and rooms left in a hurry when I entered them. Me sleeping on the new zebra-print sofa because she spread her limbs to bar me from our bed.

My son was my only comfort in this time. I only had to look into his eyes to know that I had made the right decision. I saw his future there and was pleased to discover he would be a man of firm convictions.

After seven days my wife lifted her silence. 'But what of our future?' she asked.

I heard the typical rattle as the A/C switched off, then the lights went out. I went through the darkness to our bedroom where the fuse box is located. I hit the switch and light returned, showing the room as if I was seeing it for the first time. A cosy space with all necessary features. Light. A place to sit. A window to permit a segment of the outside. The sky was a lovely shade of dark blue and despite my wife's complaints of small dimensions the room seemed big enough to contain the dreams of an entire span.

'Everything we need is here,' I told her. 'Our son is here. God's love finds us here every day, we do not need to look elsewhere for it. The money would be a chain around my soul and the demands of the job would keep me apart from my record-breaking fixture. A man must know his place, and my place was set up previously. This is my decision. I have made it for our protection and there is no going back.'

I saw my wife's eyes turn wet and knew that my words had entered her heart in effective manner. This expressed later that night when she allowed me to return to our bed. Back in the arms of my dear ones, and everything settled into usual rhythm. Before sleep came I introspected on my blessings. I had received a clear vision of the future and saw that if I took up this life bad fortune would swallow good and a shadow would fall over the legacy that I had worked so hard to plant in dusty soil. I recognised the divine warning and acted quickly to prevent this terrible consequence.

Still today I am asked from time to time if I regret this decision. Many of my younger students share a big love of the actioners, and they often fantasise of seeing me perform on the silver screen.

When they question my philosophy I always reply thus: when a donkey comes to your door do not be tricked by the gifts he carries on his back. If you pull his tail he will still drop loosies on your feet. I have stuck to this rule through thick and thin and this is why I can hold my chin high above all challenges.

Thank you.

As the sun set over the hills beyond the pylons of Vashi I climbed into a barrel and started stomping. The grapes felt slimy between my toes. I realised I'd been craving the touch of something organic for as long as I could remember.

The rooftop SkyBar was hosting a New World wines promotion. I'd come here to feel indiscreet. The corporate high-flyers pranced and flapped for a free bottle of Chilean Merlot while in the street below fatherless children clamoured to divvy the sweetbreads from eviscerated clock radios.

I was in the third barrel. The girl next to me was Korean, I think. A furious little thing in oatmeal linen, she stomped the fastest of all of us. She wanted to win. The waiters were handing out free bottles like they were the last of a tainted batch. As guests of the hotel we were owed something. A prize for having made it to the jet set.

None of them knew they were dancing bears. I was the saddest bear of all but at the time it didn't matter. I was strong and alive and I had a friend who'd die for me.

A circle formed around us. The other hotshots still in their shoes clapped and hollered. Tonight they were on fire. Far from home and swaddled in booze they'd write their own history on the sky. One of them pointed and laughed at me. He wore a pink shirt and his sunburn made his head look like a fire alarm.

I looked across the rooftops to the train station and the InfoTech park, its stacked boxes topped with Airfix aerials and dishes. I decided for the night that it wasn't a call centre at all, but a training facility for orphaned acrobats. The smudge-faced kids in the rat runs below me had once been caged there, sold by their families into showbiz slavery. They'd escaped into this darker freedom and were happy to endure its hardships if it meant no more cartwheels at the tip of a ringmaster's bullying cane.

I stomped my way to notoriety and won my bottle. I held it up like a trophy. They cheered me. I fled to the edge of the roof to commune with the hidden stars. Their music couldn't puncture the smog. I listened instead to the howling and chatter of the high-flyers and imagined myself better than them because I had a purpose worth running from.

The kick had been a breakthrough. When I'd landed my foot between Bibhuti's legs I'd heard my own bones creak and mesh into a new formation that would let my greatness out like rays of light through pinholes in a blanket. It was restorative. Bibhuti's nightly incursions were just local colour and the dogs that sere-naded me so tirelessly would one day be bonemeal for an orchid farm.

A couple of weeks in and the novelty had started to wear thin. I was always tripping over Bibhuti meditating in the darkness on my way to the toilet. I tired of the sight of him in his underpants stand-ing over me as I tried to sleep. I needed a dose of comfort to reward myself for all my hard work. Cotton sheets on a king-size bed and a break from his watching. Some carefully selected pleasures to throw a share of my money at before it got swallowed up in the record attempt and whatever life came after. I booked a night in the hotel next to the shopping mall Bibhuti had taken me to. I left his apartment in a holiday mood and promised to be good.

Bibhuti didn't like the idea. 'What if something is happening while you are there? A bomb or a fire or perhaps there is too much temptation there and you are returning to bad habits?'

I told him those things were behind me. The quiet would be a tonic and I'd come back stronger.

The lobby air smelled like a focus-grouped future and there were free boiled sweets in a jar at reception. I took a handful to last me.

I swam some lengths in the spa pool in exorbitant trunks from the in-house boutique, scraping elbows with fat Europeans on a desalination junket. I ate a fusion lunch in the restaurant that came out the other end a vibrant orange and sipped cold beers in the Tipplers' Lounge, watching an office block go up on the opposite side of the street. The scaffolding was bamboo and the unharnessed workers dangled from it like monkeys. I credited their bravery to a handed-down belief in falcons that would swoop in and pluck them from the air if their footing failed them.

I could feel Ellen looking at me wherever I put myself. I couldn't put a lid on what I'd done to her. I had more freedom than I knew what to do with and all I wanted to do was sleep and wake up again in a post-people world, where all our rivalries had grassed over and the animals ran the streets again.

I became aware of someone standing beside me. I looked down and saw a brown hand clutching the railing next to mine. I looked at her face. She was young and slender. Her native complexion looked out of place unstarched by waitress whites. In her emerald-green dress she could have been Bollywood. She smiled diffidently. The heat whispered over us and stirred something up. I let her make her proposal. I added my amendments and she suggested a price. I accepted. We boarded the lift in silence.

Our soundtrack was an instrumental version of 'Bridge Over Troubled Water' played by robots in tuxedos. The girl could have only been twenty-five at a push. Complicit eyes sharpened to a merchant's point and hair tied in a ponytail. The back of her neck was exposed as she turned away from me to guard the lift buttons and to dwell on whatever happy consolations she needed reminding of to pull her through the next hours. I watched her neck and wished the both of us animals, unthinking things unstalked by death that did what we did only because the rules of being alive compelled us to.

She checked my money under a UV lamp that she carried in her handbag. The rupees passed her inspection and she went to the bathroom to undress. She took her bag with her. I scanned the room for things I could defend myself with in case she came back with a pistol. I put a glass on the bedside table, half an arm's length from my side of the bed. I stood on the Egyptian cotton sheets and examined the smoke alarm for a hidden camera. I sat on the bed with my shoes still on and listened to my heart charging.

Outside, hammers and horns rained down. The city was rebuilding itself for the benefit of those who'd come after me. Sewer lids were being driven down against the hazards of the coming storm.

The girl came back in red underwear. She stood at the foot of the bed and let me take her in. Her flat stomach and soft limbs drew from me a gasp that sounded loud in the room. She smoothed herself down, as if to remove the static or shame from her skin. She knelt down and untied my shoes, slipped them off and dropped them on the carpet. All the while looking me in the eyes with a fabricated understanding of what it was I needed to smother my pain. I wanted to press myself very gently against her and feel her warmth, the strong heartbeat that quivered in her neck and pushed clean blood around her body, and the dreams tarnished and advanced by the likes of me.

She opened the wine I'd won and filled two glasses, put one on each bedside table. She got on the bed, on all fours.

'I can start now?' she asked.

'Yes please.'

She hesitated, poised to turn and sit down but unsure of herself.

'I'm dying,' I said as an inducement. 'I've never done anything like this before.'

'You really are dying?'

'It's alright, it's nothing you can catch. I won't ask for anything else, I promise.'

The girl did something sympathetic with her eyebrows and sat down beside me. I plumped the pillows to make her more comfortable. We almost touched. My mouth went dry. I took a drink. The wine was claggy and I felt it stain my teeth.

'You can get in if you want,' I said.

'You don't want to see me?'

'It's up to you. Only if you don't mind.'

'I will stay here,' she said.

'Do you know Tom and Jerry?'

'Yes I know them.'

'You know what you have to do?'

'Of course.'

I gave her the colouring book. She opened it and flicked slowly through its pages, introducing herself to the pictures. Her lips curled into a belittling smile and I stirred in spite of it.

The hammers stopped for the night. In the quiet they left I was monstrous.

I opened the packet of felt-tips and offered her the first selection, a boy sharing stolen cigarettes. She shuffled closer to me and picked the brown. She made a start on Jerry, resting the book on her thighs. She held the pen lightly. Her face set into enchanting concentration. I chose a blue and took it to Tom where he gave chase. She opened the book out wider for me.

Ellen was half a world away and had probably stopped mourning me by now. I'd never stop mourning her. The feeling came back to me of being alone beside her in a bed too small to kick out in. Her body immovable and unwilling to be played, a piano with the lid nailed down. Sometimes I'd deliberately touch her and feel her shrink under my fingertips. Sometimes I'd go a lifetime without touching her at all. Hearing her frightened breath catch on the air between us I'd marvel at her patience and my own. Both of us waiting for something to break, or for the darkness to spread wide enough for us to disappear into it for as long as it took to be forgotten. Our former selves were ghosts that came back to sniff at us whenever a tender song played or a need for relief prickled our clammy skin. Our youth was dead and buried in a hole dug with care and lined with wool for softness.

The girl asked if she was doing it right and I said she was. I let myself believe that I was showing her a kindness, by giving her a break from the things she was usually made to do. Her skin on mine where our thighs touched was softer than the air around us. The silence drifted over me and settled into the places where papercuts had languished unsealed for years. Watching her hands roam the page I shrank back to a boy catching bees in a jam jar.

When the morning came she was still beside me. On top of the sheet, still stripped to her underwear and watching me closely, reflecting on ageing and what it might do to her as it had done to me.

She asked if she could pleasure me with her hand and I declined as gently as I could. Instead she took me to the bathroom and washed the grape must off my feet. She had to scrub to get the stains off and she apologised for hurting me. I told her it was alright. I offered to buy her breakfast but she said she didn't eat breakfast. Hammers and horns. She pulled the blackout drape open a crack and light came lancing in to unhide my vulgar flesh. I folded my arms. She looked out on the day. There was jealousy in her eyes. The world wasn't yet as she'd instructed it. Some people still had it all and some still had nothing. She still had all her proving to do.

Between the hammer blows came drums, away in the distance. The girl took in the day and made her plans for the future.

I looked at my watch. It was gone twelve. I felt like I'd slept for days.

'You could have gone,' I told the girl. 'It's late.'

'I am staying. This is the agreement. You have late checkout, you told me this? I will go when you go.'

She ploughed a hand into her knickers and scratched herself lavishly. The colouring book lay open on the bed. I picked it up and flicked through the pages all now living in the colours we'd applied. The cat chased the mouse around. The cat played the piano. The dog snapped at the cat's heels and the mouse bent his back under a piece of cheese as big as a house.

The drums sounded louder. I thought I heard trumpets among them. The girl beckoned me to the window. Her brow was knotted in deep thought. I stood behind her and peered out through the gap she'd made in the curtains.

'Do you hear it?' she asked.

'Music?'

'It is a wedding.'

I looked down onto the street below. I couldn't see where the music was coming from. Louder and louder it came, trumpets thickening and drums beating at a festive rhythm. People started gathering outside the hotel, looking off in the direction of the music. Beggar children stood meerkat to attention, pulling in excitement at their private parts. The streetdogs barked in anger at the rival noise.

The band turned the corner and the children ran to greet them. They trailed them to a spot in front of the hotel where they stopped and struck up a new song. A corps of dancing revellers fell in around them, brightly dressed and beaming. They surrounded the happy couple, who were young and scared and dripping gold. They were lifted onto the shoulders of the crowd and bounced in time with the music. Sweets in colourful wrappers spilled from their elders' hands to be fought over by the street kids with thrilling animosity.

The girl watched all this and wiped a tear from her cheek.

'The bride is very beautiful,' she muttered.

I stood beside her on the carpet, felt the vibrations from the wedding party needling the soles of my feet. I was almost afraid to look at her in case my attention scratched a permanent mark. She was an island of undiscovered music in a sea of noise.

'Soon they will be coming into the hotel,' she said. 'They will have a banquet room with flowers and more music playing. There will be food and dancing and somebody to take their pictures. There are lots of weddings here.'

The horns had taken on a ragged quality, the trumpeters' industry slackening as the air grew thick with the spectacle wealth makes of itself.

'Shall we gatecrash?'

The girl didn't know the word. I explained. 'We're guests at the hotel, we should be allowed to join in. We'll get drunk.'

'We cannot go into the party, it is not permitted.'

'Then let's get down there while they're still outside. Come on.'

I came away from the window and dressed quickly, glad of the excuse to pack my desires away out of her sight. I checked my trouser pocket for the sweets I'd stolen. We'd need more. The girl saw that I was serious and got dressed too, retrieved her bag from the bathroom. I put the colouring book in it. She didn't look for meaning in the gesture.

We jumped up and down in the lift to make it go faster. I scooped a handful of sweets from the bowl at reception and gave them to the girl. The security guards opened the door for us and out we charged into her rightful sunlight.

The wedding party had swelled, sucking in well-wishers from the passing shoppers. Fellow hotel guests, called like us by the trumpets, were lurking at the outer circle, filming stray splinters of the procession on their mobile phones to bring back home for the amusement of their offices. Out here the drums hit me in the stomach. It felt like they were coming from inside me. Sweat from the dancers hung like flies in the air and their colours formed a fire-ring around the promised couple, a barrier to the dust and resentments of the wider world.

The girl stood and watched, her mouth open.

'I like the colours,' I said.

'These are the colours I would choose. But I do not like her jewellery, the design is very old-fashioned. I would choose something more modern, I think.'

The bride wasn't beautiful like the girl had said. She was caked and basted and frightened. The groom the same. In the eye of the storm they waited to be told what to do, their sugared lips parted in acceptance of their good fortune, their kohl-smeared eyes flea-jumping to every movement that might divert them from each other's gaze. I felt a rush of worry for them. I threw a sweet to a boy who was standing apart from the crowd, naked from the waist down, ignored by the elders' ritual scatterings. He didn't grasp my intention in time and the sweet hit him on the side of the head. He bent to pick it up without complaint.

Other children rushed in and I threw the rest of my sweets, showering them with my benevolence. The girl joined in, throwing hers more discriminately, one at a time to the little girls who reminded her of innocent times.

When they were all gone she wandered away from me through the hotel gate, unstung by the suggestive looks of the security guards. On the pavement outside she found a place for herself in the surge from where she could get a better view of the final flourishes before the trumpeters gave out. I stayed where I was, watching her back in case she was caught up in the crush and needed saving.

A prying dog snarled at the watchers' legs, causing a fall somewhere at the back. In the commotion a tourist dropped his phone and swore loudly. The dog had its foot trodden on and let out a yelp. A cross-legged infant shoved the dog muzzle-first out of the firing line and picked up the sweet that had been hiding in its shadow.

The music died and the crowd cleared to let the procession through the gate. The lovebirds were eased from their seat and lowered to the ground. The doormen swung the doors open to the advancing party. The bodyscanner was switched off, a prearranged concession to the dignity of the occasion.

I stepped aside to set myself apart from the happy ones as they filed into the lobby. I looked for the girl.

She was standing in the road watching the bride being swallowed by her new family, her face starched and covetous as the gate was wheeled closed. Our eyes met and I gave her a little smile. She didn't return it. She didn't have to. My money was hers now and she could do what she wanted with it.

'I know where there are butterflies,' I said. 'I can take you to see them.'

'I must go,' she said.

'Okay. Thank you.'

'I hope you don't die.'

'Thanks. You too.'

She turned and crossed the road and kept on walking. I waited until she was a speck and then I went back to the room to get my things together. I smelled her as soon as I walked in. I cried briefly for my loss.

I took the train back to Airoli, breathing in the dust from the open door and thinking about the approaching rain. How heavy it might be and how fast it might fill me up if I stood very still with my mouth wide open to the sky. I bought a bunch of blackened bananas from a child with eyes dimmed by illiteracy and the smoke of rubbish fires. I gave them to Bibhuti's neighbour when I got back, to feed his addiction to beauty.

Bibhuti was on tenterhooks. I told him I'd behaved myself and he embraced me like a long-lost friend. He hadn't been convinced that I'd return.

'What made you think that?' I asked.

'I imagined you might go home and leave me without hope. It has been a difficult time for you.'

'I wouldn't do that. I made you a promise and I'm gonna keep it.'

His relief was startling and I had to sit down. It felt good to be missed.

22

I was beating the life out of Bibhuti with a baseball bat when my first monsoon broke. Jolly Boy was timing me on his stopwatch.

'Faster, Uncle, faster! Hit him more harder!'

'It kills your arms though.'

The sweat was falling off me in waves. I felt sick to my stomach but I'd come too far to give up now.

Bibhuti was standing with his legs spread apart for balance, his body tensed like it was holding a high note. His face holy cow serene as I piled into him, bouncing the bat off his shoulders and his shins and his thighs, his back where the crocodile bites were shining. He made a tree of himself and took it, let out a satisfied little grunt whenever I hit a sweet spot.

The black clouds spilled their first drops. Big rain. Birdshit big and hot. A drop landed on my head. Itchy. Then another one. Everything went dark. The courtyard sagged and sang under the weight of it, all that enraged air. I couldn't get the right grip, my feet were slipping. Everything hurt and the raindrops were burning.

'Keep going,' Bibhuti said, his voice quiet and steady. He sucked a fat raindrop from his moustache.

'Twenty-four seconds!' Jolly Boy shouted, jumping up and down with the turmoil of it all. 'You can break it! Hit him!'

I lifted the bat up higher, tightened my grip. I thought I could see a hairline crack but it wasn't enough, it still felt too solid. The fear was a coal in my throat. I looked at Bibhuti's shin where it had come up red and swollen. I didn't think it would be this hard to break a man.

'Come,' Bibhuti said, waving me in. 'You are almost there. One more hit only, I can feel it. Come.'

His voice was soothing. Like Mum rubbing calamine lotion on my wasp sting, that time at the Mumbles when I was a boy. I was as helpless as a boy again. A prisoner of the moment and its keeper, weak and drunk on daring. I couldn't let him down. I lined up another shot across his shoulder, closed my eyes and stepped into it.

A great scream like a wrecking ball split the darkness in half, and I fell forwards into empty space.

There was a moment of nothing when I could have been anyone and anywhere. It was beautiful and it made up for every lie I ever told.

'Lovely hit!' Jolly Boy shouted, and I opened my eyes. The bat had been ripped in two, the grip end splintered in my hand. Jolly Boy was grinning at me in demented wonder. Bibhuti rubbed the spot where I got him, the bruises spreading over his skin like a wild virus. He looked at himself in grim adoration and slowly shook his head, taking in some obvious and binding truth about his new place in the universal order of things. Then came the smile, and he grabbed me in a bear-hug and lifted me up, summoned Jolly Boy in between us. I was squeezed against Bibhuti's hard unbreakable body, his son's adolescent softness. I was weightless. The three of us danced and spun in the rain, laughing at each other, warped survivors of an unreported war.

'Kudos! What did I tell you, I knew you could do it!' Bibhuti broke free, took the broken bat from my hand and snapped off the last splinters. Dripping wet and buzzing, he wore the look of some crazy apparition, an elephant-headed eight-armed angel wriggled free of earthly shame, and wherever he went I wanted to go after him. I wanted to see the place where pain runs away in rivers.

'What did I tell you?' he repeated. 'If you can break one bat you can break fifty bats. The method is the same, only the number is different. But you must go faster, thirty seconds to break one bat is too much. You must relax.'

'I don't want to hurt you though.'

'You cannot hurt me, it is impossible. Clear your head of this clutter and think clean. There is no need to worry, we will have a great success. This is God's choice and we cannot argue against it.'

Jolly Boy wiped the stopwatch dry on the thigh of his jeans. Another laugh dribbled out of me and it tasted like my own religion. The rain was lashing down now. The noise filled me up from the inside. It scoured the colour from the buildings and sent the shutters rattling down on Suresh's dosa kiosk and the Ayurvedic health centre across the road. Streetdogs settled in under parked Marutis and Hyundais, lumbered to the shelter of quaking palms. The world felt furious and free and we stood there watching it, me and Jolly Boy daring each other to stick our heads out, to stamp our feet and wash our faces. The boy made a run for the open sky. I crossed my fingers and followed him out into the downpour.

I felt the falling rain, let it soak into me. I remembered how far away I was from home. But I wasn't scared, not like I thought I'd be. I felt nothing but relief.

'Come. We will rest and hydrate, then we will practise some more.' Bibhuti dumped the two halves of the dead bat in my arms and stumbled to the stairwell. He flinched when he took the hand-rail, his moustache drooping at the edges. Jolly Boy looked anxiously to him.

'Baba, your leg is broken.'

'Nothing is broken. Your Baba cannot be broken, remember?'

The boy took his father at his word. They left me to stand there in the rain, alone with my thoughts. The neighbours had taken to the streets. They danced around me in circles, faces lifted to the sky in joyful communion. It had been a long dry season and the coming of the rain had triggered something in them. Spirits left the earth and flew.

I still couldn't believe how I'd ended up here, whether I'd made it happen or let it happen. I mouthed thanks to India for giving me my breath back. This must have been the first time I'd been happy since I died.

23

Ellen wouldn't have known what hit her. At the time I thought there was a mercy in that. I thought I was doing her a favour. In the weeks between deciding and going I did my best to keep my excitement from her. We slept on our own sides of the bed. She still made my lunch and I still took it with me when I left the house in the morning for a job I'd already walked out on. Instead of working through the day I'd drive one junction up the motorway and sit in the services putting my escape plan together. I grew my shell there watching the rain trickle down the windows, talking myself into the stubbornness I'd need to get on a plane without her.

I made my pilgrimage to the visa office and emptied my bank account. I bought chewable vitamins and practised going hungry.

When it was time to come home I put my tie back on and turned the key slowly as if I was walking into a stranger's house.

At night when Ellen went up I'd go out into the garden and X-ray specs the bones of all the animals buried there. The pets of the children who'd lived in the house before us, the orphaned hedgehog we'd rescued from the cats. My pheasant. I hoped the animals I'd known had liked me. Listening to the star music while

Ellen dreamed herself a musician above me I'd mentally rebuild the tiny skeletons and clad them with new flesh. I'd blow into their nostrils and bring them back to life, and they'd thank me and go scurrying back into the forest to tell their families who'd given up on their returning that magic still lived in the hearts of selfish men. I'd tell myself I was sparing Ellen a sharper pain to come by getting away while I still could.

With me gone she could be light again. I'd take my weight and my plans with me and in their place she'd put a dance floor where she could swirl unseen and not have to fret about being in anyone's way.

I made all the bookings and got my travel things together in secret. The house grew cold under the deception I'd laid and every movement of mine through it became fraudulent, head up and shoulders straight for the cameras. I moved the heart-shaped pebble I'd picked her from Brighton beach, to give her something to find unexpectedly and cry over when I was gone. I stole her favourite nail polish, the plum colour she always wore, to have something of hers with me that felt random and meaningful.

The night before I left I asked to put the conditioner in her hair, and feeling it turn from wire to silk I fell in love with her again. I dug the stray foam out of the folds in her ears and kissed her as softly as I could. She looked at me intently, her eyes bluer than I remembered them. I saw myself in them as I'd once been and I saw how much she missed that earlier me. The man who was leaving wasn't the same man she'd once pinned her hopes on and he didn't deserve her pity.

In the morning I left her sleeping and drove to a Travelodge on the edge of the known world. I listened to a consumer affairs phone-in on the radio while I ate up the lonely miles. Someone was having a problem with a leaking conservatory door. Someone else couldn't get the manufacturer to honour the guarantee on their faulty microwave. The host of the show gave his sympathy and promised results. He spoke to them like a parent talking their child down from a nightmare.

I stopped to pick some motorway blackberries, parked up on the hard shoulder with the hazards on. The blackberries were shrivelled and they tasted bitter. I had to spit them out. Nothing much else had changed. The sleeping robots woke up and bent down to see what I was doing. I waited to be picked up by their talons and thrown skyward. The anticipation of it prickled my neck. I was very scared. I'd always been very scared. They let me be. I waved goodbye to them before I drove off again.

The birds were singing backwards when I woke up and I could feel the weight of Mum watching me from somewhere above and the panic of having left something behind. It crossed my mind to turn around, drive back up the motorway and sneak back through the door before Ellen had a chance to find me gone. But it was too late.

She had to believe me dead. To protect her. To stop her coming after me.

I made myself a cup of tea with two of the little tea bags they give you on a string and I counted the hairs on my ring finger until it went cold. The room was all hard surfaces and straight edges and I pined for the feel of something soft under my feet. Sand or grass. There was a voice to the room, a hum. I could hear it coming from the radiator, from the kettle as it was boiling. It was under the duvet when I lifted it up to look for the little diamond-shaped stains of bedbug shit. I thought it was the accumulated noise of all the people who'd been in the room before me. An echo of all their sleepless hopes and recreational arguments. I wondered how many of them had come here to fake an ending or to enact a real death.

Their voices gave me comfort. They persuaded me that I was leaving something unremarkable behind, going to find something miraculous in the place Bibhuti had prepared for me.

Outside the wind bit into me and the cold made me feel important. The weather knew it was a big day for me and it had come to see me off.

It was you, wasn't it? You were the weather. I didn't know it then but it's pretty obvious now. Your hands raiding my pockets, your teeth scratching at my neck. You were telling me I was alive and doomed and so was everyone else. You were telling me to slow down, to listen, to take it all in. This would be my last chance to feel abandoned and you wanted me to savour it. And so I did.

To leave a witness trail I stopped for a chat with an old-time biker who was warming up his hog in the hotel car park. He called himself Big Bear. He told me that at the age of seventy-three the longest word he'd learned was yes. It was a word that unlocked doors and won people over. I took his intervention as a sign that my mission was an honest one.

'I've never been scared of anything,' he said. 'If you're gonna be scared you might as well shoot yourself in the head. I'm gonna keep riding till the wife says I have to stop. And that'll be never, right, Little Bear?'

The old lady sat on the bike beside him gave Big Bear a smile full of plastic yellow teeth and twisted her throttle. This action was repeated by the rest of the squadron, a dozen leathered misfits straddling their Triumphs and Harleys. The noise of revving engines cut through the wind, two arthritic fingers up to the Travelodge and the barren earth it was built on.

I told them I used to have a Lambretta, when I was nineteen. I sold it to buy a guitar and an amplifier. I was going to be in a band. We were going to be called The Navigators. It didn't work out.

'You should get another one,' Big Bear said. 'Or get yourself a proper bike.' He patted his ride.

'No, I'd kill myself. It's been too long, I wouldn't know what I was doing.'

'Don't be daft,' Little Bear said. 'You never forget. It's like riding a bike.' She laughed at her own joke and they wheeled themselves to the head of the pack. Engines revved again and I got out of the way to let them all past. I waved at Big Bear and Little Bear and they waved back.

'See you on the other side,' Little Bear shouted over the noise.

'I'm not crossing the bridge,' I said, but she didn't hear me. They crept out of the car park in a careful procession, then gunned it on to the slip road. The wind when it returned was laced with their exhaust fumes and I was lonely again.

I went across the grass to the main services and had mini pancakes in the Burger King there. They didn't give me enough maple syrup. When I asked the boy for more he said I'd have to make do with what I'd got. The amount was predetermined by computer and no one ever asked for more.

The bridge was lower than it had been the last time I'd seen it. The Severn was smaller and it seemed to flow with less conviction, as if a build-up of holiday memories tossed out from the crossing cars had formed a silt that snagged the current and held it back from its quest of the sea. Wasp stings and broken bikes, swingball beatings and early escapes cancelled at the last minute when the weather took a turn. Mum and me used to screw them all up in a ball and lob them out the window at the halfway point between countries. It was a pact we made so we could start again fresh when we got home. If we left the bad stuff behind us every time we crossed the river then the next time might be different, the sun might shine and the sandcastles might last all week.

Ashes. That's all she is now.

I stood on the grass in the same wind that had taken Mum away, searched for something of her between the raindrops. I wondered if she'd felt the exhilaration of being scattered.

I told her out loud that I loved her. I told her I was sorry for never getting round to an impressive life while she was still here to see it. The wind took my words away. Then I turned my back on the bridge and walked back to the car where it was parked outside the hotel. I wrote a Post-It note and stuck it to the steering wheel. 'Gone to the bridge'.

There were some things of Ellen's in the glove box, her disabled parking badge and some bingo pens. I put my wedding ring in there. Missed calls and unanswered texts, she wanted to know where I was. She was worried about me. I took the SIM card out and left the dead phone on the passenger seat. I abandoned the car to fate and the weather.

The taxi pulled up just as I was locking up the car, making a meal of it to generate juicy fingerprints that would pin me fatally to the scene. The driver didn't ask any questions. No cameras recorded my removal. I slept in fits and bursts between the red lights on the way to the airport. Bibhuti came to me as I drifted. He was in his white karate suit and he was breaking himself for a good reason. It made perfect sense, to want to punch a hole in the world before you left it. To be as big as you could get while you still had the strength. I could feel that I was under a spell he'd cast. It was like being drunk. I couldn't wait to meet him and make his story mine.

24

World Record Number 5: 31 water melons
dropped on stomach in one minute
from height of 10m (2002)

After getting my fingers burned in Bollywood saga I became
convinced that I should approach my next record in simplest spirit.
I had been tempted away from the correct path and in punishment
for this I must humble myself even further. I had almost turned my
back on the common man when he most needed my example, so
only way to win back his trust was to return to earliest source. I
must deliver my message directly into the minds and hearts of
youngest saplings from where the trees of my country's future
would sprout.

I decided to perform my next record in DAV Public School and
Junior College, Airoli, close by my residence. Significantly, my son
would later be a student of the school and I had been imparting
training of martial arts and gymnastics to the whole lot of students
for over one year hitherto. The principal watched me perform a
few records in the past that motivated him to accept my offer so I

could inspire his kids to embrace sports and fitness culture for overall development of a child.

We arranged the day sans hassle, and my pure motivation was restored by the thought of so many children from my locality now waiting to be instructed in the golden tenets of the dedicated sportsman's philosophy. To include them at a deeper level Mr Kota the principal ran an essay competition among the students with winning child receiving the honour of assisting with the record attempt. Lucky winner was ready to perform after only short briefing from me. He could not contain his excitement in fact. To be the first child and non-professional to assist in one of my records was a great honour for him and he eyed the melons like a hungry snake eyes the antelope before he swallows him. Ladders arranged in gymnasium for all the student body attending. A previously existing record so ratification was guaranteed.

The boy climbed to the top of the ladders and I lay in position beneath. Melons were passed to him by Mr Kota himself from parallel platform. Melons had been inspected and confirmed to be the genuine article, no trickery or hollowed segments and all nice and ripe for ultimate delivery.

I had gone up the ladder previously with the star student to show him where to drop the melons. Gopal Dutta stood in for me lying on the floor below and I helped the boy line up his aim in conjunction with Gopal Dutta's solar plexus area. At this point Gopal Dutta had recovered from his tumour after several months of my close supervision and he was eager to play a hand in the attempt as marking his return to full fitness. In this instance the boy dropped a soccer ball only to replicate the trajectory and preserve Gopal Dutta from potential harm. He scored a direct hit in the intended spot. He was very happy with his success. I advised him to copy this motion closely when the real attempt began.

Lying under the ladders I received tremendous feeling of bliss. I was returning to the roots of my pure actions and all memory of my recent temptation was fading into darkness. Soon I would no longer carry the shame of it. It would be wiped out completely by my latest success under glorious banner of the children's loving support.

Mr Kota passed the first melon to the boy and he dropped it with only slight hesitation. It scored a direct hit as practised. Next one likewise. I retreated into calm shell to absorb each impact. It was very peaceful there because I knew my meeting with the devil was over. He was far in the distance behind me and under no illusion that he would ever be welcomed back. When Gopal Dutta called time and I stirred from my trance I was a whole man again. With another World Record under my belt and pride of my community restored.

After the felicitations and photos with the student body I was invited to address the students. It was my pleasure to convey to them my advice on the best way to grow strong in body and mind. This was in years before the explosion of mobile phones and computer when the couch potato lifestyle was less of a problem and there were no malls in my locality to encourage eve-teasing and idleness of later fast food boom. My duty to instil positive habits was more easily achieved. In fact from this visit I was able to recruit many children to my karate school and some have stayed on to become black belts in adult years. My first successes as record trainer came from this batch. Six of my students created Limca records in various disciplines like step-ups, jumping jacks, cartwheels, thumb push-ups, hand rotation and forward rolls (somersaulting). All juniors from ages of six to fourteen. Over the years I have helped them develop into young people of the highest attribute owing to natural elastic quality of young limbs and lack of fear.

This can be taught only if the student is willing and my role in their success is bringing me much satisfaction.

I was glad that I could motivate the youngsters to get into the competition arena. Life has certainly changed for better after having stepped into the record books as a small-time celebrity unlike film stars and cricketers. I feel great to be a person with extraordinary achievement which has been dream for others in the neighbourhood. People who know about you respect you very much for your additional calibre. That may not be sufficient to feed your stomach and family. But the passion to do something different kept me alive with utmost dignity. Clubs, institutes and associations invite you as chief guest and motivator because of your feat. I enjoy the recognition to the fullest as a common man becoming a celebrity of sorts gives me immense pleasure. I celebrate myself every other day on my own as a person having uncommon ingredients. For me every day there is a new challenge to survive and keep doing the good work to live up to the expectations of your well wishers.

At one time it was my sincere hope that my son Shubham might follow me and the young people I have trained into the record-breaking mould. He was six years old when the influx of child students first bombarded my classes and naturally keen to spend time with his father in the training. This began earlier with him imitating me while I performed my routines at home. I bought him a karate suit like mine but in small size and with a white belt to signal beginner. Shubham would wear this night and day and never take it off until he fell asleep and his mother removed it very carefully to allow washing. He was like a copy of his father in tiny scale. The kicks and punches he saw his father perform he would mirror with fine enthusiasm though technically they were inferior brand. I asked him if he wanted to join my class and he agreed sans delay. First weeks and months were a lovely time with my son never leaving my side during practice sessions in Navi Mumbai Sports Association. Many children's voices could be heard ringing through the air in spirit of dedication but Shubham's was the loudest because he was closest to me and his heart was full up with trying to impress his father like all boys do at this age. What a lovely feeling to know that he had chosen to make my passion his own.

I spotted the perfect chance to cement a role for him in the extreme sports field and ensure the hearts of father and son were combined for all days ahead. His great pal in the class was a boy called Dilip, who had just set a record of 6km somersaulting endurance thanks to my efforts in training him and his own indomitable thirst for excellence. Shubham was as impressed by Dilip's achievement as anyone. This is when I asked Shubham if he would like to follow his father and his young friends into record-breaking arena. I would help him to select a suitable record and make sure he had every ingredient needed to smash it. Not only would this give Shubham a taste of the superior feeling I had enjoyed when each record fell but also would clinch a lifelong habit for the clean living and sacrifice which allows a sportsman to walk unafraid through all weathers. I told him this would make me very happy and that he would be happy also. I told him to think of a record he might wish to master. We could begin preparations as soon as he decided.

Shubham was quiet for some days after this. His tiny face clouded in high concentration as he introspected on the count-less joyful moments which would open up to him when he landed on his selection. God was talking to him at this time and I did not interfere. Their conversation was private and I had no part to play in it.

This was nail-biting time for my wife. She did not understand why our son was so serious when just days before he had been running and laughing through the home. When she tried to stroke his hair he would not let her, turning his head away and going to sit on his own to facilitate clearer thinking. This made my wife cry many times.

'Not to worry,' I told her. 'The boy is deciding his future. The man he will be depends on these moments. It is something all boys must do. I myself went through similar process. When he has decided he will come back to you. All will be well.'

My head buzzing with ideas of the record he might choose and how I might play my role in glorious achievement. First of many, God willing.

Then the fateful time arrived for Shubham to deliver his verdict. I freely admit to you that my heart was beating like a drum waiting to hear his destiny conveyed to me. When it came I almost fell to the floor in state of shock and disappointment.

He did not want to be a record breaker, he said. He had decided that this was not the path for him. No interest in following his father. He just wanted to play cricket or soccer or design cars. No record came to his mind and no burning desire was there in his heart for the life his father had made.

I asked him if he was sure. Had he heard God's voice clearly on this matter. He replied that he had. It had felt warm in his ear like a wind. This is how I knew he was telling the truth.

I went away to my bedroom to meditate on this momentous event. Some tears were shed of surprise only. It had not been the news I was expecting. I watched the future I had been planning for fall away and saw another one rise to take its place. This took several minutes and I waited patiently for the new world to build itself as the almighty commanded it. Then I went back into the room where my son was and held him in my arms for a precious stint. I told him I was very proud of him. He had listened to his heart and followed its advice like a man, with no fear or hesitation. His heart was like a lion's.

My wife was very happy to know the outcome and we celebrated with rare trip to the dosa kiosk across the road from our apartment for muttai dosa.

You may be wondering how I could handle the disappointing news in such a positive spirit. The answer is simple. My son is his own person. He is as different from me as two oranges from the same tree. The tree may be common to both in the nourishment it provides but each fruit is separate and must occupy its own space accordingly. Also Shubham is my best friend and I love him. This means that I must allow him to follow his own path. He does not have to be like me. I will bear the differences between us as well as enjoying the binding qualities. God has a different plan for each of us. When you love someone you should not stand above them as the leaves to shade them from the burning sun. You should stand back and give them a clear sighting of the sky. This way they will grow to their full height. You can watch the journey in comfort and take great pleasure in the shapes they make.

Thank you.

The rain fell. It roared and kicked and pulled the breath out of me. Already I couldn't see ahead to a time when it would stop. The world cooled and filled itself in, everything that was once empty became swollen and precarious. Shoes and silences drowned. The sunglasses sellers left their intersections for higher ground and second jobs weaving placemats out of the hair their wives had harvested from unsuspecting sightseers in the high season.

The birds and the butterflies all went away. The street danced and life moved inside.

Bibhuti plastered his leg. It was a clean break and he was skilled in repairs. It would heal in two weeks, he said. I needn't be worried. He'd broken every part of himself in pursuit of his sport and he'd always healed himself to full satisfaction. The break was a good thing, it meant I'd overcome any fear I'd had of hurting him.

'You are ready now,' he said.

'I don't feel ready.'

'You will. I am very proud of you in this moment. I knew you were the right man for the job.'

His wife made draughts of turmeric and milk for the pain. Jolly Boy brought a sack of rice for him to rest his foot on. The TV consoled him in his time of inactivity. He played the tapes of his record-breaking history, and mesmerised himself into a rapture from which all future spells would rise. Visual proof of his superpowers gave him nourishment and he hit the phone, calling in favours and spreading word of the record attempt like a boastful smog through the city. He set a date, four weeks away to allow for his recovery. There'd be advance notices in the city and sports sections and Bibhuti was promised an interview in his own paper.

After tense negotiations the venue was confirmed, the temple where his wife worshipped. She'd pushed for it as the only way of guaranteeing his safety. At the closing of the deal she dashed out in the rain to give her thanks to the priests in person. She came back spattered in caramel-coloured mud, bags of food swinging from the handlebars of her scooter. She cooked a celebration thali of dhal and gobi and something with cashew nuts.

The new school term started but Jolly Boy stayed at home. He confessed between our courtyard shuffles that he'd been expelled for fighting. Another boy had questioned his father's sanity. The privilege of being Bibhuti's son needed constant defending from the book-shy dullards of his class. Until a new school could be found he was mine to lean on. His laughter was my medicine whenever my belly ached or my legs started to shake under the stress of his father's expectations.

Bibhuti still hobbled down to the courtyard to put me through my daily paces, sitting on the bonnet of his car spitting motivational slogans at me while I brutalised a man made of rice sacks, perfecting my swing and sharpening my taste for his blood. The rain pinned us to the walls and sprayed the face of Jolly Boy's stop-watch whenever he tried to get a reading. It kept putting out the flames at Gopal Dutta's funeral. The smell of him roasting made me hungry. It stuck to me for days.

His death came as a shock. I'd supposed it was the return of the cancer Bibhuti had banished all those years ago. I expected to be revisited as he'd been. Bibhuti claimed natural causes, just his age catching up with him. His reaction to the inevitable was to pine for a day behind the locked bedroom door. When he came out he was himself again.

He took a practice bat to the cremation to use as a prop. It held him upright when he stood at the pyre to mumble a farewell to his eldest student. He hoped also that it would remind the mourners that Gopal Dutta had been an ally to our grand plan. In his absence life would go on and greatness would follow.

He'd wanted to be a woman next, his daughter told me. He liked the idea of carrying children who could eat his sins while he slept.

Every day a suspension of disbelief. A brave front against the constant chatter of gods and reincarnations. Everyone was wired in to your presence but I hadn't seen you yet and I couldn't feel you coming. I looked in the rain and I looked in the dead face of Gopal Dutta. I looked in the scars on Bibhuti's back from a decade of self-flagellation. I saw nothing there that inclined me towards you. Darkness still awaited me sooner or later and my occupation became sandbagging myself against the fear of it.

The air con flitted like a restless bird from off to on to off, and I was a bird to be fussed over between the customs of the house. Every so often Bibhuti would look up from his laptop, the secret write-up he wouldn't show me, to ask if I was comfortable and had everything I needed. He'd consult with his wife who'd retreat to the kitchen and return with another plate of mango slices or another glass of water.

Bibhuti brought a bat inside and took to bunting it absently against his shoulder or his unplastered leg as he sat thinking between stints at the keyboard and in the quiet times after meals. Every impact set the teeth of the room on edge, all but his. He was blissful in these moments, fantasising about the places I might hit him and the pleasure it would bring. He beat out a guillotine rhythm that had his wife fleeing to the kitchen to scrub the pots with audible force.

Then silence would wash in again and all would seem as it should be. I decided that his faith was just a wilful act of forgetting. He needed to forget that should he fail his death would stain other lives. That was how he bartered his own fear down to a whisper in the dark that nobody else could hear.

Vijay Five came to interview Bibhuti for the newspaper. He didn't ask Bibhuti any direct questions beyond the date and location of our attempt. He already knew Bibhuti's story and had made his peace with it.

Bibhuti asked for the front page. This would be his crowning achievement and he wanted everybody to see it and know what could be done with the right attitude.

Vijay Five said he'd try but it wasn't in his hands.

I posed with Bibhuti when the Turbanator arrived, bowed and tested by his journey through the new rivers that had sprung around the city as the rain kept falling. I was a front-page story and the city welcomed me. I represented hope in a time of siege.

The news had moved on from a crashed plane to the monsoon's more predictable death tolls. No slo-mo or strings for them. People had already started drowning in uncovered sewers and falling from crumbling bridges. Mostly on the mainland where things were older and order hadn't been planned into the fabric of life. Nature, we agreed, had no sympathy for the underdog.

Vijay Five asked Bibhuti if he'd include me in his book.

'You're writing a book?' I said.

Bibhuti was bashful. 'It is a timepass only. I might not publish it. It is the story of my life and my record-breaking achievements. I began to write it some months ago when it looked like I had set my last record. It was a bleak time and I wanted to record my journey so that history would not forget. Then shortly after you are arriving and all is saved. I am carrying on with it so that I can look back in the future and remember this precious time with full details and emotion. We can look back together.'

'Am I in it yet? Have you made me look good?'

'You will appear soon. I will describe everything as it is happening in reality. You will be very pleased with the outcome.'

I said I hoped so.

The rain's spectacle fixed us to our place. The longer it kept falling without our consent the surer we became of our debt to it. It was a reminder of scale and a quickener to the senses. Watching the water tumble and rise we reckoned ourselves key pieces of something bigger and beyond us, two of the plumb twigs that held the nest together. We owed the rain for the liberating smallness it gave us. To be small to a storm, but fearlessly and through prior arrangement, was to be a splinter in its eye.

A week of flooding and healing and Bibhuti kept worrying his plaster, feverish with the urge to tear it off and be free again from the weight of caution. One afternoon when we were stranded on the stairs we saw a Maruti Swift come limping down the flooded street, pulled towards the pothole that had opened up outside the dosa kiosk. It slid to the pothole's mouth, tipped its nose in submission, and fell in.

Bibhuti stroked his moustache and shambled down the steps to conduct a rescue effort. I went after him.

The driver of the Swift clambered out of his window all elbows and knees and plunged into the water. It was waist-deep where he fell. He waded around the prow to the passenger side. He coaxed and pulled his wife breechways through the window, her behind snagging on the door and then shucking clear in a moment of lewd release. Her sari dragged in the muddy water and she found her feet. The husband tugged her to the rear of the car where it perched on the crater's edge. He lifted the tailgate and started salvaging its cargo, passing boxes to his wife where she stood on the higher ground beyond the rim.

Their little girl sat in the back seat. Her eyes shimmered with fear. She kept trying to open the door and her mother kept barking at her to stay put. The car was listing to one side and the water there was window-high. The girl scrambled to the safer side and waited to be freed.

Wading was heavy going for Bibhuti with his plastered leg. Jolly Boy skipped ahead to guide us to the car. We held hands and formed a chain. I stepped ankle-deep and my shoes flooded. I imagined myself immune to the waterborne nasties.

Bibhuti slid to the husband's side, took hold of the bumper and lifted, trying to haul the car clear of the crater. The wife started moving the boxes from the kerbside to the step of the Ayurvedic clinic where the water couldn't reach them. They were all of the same dimensions, taped shut.

The little girl beat her fists against the window and started squealing.

Her father picked his way round Bibhuti's heaving arms and carried on plucking boxes from the back. His wife received them from him and carried them to safety. Their focus so intent on preserving their treasures that their child's terror went unregistered, her screams snatched away by the clattering rain.

I waded to her and told her to open the window. She didn't understand. Jolly Boy repeated the instruction in their language. She tried the handle but it wouldn't move. I forced the door open and grabbed her. Water flowed into the car. The husband wailed at me for ruining his upholstery.

I lifted the girl onto the roof of the car and told Jolly Boy to stay with her. He reached for her ankle and stilled her, murmured something comforting. She stopped her squealing, shocked into herself by her sudden exposure to the sky's fury.

Her father dropped a box in a rushed handover and I heard something shatter inside it. He swore. The girl yelped and threatened to cry. To placate her, the woman passed another box up to her for safekeeping. This one was open. I peeked inside and saw that it was half full of snowglobes. The girl wrapped her little arms around the box and clung to it, her young face twisted into something ancient and worn down by life's misfortunes. Her legs dangling and her hair getting drenched, she held on for dear life. She put all her passion into being a safe pair of hands.

I saw more snowglobes when I joined Bibhuti at the lifting. Some of the boxes in the car were open and they were all filled with them. Every one contained a tiny model of a power station, roughly detailed in plastic. The cooling towers looked so out of context in their childish shell that I thought I might be dreaming. I picked one up and shook it to make sure it was real.

There could have been more snow. The volume of glitter was disappointing.

'I only just took the delivery,' the man griped, clawing at a box and dumping it in his wife's arms. 'This is in my native place. My father worked there and so did my uncles and two of my brothers. I worked there also before I moved away to make my own business. I had these made to commemorate them, custom order from China. I sell all kinds of novelty items in my store, all high-quality and best prices. These will be a good seller, many people will want to pay tribute to the men who made our country the new super-power in the world. This power station is a symbol of our future. I cannot lose them.'

'You could have done with more snow,' I told him. 'Look, when I shake it. There's not enough. They should have used more glitter.'

The man stopped what he was doing to watch as I shook the snowglobe again. He was unmoved. 'No, this is just right. If there is too much you will not see the power station clearly.'

I was irritated. I was trying to help him and he wasn't listening to me. 'No, people want to see plenty of snow when they shake it. It's no good otherwise. They can still look at the power station when it's sitting there, you can see it all the time. But when you want to make it snow it needs to snow properly or there's no point.'

The man picked up a snowglobe and gave it a shake. He watched the glitter swirl sparsely over the cooling towers.

'See, it's not enough, is it? It's not satisfying.'

Bibhuti lifted the back end of the car clear of the road. The car tilted away from him and I heard a scream.

I turned to see the girl sliding off the roof. Jolly Boy had recoiled when the car had moved and lost his hold on her. The girl let go of her burden and the snowglobes she'd been holding fell over the side, some smashing and some bobbing away down the incline in the road.

Her mother balled her sari at her hip and splashed after them.

I caught the girl just before she hit the ground. I stretched myself as tall as I could go and kept hold of her. Her little wet hand clutched my neck and I felt my skin prickle from her touch. I carried her to the step and showed her that we were safe from the water. I told her it was alright. She bawled.

I hated myself for not knowing the words that would make her feel safe. I loved myself for saving her. I was a good man. Everyone who was looking could see it. She was my proof, right there in my arms.

She squirmed and her father was there to take her from me. He croaked a thank-you and went trotting after his wife and their fallen goods, the girl bouncing on his shoulder as he stooped to gather up a straggler.

The car rose and lurched forward. Bibhuti stepped the back wheels out of the crater, dragging his plastered leg in a wide radius to keep it clear of danger. He was steaming and pain flared from him in visible flashes. I rushed to his side and bent to grasp the bumper just as he set the car down on even ground.

When I looked up Ellen was standing on the kerb, unsteady and lifelike under the rain. Harshad, straddling his scooter, passed her walking stick to her and waited while she corrected herself. Ellen looked at me. She parted her lips to say something but no words came. I leaned into the car to still the trembling in my legs.

Bibhuti's wife came out and draped a shawl over Ellen's head. The women turned and went inside. Harshad rode off through the floodwater, a shameless conspirator. I let the rain fall on me. The bite of it was pleasant on my skin. I breathed my special breath and got ready to explain myself.

Ellen threw my wedding ring at me but her aim was poor and it fell at my feet and spun woefully on the floor tiles. I picked it up and slipped it into the pocket of my workout bottoms. They were sticking to me and I didn't know what day it was. I'd stopped recognising the differences between them. It had felt liberating when she wasn't here. Now it felt pitiful, a sad sign of the distance I'd strayed from the routine things that had once given me shape. The meals Ellen had cooked for me, the little traditions we'd invented so we could feel like a part of each other despite how far we'd come unstuck. Movie night and bingo and the weekly shop. Sunday night pill counts and Chinese Wednesdays.

I realised, powerfully, that we should have made children when there'd still been the chance of them. I should have given us other things to love that wouldn't rust shut over time like we had.

Ellen had brought the rain in with her. It hung over our heads in the living room while we all sat dripping in a stiff arrangement, blowing the skin off the tea Bibhuti's wife had cooked. Ellen's walking stick stood between her legs. Her special shoes were soaked through and puddles were spilling out from underneath them.

'I didn't do it to hurt your feelings,' I said.

'What, the walking out or the pretending to be dead?'

Her thin lips trembled as she said this and inflicted the words with a sharpness that had been filed over weeks and years of untold resentment. The sound they made came as a shock. Something hateful floated like wreckage in the blue of her eyes. Her patience for me had died and we were both compelled to mourn its passing with verve and uncustomary honesty.

'Both.'

She told me I looked like shit. I didn't argue. Barely any time at all had passed since I'd last seen her, but we were strangers now and I supposed we'd die that way.

'Was there a funeral?' I asked her.

'No. You're not dead yet. Not officially. The police couldn't find you. They said you'd probably been washed out to sea.'

'How did you find out?'

'Your bank statement. The flight and the hotel, it was all there. You didn't exactly cover your tracks. I booked the same hotel. The man said you'd be here.'

'I should have paid in cash. I wasn't thinking straight.'

'Obviously not.'

I told her she shouldn't have come. Not in this weather. What if the plane had skidded on landing? How could she come all this way on her own, without me to look after her?

She flushed, squeezed her stick tighter. She wasn't an invalid. She had as much right to be here as I did.

I looked round at the faces of the family and saw that my lie had burned them. Bibhuti was stroking his moustache mechanically, lost in the effort of recalling the last time he'd been so carelessly betrayed. Jolly Boy sat on the floor at his father's feet and snapped through the pages of the car magazine I'd bought him from the newsstand across the road. He whispered something irreverent to himself that sounded like an assessment of my character.

Bibhuti's wife was unchanged. I'd offended her irreversibly the moment I'd decided to take a bat to her husband and reconciliation had never been on the cards.

We listened to the wind and the rain battering the windows. When Ellen finally spoke it was to ask me if I was coming home.

I told her I couldn't.

I told her things had changed and my place was here. I'd promised to do something and I couldn't leave until it was done. It was something she might not approve of or understand, but it was a special thing, mine and Bibhuti's, and if I turned my back on it now I'd die a liar.

I told her our plan and waited for a reaction. She said nothing.

Jolly Boy read aloud about the AMG Mercedes and its gullwing doors. His mother went out to the kitchen to bang some pots together.

'I know it sounds impossible but we will do it,' Bibhuti said.

'He's got this gift, he can't feel pain.'

'I can control pain,' Bibhuti corrected. 'I have learned to master it. Also I am very strong.'

'It's destiny,' I said.

Ellen coughed up a hairball.

'I am giving him a cure,' Bibhuti said, anxious to help my cause. 'It has worked on others and it can work on him. There is no need to worry. I will save him. But he must stay to complete his treatment.'

Ellen looked at me fearfully. I told her about the cancer. I went through it all, how I'd been feeling and what it was building up to, making the appointment behind her back and feeling the doctor's hand up there digging around for evidence. Then the referral and the tests and the news. The brave decision I'd made to run before the news could spread and infect her.

'Why didn't you tell me?' she asked.

'Because I didn't want you to have to watch me die. I couldn't put you through all that. You had your own problems. I just had to get away. I'm sorry.'

She levered herself up from her seat, swatting away my help, and clicked to the kitchen to unleash her feminine sorrows on a sympathetic ear. She paused at the doorway and looked at my face. 'You should get rid of that,' she said. 'It makes you look like a pervert.'

I felt my lip, the patch of fluff growing there. I'd decided to stop shaving in a moment of whimsy, as ham-fisted homage to Bibhuti and as testament to my resurgent manhood. I'd regretted it when the itching had started but I'd kept going with it to save face.

'Why didn't you tell me it looked bad?' I asked Bibhuti.

'Some things are not meant to be,' he said. 'You must discover this as God reveals it to you, I cannot negotiate.'

'I liked it,' Jolly Boy said, having worked through his anger and befriended me again. He followed me to the bathroom to watch me get rid of it. The process was fascinating to him, as if I'd given him his first taste of a bullfight. I was the bull. I shaved the thing off and came back feeling brighter.

When the rain stopped I walked Ellen back to the hotel. She felt her way through the thick Indian darkness, along a path littered with the latest treasure from the overrunning sewers. Dead sanitary devices and lost costume jewels and various incarnations of shit. She was the flypaper my lies stuck to and seeing them on her shamed me. I steered her by her elbow to the spot where the old man once traded his gods. His absence hit me like a kick in the stomach. He was gone just like he'd said he'd be. He could have been any one of the raindrops that had fallen on me in the last few days. He could have been a god himself by now.

The picture was gone too. Harshad had whitewash on his hands and the wall was scarred with wire-wool scratches. The heroic figure and the defeated snake had been buried. A sense of jeopardy stung the air, the turpentine smell of dreams given the boot.

Harshad fussed at some paperwork behind his desk, bowed to the books. He couldn't look his vandalism in the eye. The glass of whisky at his side was full to the brim, a dare.

I asked him what had happened.

'It was a mistake, I see this now. I do not wish to be reminded. My wife is gone. My friend is gone. The rain has taken him away. Twelve years I am knowing him. I see him every day. Now I will never see him again. I do not want to remember anymore. I do not want to remember anything. I never knew where he went at night. He is happy where he is now but I am in great pain. If I look at this picture every day for one thousand years it will not bring back the things I have lost. I just want to forget them.'

Amrita came out from the back room, clutching a whisky bottle in each hand. She held them up for her father, a prideless catch. 'This will not make you forget. It will only spoil their memory.' She let the bottles go. They smashed on the ground.

Harshad flinched. He looked for somewhere to run to but he was stuck in a moment of grim revelation.

'You are a foolish man,' Amrita declared.

'I am a lonely man,' he said. 'I am old and tired and I have run out of dreams this morning. They are no good to me. Go now. I will clear up this mess. Go.'

Stubbornly Amrita went to pick up a shard from the broken bottles but her father shooed her away. She stormed out and in her absence Harshad let himself weep, a brief appalling rush of pain that leapt out from somewhere deep down and broke on the air like the snap of a bone. When he looked up it was over. He fetched the mop from out back and began dabbing at the broken glass. My offer of help was dismissed. I stepped aside.

I resolved finally to keep to my pledge of sobriety. I'd never touch another drink again.

'It was beautiful,' I said. 'The picture, I liked it.'

'Foolish man,' Harshad murmured. He pushed the mop around until it was sugared with glass.

Ellen turned away when I tried to kiss her cheek and swayed past me into the room. It was identical to the room I'd had. The same brand of loneliness dusted its surfaces. The loneliness of unaccompanied travel and clothes that had seen better days. She didn't belong here. She belonged where there was comfort and the climate was temperate. She'd never got on well with the heat. Her face was red and her breath came loud and shallow. She slumped onto the bed. I asked after her feet and her blood pressure.

I hadn't helped with either.

I couldn't say it, but I was proud of how far she'd come to put a spanner in my works. It couldn't have been easy, the travelling. If she'd fallen I didn't want to know. The image of it would be too horrifying to gloss over.

I felt my bad cells tearing round inside me, and I knew I wasn't going to recover. Bibhuti's methods weren't working. There was still pain. You hadn't bought my argument for mercy. Ellen wouldn't either. My impatience to live was a betrayal of her. She was too slow and I couldn't take her with me.

'If you want to wait for me you can,' I said. 'I'll come back with you when it's over.'

She shook her head at me. She told me I was going to make up for all the trouble I'd caused. I was going to put things right.

I tried not to touch her while she slept. The hairs on my forearms shivered when she moved. When she started snoring I cried with gladness. In the darkness she was a ship to sail away on and an anchor to my name. Her nightdress was faded from over-washing and she was the only woman I'd loved.

The plaster came off and I hit Bibhuti again. I carried on hitting him until my arm got tired and I had to stop. I stayed away from the bad leg, mixed up my targets to avoid another break. I made his back shine red. Jolly Boy timed me and touched the marks I made.

'Twenty-two seconds!' he yelled.

Another bat lay broken at my feet. My hands trembled with something elemental as the rain fell around us.

I hit him. I stretched and swung and every time a bat broke I felt proud. Out in the scorching rain or under the cover of concrete I hit him and hit him and hit him. The neighbours gathered to watch, huddled under their eaves, yelled to us from across the street of the latest landslides and blackouts. Roars went up when another bat was broken. Children were dancing on water, the roads were rivers and we were marooned on an island of splinters. The world twisted under our feet with every collision and we widened our stances to keep from slipping. We kept going until I had no more fight left in me.

I hit him. I got it down to two strikes for a break, across his back. His joy was absolute, a force that rushed in from somewhere hidden and buried our differences. He took everything I threw at him. He was real and alive and he liked it.

I was starting to believe in something, I could feel it growing in the places where my old complaints used to grind. Nature, or Bibhuti, or my body and the things it could do in its last hurrah. My own human fire. I don't know. But something fell with the rain in that sunken courtyard that made me dominant over the beasts of the earth. I pushed the sky away and you with it.

The nurse refills Bibhuti's drip and he recoils when the morphine hits. His lips part to release a startled breath. Everyone jumps. His wife reaches for his shoulder where a break in the plaster exposes it and tries to shake him awake. Bibhuti flops around inside his casing and Jolly Boy lets out a cry. The nurse coaxes his wife away but she shrugs her off. She thumbs Bibhuti's eyelids open. The eyes beneath are blind.

She jabbers something in her language and shakes him again. She shovels a hand under his back and tries to lift him. The plaster creaks and more of him splits. The nurse cuts in and prises his wife's hands clear. Bibhuti falls back onto the bed and lies still.

He sleeps, relentlessly.

His wife sits back down by his side, her face sheened with sweat from the effort of wanting him back.

'He's coming back, I can see it,' Ellen tells her. 'Any time now.'

'It's like an engine starting from cold,' I tell Jolly Boy, 'he just needs a few goes, that's all. He'll get there.'

Jolly Boy is frozen at the window. Not man enough to grind his heels into the days with the weight needed to change their course, he has stood and watched and hoped boyfully, waiting on tiptoes for the walls of his world to cave in. The room smells of his childhood's fading, the fat-flowers that bloom on forgotten chocolate.

His father wired up to a painkiller gives me a glimpse of what awaits me. Tubes sticking out of me keeping me just alive enough to suck the air out of a room, to ruin it for everyone else who still has plans and places to be. Too asleep to feel the loss of life while everyone else gets to watch it drip away. That's if the painkillers work. What if they don't and I feel every scratch? What if the memories hurt on their way out? That's a lot of hurt.

I don't tell Ellen how sick I'm feeling. I don't tell Bibhuti's wife either. We're not talking anymore. I'd tell her I was dying again if I thought it would console her. But she's too good at being human to take any pleasure in it. She tries to stop Jolly Boy following me out the door but he's set on getting as far away from his father's zombie show as his feet can take him.

We find Zubin in the orderlies' room, playing Paplu with the night-shift mortuary wallahs. We wait until the hand's played out. His nemesis is a moonfaced man who wears Shiva's trident in fraying ink on the inside of his wrist. He touches it for luck before each draw. The luck rubs off more often than not. Moonface calls rummy and slaps his cards down on the catering-size ghee drum they use as a table. The other players curse him. Zubin shakes the mystery from his hair and asks what he can do for me.

It was here that Zubin led me when I first tried my hand at bribery. I needed underpants and a razor and a clean place to make my ablutions while the siege rumbled on. I caught Zubin in passing and confided my needs. I jiggled my money bag at him as a sweetener. He took me to his hideaway and made a log of everything I could think of asking for. The things appeared an hour later as if conjured from the cracks in the walls. The razor had four blades for glide and closeness. The channa tastes good shovelled down behind closed doors and my trips to the basement give me regular breaks from the monotony of the bedside watch.

My attempts at corruption were clownish. Zubin never asked for money and my ungainly offers horrified him. He's immune to flattery and subterfuge. He just wants to help me out of respect for his elders.

'I've come for the key,' I tell him.

'Of course, sir,' Zubin says, and he frees the key to the staff bathroom from the chain at his hip and hands it over.

Me and Jolly Boy take turns in the bathroom, one guarding the door while the other labours under the anaemic shower and makes the most of the sliver of mirror to rub the soot from woe-tired eyes. I hear sobs coming from inside. I hold my breath and listen for him spending himself and when he taps on the door I let him out. He hasn't washed. He's bone-dry. He smells ripe and war-torn, his eyes mad with the terrible things they've seen men do. His oath to his father is to stay mired in grief for as long as his sleeping requires it. I don't mention the smell.

When it's time to sleep I lead Ellen to the room next to Bibhuti's, leased with a signature on a form and a show of big-number rupees. I catch snatches of rest with Ellen still beside me, keeping one ear on the crowd outside and dreading what might come through the window until darkness and the rain subdues them. Their placards become umbrellas and their brimstone hymns grow faint, rising like smoke to lull me into sleep.

The old man is back. Without his gods he stands stranded in the car park, his orange beard glowing. He holds his watering can at his side. The rain has stopped and the sun burns the world white. The old man's posture, poised and exhausted, suggests he's reached the end of a long and gruelling journey. He's walked in solitude with only his disappointments for company, having failed to turn into rain as he'd expected. He holds his head up straight in defiance of fate's deception. The protesters bow to him in deference and form a circle around him.

He raises his arm and empties the watering can over his head. He douses himself, shaking out every last drop, and then he lays the can down on the ground. A query to the crowd and a monk in saffron robes steps forward to consult with the old man. An agreement is reached and the monk scurries away to the fringes of the camp where a fire's burning. He lights a torch. He comes back and hands it to the old man. He holds it up in front of himself like a ceremonial relic. The monk joins the circle again and the circle widens, leaving the old man an island again.

A chant goes up, urgent and lascivious. The old man makes a brief concluding statement to the god who abandoned him and then he lifts the torch to his head and sets himself on fire. He blazes instantly and the crowd leaps back, their song caught in their throats. I leap back too. I want to cry out but I can't find my voice. The old man staggers around like a matinée mummy wrapped in consuming flame. Skin and memory fly from him in filmy shards. The window is open and his sparks fill the air with the sweet smell of barbecued meat. No one tries to put him out. He falls to the ground and rolls. The demonstrators clear a path for him.

I become aware of Jolly Boy beside me and I ease him away from the window. It's too late, he's seen everything. Shock has aged him and stolen his tears.

The old man rolls and rolls and then he's still. His dance with the elemental is over. He's found his peace at last. They let his body burn. They take up the chant again, sing their hearts out for the sacrifice he made. Children frolic in the old man's spillage. His flesh sticks to the soles of their feet. I see my beggar kids, all run out of things to sell. They chase each other laughing through the slick of the old man and disappear out of sight.

The demonstrators lift their voices higher when they see the orderlies emerge with a blanket and bundle the charred corpse up, skipping around the flakes that rub off him like black feathers. They run the remains inside. The police guard clamps shut again behind them and I'm spotted. It's the children who see me. They point to my window and the crowd follows their fingers. I duck, pulling Jolly Boy down with me. I hear the surge as the crowd lets its rage spill over. I saw a machete being shaken and it has my name on it. It looked blunt and terror shoots through me.

'You've got to do something,' Ellen says.

I rush from the window, past where Bibhuti sleeps. I push the door open. The TV reporter's slumped in her chair fingering her iPhone and Vijay Five's pacing lethargically, each step his attempt to set off a gentle earthquake that might stir his friend awake. I ask them to come with me.

'They will kill you,' Vijay Five says. 'A man has just immolated himself for you.'

'I knew the man,' I tell him, the horror of his death still smouldering before my eyes. 'I saw it happen. I don't know he did that for me, he had his own stuff going on. This isn't what I wanted.'

The cops give me a chair to stand on so I can be seen above the wall they've made for my protection. The radicals in the crowd make their lunges for me and are beaten back. I look for the machete and see it being wrestled from its owner's grip. A cop runs away with it and is chased down. He falls, and the crowd sweeps over him. He bobs up still holding the machete and his colleagues swarm in to shield him back to the holding line.

The TV reporter introduces me to camera. There are jeers. Signs are punched skyward that call for my hanging. Every face in the crowd is twisted in hatred. I talk into the microphone. I tell the reporter and her viewers that I'm an honest man.

'Bibhuti's alive. I'm his friend and I didn't mean to hurt him. I've given a statement to the police and they've let me go. I've done nothing wrong. There's no need for all this. You should go home, get back to your lives. I don't want anyone else to get hurt.'

I can't hear myself above the heckling. The police pull in tighter around me, lash out at the bravest to keep them honest. Children snake between the clashes, playing in a world at war. The torches are all lit. The spot where the old man went up has been filled in by the living sea. Men churn in a common swell, sticks and tempers all raised against me while the women on the outskirts cluck their tongues and weep. All this for me. I'm a god of chaos.

I feel like I should apologise for everything a white man has ever done in the name of ambition.

I tell them again that I'm Bibhuti's friend. I love him and I'd never wish him any harm. I only did what he asked me to do. I made him happy. I look out over the crowd. I don't know what to do with my face to show them that I'm sincere. I just hope that they can see it in me.

'If he dies I'll give myself up. You can do what you want with me then, I promise. I love your country. Please just leave us for now. Thank you.'

The reporter ties up and hands back to the studio. A policeman helps me down from the chair. A bottle thrown from the crowd screams through the air above my head. I don't hear it smash. I turn to see a nurse has been hit. Blood trickles from a gash above her eye. She's wailing and she doesn't care who sees it.

Bibhuti cried the way he laughed, with his whole body. He shook and shivered and let out a noise that was harrowing and inhuman. It shredded the air and scarred everyone in the room. The Guinness official reached for the bowl of food on his desk and held it down until Bibhuti was done.

'Sir, you cannot do this to me,' Bibhuti said. His lips trembled and tears rolled down his cheeks.

For the first time I thought of him as a weak thing, prone to the same disappointments as any other man.

'I am a sportsman of high standing, my record is there for all to see. You are mistaken if you think I am not up to this task, nothing is beyond my abilities. Please, sir, you must listen to your conscience. You cannot deny this to me.'

The Guinness man picked at his food with fingers yellowed with turmeric. He told Bibhuti that he lacked the power to intervene on his behalf. The decision had been made above his head. The Guinness organisation took the safety of its applicants very seriously. Our record was considered too dangerous to ratify.

'I have achieved many dangerous things before with no bad consequences,' Bibhuti argued. 'This time will be no different, I assure you of this.'

'We are not satisfied that this record can be achieved without serious injury. We would not wish to see you meet an unfortunate accident.'

'My Baba cannot be hurt!' Jolly Boy shouted, his eyes welling with tears. 'You are stupid!'

He ran out of the room, tearing a book from a shelf as he passed it. A three-year-old copy of the *Guinness Book of World Records*. It landed with a slap on the floor, spine up and splayed like a banana skin.

'Have you considered applying to Limca?' the Guinness man suggested. 'Perhaps you will have better luck with them.'

Bibhuti smoothed his moustache, composed himself. His voice took on an even instructive tone, a grown-up explaining a law of nature to a child with cloth ears.

'This will be my final record. After this I will have nothing left to give to the world. I know this in my heart, I have heard God tell me this in the nights when I am waiting for sleep to come. Sir, Limca is not the place for me. My last record will mean nothing without the name of Guinness behind it. I have had a long and distinguished career as staunch promoter of the Guinness philosophy. I have shed one thousand drops of blood and broken many bones to share your message far and wide. I must have your blessing.'

He stuck his hands together in an earnest namaste.

'Sir, tell me what I can do to make you believe. Anything you say and I will do it. Sir, please. I am begging you.'

The Guinness man stared at him unconvinced.

I went to the car and got a bat out of the boot.

When I came back Bibhuti was still rooted to the spot. Jolly Boy had returned and was picking absently at the prayer bracelet round his father's wrist. They both rose up rebellious when they saw what I had in mind.

The Guinness man tilted back in his chair, dodging a phantom swing.

'Let me show you what he's made of,' I told him. 'Watch closely. Then you can tell him if you fancy his chances.'

Bibhuti took up his ready position, his legs spread in front of the desk. I made myself some room and bunted Bibhuti across the shoulder, a short backswing just for example.

The Guinness man flinched as the bat hit home.

'It's okay,' I told him, 'it doesn't hurt him. He broke his leg three weeks ago, now it's better. You couldn't even tell. Look.'

I hit the leg. Nothing snapped. Bibhuti smiled vaudeville and I got a flash of us as a double act on a sepia stage, busting our guts for the amusement of some dozing philistine.

'You see?' Jolly Boy yelped. 'My Baba cannot be hurt! He is strong! He will win!'

'You may hit me if you wish,' Bibhuti invited.

The Guinness man waved his hands no.

I hit Bibhuti again a couple of times to prove our point.

The Guinness man knitted his fingers into a roof for his thoughts. Throats were cleared and the rain threw itself against the glass. The ceiling fan chopped at the resinous air. I said something I thought was key in the circumstances.

'I'll stay away from the head.'

'This is how we have practised it,' Bibhuti confirmed.

The Guinness man let out a weary sigh. Bibhuti swayed on his feet and I grabbed his elbow to steady him.

'It is a man's dying wish also,' Bibhuti added, and explained that I had cancer. The Guinness man raised his eyebrows.

'It's true,' I said.

Bibhuti told him how I'd come all the way from England to help him. That I was running out of time. Jolly Boy picked up the book he'd felled, put it back on the shelf with care.

'I cannot guarantee that your request will be granted,' the Guinness man said.

'Just ask them,' I said. 'There's no harm in trying. It's our destiny. I've got money.'

'That will not be necessary,' the Guinness man said. He picked up the phone and dialled with a fat middle finger.

Bibhuti sang all the way home. Cars were babystepping in the darkness. Their tail lights smeared blood on the road. The horns sounded fretful, all their cocky exuberance muffled to a whimper by the drumming of the rain.

A giant Ganesh glided past us, trussed to the back of a pick-up. Bibhuti's dashboard Ganesh averted its gaze as if ashamed of its brother's capture.

The rain stopped abruptly, a tap twisted shut.

The women were waiting in the courtyard to hear the verdict. The tension had infected them in different ways since Bibhuti had received the call to say that Guinness was withdrawing its support for the attempt. Ellen had been outspoken in hoping some bureau-cratic intervention would bring our madness to an end. The untold difficulties of her journey had made her impatient of our foolish-ness and she nipped at our ears with reminders of my abandoned life and the pressing need to go back and fix it.

Bibhuti's wife had kept her distance, straying to opposite corners of the rooms Bibhuti occupied, turning her face away whenever he looked to her for understanding. Sometimes I'd hear her humming a low honeyed lament for her former years of anguish. She coloured her hair while her husband locked himself in the bedroom to meditate on his options. While he scrambled for God's guidance she dashed to the arms of the woman she'd been before his sporting mania had unsweetened her. A hurried reunion while the hope flared that Bibhuti might come back to her as a man uncomplicated by ambition.

She greeted the news without comment. She was up the stairs and the door was slammed shut behind her before Bibhuti was out of the car.

Ellen had been introduced to the neighbours' feeding ritual. She held a striped tiger in the palm of her hand, watched it suck on a piece of banana. It tired of feeding and fluttered away, came to rest on a black skin dangling from the washing line. The neighbour's wife consoled her with assurances of her butterflies' loyalty. They'd carry on making visits as long as there was food for them and kind hands for perches.

'You're staying then,' Ellen said.

'Destiny cannot be argued with,' Bibhuti said.

'I suppose not.' She shuffled away, her special shoes squeaking on the damp concrete. She pulled herself slowly up the stairs. A butterfly rode her back. It fanned its wings in praise of itself and the sun that warmed its blood. She didn't know it was there and I didn't tell her. I wanted her to be something beauty felt a kinship with.

29

The roundabout statues of imperial patrons pricked at the night sky, their paternal reprimands shouted down by the traffic. We cruised by the forgotten ones sleeping top to tail in the park across the road from the Victoria Terminus, street traders catching some shut-eye between shifts selling cigarettes to the white collars. Bibhuti stopped the car and we got out to breathe the air and gawp at the grand building, its halls still ringing with the ghosts of terrorist gunfire.

Bibhuti's wife stayed in the car, singing lullabies to Jolly Boy in a secretive tongue.

Bibhuti had insisted on giving us the tour of Old Bombay's landmarks as a gesture of welcome to Ellen, and for us a dip into normal pleasures before we departed for the wild lands. Decency had demanded it be a family affair and Bibhuti's wife had caged her disenchantment for the night. Still it was there with us, a muted bird that shamed us with its silence.

'It is very beautiful,' Bibhuti prompted, and Ellen agreed.

'My city has not yet recovered from the damage. People are still afraid that another attack will come without warning. Fear is harming them as much as bombs and bullets. I would like to show them that fear can be dismissed. It can be blown away like a seed on the wind. When they see this the joy will return to them.'

'Aren't you scared of dying?' Ellen asked him.

'I am never afraid. I am in God's hands. He holds me like a bird. I am always safe there. When he releases me I will fly directly to my heavenly abode. No pain is there. Everything is the way it should be.'

The ghost bullets faded out and I found a quiet spot on the border of the park to be sick in. Then back in the car and on to the next point of interest, Ellen granted the passenger seat and me shameful in the back with Bibhuti's wife, placid as a lake that hides a nation's corpses.

Today was a surgery day for the god of the rain and Bibhuti's wife had come to bargain with him for an end to the destruction. At the temple she'd kiss his statue's feet and say a prayer that would scare the stormclouds into disbanding. All the floating atrocities spat from the flood would be auctioned for good causes and peace would return to the land.

'You do not kiss the statue,' she corrected. 'Only lay flowers.'

Bibhuti was scornful. 'People are praying to one god for the monsoon to come and asking another god to stop it when it becomes too wet. They are very undecided like this.'

We slowed to a crawl behind a relay of buses sprinkling pilgrims onto a street lined with food sellers and women sitting on the pavement spinning garlands for the latecomers. We parked up at the kerb, stretched our legs among the dying dogs and shitting cows. The queue for the temple snaked half a mile up the road and there were machine-gun nests at every corner, the privates watching from behind their sandbags for any scattering or thunderclaps that might spell trouble.

So many people all waiting patiently to beg for their lives with a plaster mediator. All stepping softly around the toes of their neighbours as they shuffled towards the temple, hanging on to each other's shoulders, clutching their flowers and their children. A sea of pepper, no two grains either separate or alike. Bibhuti's wife bought her offering flowers and joined the line. Jolly Boy and Ellen were wary accomplices. Bibhuti led me round the corner to a small square that skirted one side of the temple. We'd wait for them there unaccosted by their beliefs.

'I do not need to put flowers on a statue's feet to feel close to the almighty,' Bibhuti said. 'The almighty is everywhere and all around us.'

He took a sweeping look around the square to illustrate his point. I copied him. I saw the pineapple patterns on the bark of a palm tree, heard the low trill of secular lovers as they strolled past, untouching hands hung formal at their sides.

'I've never believed in anything,' I said. It was the first time I'd confessed out loud to being empty inside. It brought on a wave of remembered loneliness from days and moments past, a wave so strong that I had to sit down before it took my legs from under me.

Bibhuti's eyes misted with pity. He sat down beside me, smoothed his palm over the damp grass between us.

'Do you believe in me?' he asked. 'Do you believe in what we are doing?'

'It's crazy when you think about it.'

'Nothing is crazy. The world is full of mystery behind every door. Only few people open this door because they are afraid to see the truth. I am not afraid. Neither are you, or you would not come here. Together we will bring another truth into the world for everyone to see. They will use our example to live their own dreams. This way happiness is spread throughout the globe. I am very happy to be here. I will thank you for the rest of my life.'

I listened to the traffic circling the park, horns blaring to assert their dominance over the insects.

Bibhuti's wife came back from paying her respects, still veiled in the silence of the temple. Ellen wore the glazed-eyed look of someone who'd witnessed the acting out of a miracle by children with tinfoil halos. Heads bowed, we walked back to the car, our closeness making the air we breathed heavy and sweet as rotting fruit.

Bibhuti steered us towards the sea. I could feel it as it got nearer, the slow pull of something historic. When we made the coast I looked out and saw the sweep of the harbour behind me, a string of pearls glowing orange under the black sky, stretching away to a distant anchor point where the twenty-first century must have been born.

Marine Drive sparkled with sightseer horses, their heads bowed under festive plumages. Neon-dripped carriages pulled expectant romancers through a night of negotiated mystery. We sailed gently around the hooves and parked up in front of the Gateway of India, shining gold against the black wash of the bay.

Bibhuti stood us between the Gateway's legs and took our picture. I gave Ellen's stick to Jolly Boy to hold and put my arm round her shoulder. There was a stiffness that incriminated me.

'Smile,' I said.

Bibhuti aimed his phone at us and I held my pose, listening to the sea whispering at my back. Bibhuti persuaded his wife and Jolly Boy to flank us for some group shots. He gave the phone to his wife and got in on the act. He hugged me with more meaning than Ellen had done. He had the luxury of never knowing the real me.

When I saw the images we'd made my chest fluttered with the small wings of belonging, as if I'd swallowed a songbird whole.

I patted the nose of the horse Ellen had chosen, a grey mare with a pot belly and egglike eyes opaque with sadness. I whispered soothing noises to her and told her my name. We set off in silence. The first pothole we hit jolted Ellen out of her seat and I took her hand to steady her. She kept it there. I watched Mumbai wash over her and leave no visible traces.

I told her I'd wanted her to follow me. I couldn't face dying without her by my side.

'I know,' she said. 'That's why you made such a pig's ear of leaving.'

'Do you mind?'

'You could've just told me the truth. You could've said you were scared and you needed time alone or something. I might've understood that. I'm scared too. You didn't have to make out you were dead already, that's like you've given up. It's like you want to be dead. That doesn't make me feel very important, does it?'

'I know. It was stupid. Maybe I wanted to see how upset you'd be.'

'Did you get your answer?'

'I'm sorry.'

It seemed to make no difference to her. She only had eyes for the horse and the whip that drove it through the night.

I didn't know how much of me was left or how quickly I might fade. I didn't know about you then. Maybe the only way to die as myself was to get Ellen's love back. I needed to be gentle again once I'd broken Bibhuti the way he'd asked me to. Maybe it would be easier to be gentle after we'd scratched that itch. Cheating his death might brace me against my own and with that strength I could be a balm to others. I rested my hand on Ellen's. I'd put my ring back on and it felt loose. I fell into the Indian night with her and drifted to the sound of hooves.

30

World Record Number 6: 27 one-arm
chin-ups in 42 seconds (2003)

It is always a painful lesson to learn when a friend you once were trusting with your life turns and bites you. I experienced this only twice: first time as young boy in my native place when my best friend Adil tried to kill me, and again much later when Rajesh Battacharjee did the same.

First time was actually more painful than the second. As a young boy in Cuttack I was always very gymnastic, developing strength of fully grown man plus great flexibility from very young age. This was due to the work I did with my father on our farm. It was very physical and I enjoyed it for practical benefit of my family. When the day's work was done I would perform tricks for my own pleasure, doing chin-ups around my village. This came about quite naturally as there was an abundance of locations there: lower branches of tree or bamboo roof of orange seller or railway bridge over banks of Mahanadi River. Many arms of goddess Durga statue made a lovely spot for practice before their requirement in Durga puja which Cuttack is famed for across the nation.

The other children could only watch with much admiring. Each day they would set a new challenge for me, higher numbers added to my target, and I would break every one. Only Adil, my best friend of all, did not like the attention this brought to me. He became low in spirits and stopped walking to school with me. When the other children gathered to give me my latest challenge he was on his own at the other side of the yard. Final setback occurred when Adil brought a surprise challenge to me after weeks of no communication. He proposed a contest to see who could perform the most chin-ups from the railway bridge. He had been training in secret and wanted to prove that he was now stronger than me.

At first I did not accept his challenge as I was worried for his safety. He was not as comfortable with big heights as I was. But Adil would not rest until I had given in to his request. As his friend I had to accept that his desire was serious and based on personal honour. We would not let the adults know. We would go out to the bridge on a chosen day and there we would learn once and for all who was the stronger. Our friends would be witness and the result would put all quarrels behind us.

Chosen day came calling and we all took the long walk out to the bridge. Heavy feeling of guilt hung over us and also great excitement. When we arrived at the bridge and saw the river lying in wait below I gave Adil one last chance to drop his idea. But he would not.

'I am stronger than you,' he said. 'Everyone will see it and then they will follow me instead.'

'I do not care who they follow,' I told him. 'I just want you to be my friend again.'

'We will never be friends. I will beat you and then we will not speak again. I have decided this and you cannot change it. Now hurry.'

I wanted to cry when I heard his cruel words but no tears were coming at this time. Perhaps my heart was broken but I was too sad to hear it snapping. And so we went together to the bridge where it began its span across the river. We climbed down to the spot where the railing provided the best place to hang from. Friends staying on the bank to watch with much trepidation. We lowered ourselves together from the railing. Adil could not swim so a situation over the water was not on the cards. The sand fifty feet below which would make a painful landing if we should fall. We looked at each other hanging there and promptly began the chin-ups in matching sequence.

All was fine at first as we kept nice pace without tiring. Adil had indeed been training hard, as I could clearly see his strength had improved from steady motion of each lift. It was actually a great feeling to be exercising God-given energy alongside my friend in surroundings of nature, with the sun shining on the water and a fine current from the air tickling my feet. I let out a laugh. But Adil did not share in my joy. He was very serious, concentrating hard on beating me.

I realised at this moment that my only hope of restoring our friendship was to win the contest. If Adil won he would keep his promise to shun me. To win my place back in his heart I must teach him valuable lesson of his limitations and the peace to be found in accepting the role the almighty had laid out for him. So I pressed ahead with greater purpose, putting more effort into my lifts. He looked across and saw me outstripping him with ease. I hoped he would be disheartened and stop his foolish pursuit of me.

Instead he became very angry and upped his speed. This proved too much for him. His strength left him and he began to struggle. He could no longer lift himself in smooth action. His arms wobbled and he was forced to slow down. Still hanging there but in no fit state to support himself. He looked down at the sand below and his eyes filled with panic. But he would not climb up because it meant declaring himself beaten. He hung there like a twisting rope and refused all my efforts to relieve him.

The ground fifty feet below was looming and my confidence extinguished. I had to stop my chin-ups to focus all energies on maintaining my grasp. I was forced to climb up in order to preserve myself. I reached safety and turned around to pull Adil up: he was no longer there. Only a scream where he had been.

I felt a sickness and looked down expecting the worst. Adil was lying in the sand below, perfectly still like he had been painted there. Our friends clambering down the banks to aid him. Time became shrivelled like apricot stone. I made my way down to the river in state of shock to find Adil already expired. Nothing could revive him, it was too late.

Seeing my friend broken in the sand brought many feelings rushing in at once. Anger that he had not listened to me. Sadness that death must bend its grip around us even before we have prepared for it. Most of all I felt a powerful desire to give up myself to the almighty's pleasure. I said a promise at Adil's side that I would gain revenge for his expiry by living my life in the right way, making full use of all the opportunities at my fingertips.

After my painful experience with Bollywood I was very keen to rediscover old self, and this is why I poured all effort into breaking two records in close succession. The first of these was detailed in previous chapter. In quiet period between them I took a trip to

Tadoba Tiger Reserve in Nagpur where Shubham had long expressed his desire to visit. This to show him his father still loved him despite my decision to remain in old conditions instead of grabbing Bollywood riches. Sighting of majestic big cats brought revival in possibilities and restored the family love to previous level. Shubham provided one moment of anguish when he tried to touch a tiger as it crossed the track behind our Gypsy. Fortunately the tiger was too far away and I pulled his arm back inside before any harm could come.

Shubham was happy to have his father back and this time also allowed me to patch things up with my wife. With every effort peace was returning to our home and my decision to keep the next records simple met with approval all round. No special training required and no risk to my person. No complicated measures or preparations. This record was conducted in Mumbai's historic Victoria Terminus, a proud landmark for all attending (the happy event took place some years before unfortunate scenes at same location which sent dark echoes around the world), and received live telecast on New Delhi Television and Star TV. To this day I cannot pass the magnificent building without recalling to that time and reliving the joyful emotions which accompanied the day.

Twenty-seven one-arm chin-ups in forty-two seconds.

I heard the words spoken by Gopal Dutta and echoed by Adil from his viewpoint above. This record holds special importance for me, because it was to honour the memory of my best friend Adil. He died while trying to kill me but also provided strong inspiration for me to move forward through my span in determined and positive manner.

The world is full up with hidden traps in every direction the eye can see. You must be watchful and ready to leap if your foot touches on unfamiliar ground. When Adil came across a strange twig his desire was to test it. He jumped upon it to discover what was underneath, and underneath was nothing. Just a deep dark hole that he fell in. He was not satisfied with the place in which he was born. He wanted to take my place. The outcome was calamitous.

Such a calamity almost took me personally when Rajesh Battacharjee came calling. I had not associated with him for long time since the Bollywood scandal. I did not like the company he was keeping and he had lost face to the Bollywood producer when I walked away from the filming. There was a rift between us. However I welcomed him into my home as he was in state of disarray. I cannot turn my back on a person in need.

I listened with disbelieving ears as Rajesh Battacharjee told how he had reached a low point due to financial need and various projects failing to take off from the ground. He had become indebted to Mr Karkera, the Bollywood producer who had caused me such distress in past encounter. In order to repay debt and avoid a sticky end he had devised a plan for which he needed my help.

'Mr Karkera is a very powerful man,' Rajesh Battacharjee said. 'You think he is just a Bollywood playboy but there is much about him that you do not know. You are fortunate, BB, you have rare skills which you can make into gold. I do not possess these gifts, all I have is my nose. I must follow it where it leads me to sniff out the best opportunities. Now we must both make up for these losses. It is lucky for us that my nose has found an alternative option.'

He told me quite frankly how he had been diverted from the straight path by his involvement in political world of Mumbai. In his role as elected corporator he had many opportunities to serve the needs of his community and advance conditions for the common man, but unfortunately greed had got the better of him. He had been using his position exclusively to fill his own belly. He confided to me sleazy details of his activities within office of development, accepting illicit payments to grease the wheels of several construction projects around my city, including fancy apartment complexes and retail sector. In return for these payments he would award contracts and fix paperwork so that work could begin without proper checks and assurances. Because of this many projects were halted midway through due to exhaustion of funds and others were allowed to progress to completion despite severe gaps in quality of materials and safety feature. Thus my city is looking like a concrete jungle with many broken branches, office blocks half built and standing empty, residential towers collapsing without warning due to low-grade concrete and many unfortunate souls crushed in the rubble. Only people to benefit are contractors and Rajesh Battacharjee and his fellow conspirators on planning board of municipal corporation.

This had been going on for many years and the thought that my former employer, who once lifted me up on his shoulders when times were hard for me, could be involved and happily profiting from this evil function brought tears rolling down my face.

'Why did you do it?' I asked.

'Because it is the way things are done,' Rajesh Battacharjee replied. 'I am a family man, BB. I am just like you. I will do anything to protect my dear ones and make them happy. I came from nothing. To be born poor is no sin, but to die poor is foolish. I will not make that mistake.'

'I too have come from nothing. But my heart is not filled with greed. This is a lonely path and it leads only to ruin.'

'Not quite from nothing, BB. I gave you a job when you first arrived here. I gave you food when you were starving. Everything you have become now is because of me. This is why you cannot turn your back on me now.'

I was silent. Rajesh Battacharjee told me his plan for recovery of fortune and release from Mr Karkera's jaws. He intended to announce through his contacts in construction industry a major new residential complex for the mainland, on undeveloped site in Andheri. It would attach all top features of modern standard, including state of the art sports facilities onsite, and would offer splendid accommodation to high-class residents from elite of Mumbai. The gymnasium would be named in my honour and he would like to use my image and the recognition I had achieved in my extreme sports career to promote the project. He said this would be a big boost in attracting the people to invest in the apartments. With my name attached they would be clambering to sign up for every available unit in the block. No work involved my end except lending my name and image and perhaps appearance on website conveying benefits of all the fitness equipment on offer. In return I would have satisfaction of knowing I saved his life from the clutches of bad men and perhaps a cash sum from pool of deposits when all the units were claimed.

At this point you may be thinking that this was not such an unhealthy deal. I would agree wholeheartedly were it not for the fact that no such apartment block would ever exist in reality. Rajesh Battacharjee planned to pocket the people's deposits then make an announcement that the project had stalled due to unforeseen hitch-up. People would have no luck recovering their money as it was not legally protected. He might employ a fellow as front man to make the announcement, who would then flee when the back-lash came. This way no public outcry would stick to him and his reputation would be preserved.

Also he asked me to provide muscle to protect him from Mr Karkera and his henchmen in duration of the scheme until it had been successfully completed. For this there may be a salary.

Needless to say I was shocked by this idea. I told Rajesh Battacharjee immediately that I could play no part in it. With a heavy heart I decided to remove his name from my history for ever.

'It is wrong,' I told him simply. 'You cannot go through with this.'

'I have no choice. He will kill me.'

'I do not believe it. He is not so powerful that he can decide your fate in this way. Only God can do this. I will ask him to pick you up from this path and set you back on the correct route. When he has done this no harm will come to you. Now you must leave.'

Rajesh Battacharjee left my home vowing to proceed without my help. In the next days I spoke to him constantly to try and talk him into dropping his plan. But to no avail. Therefore I had no choice except to expose him. I could do nothing else, if only to protect the dignity of the common man whose pockets he wished to plunder.

Even knowing this would bring assassins to my door I would still have splashed the story. Such was my disappointment in Rajesh Battacharjee and the dishonour of men in general. I immediately began investigation with burning sense of commitment to the righteous cause. Using the words Rajesh Battacharjee had confided to me and my knowledge of Mr Karkera's dealings gleaned from my time on set of *Vengeance at Midnight* I painted a sensational picture of corruption and violent lawbreaking at the heart of my city's corporation. Some colleagues on my newspaper told me to leave this wound unpicked for fear of reprisal from powerful men but I was adamant the power of a truthful man would always be greater. My editor was unsure at first whether to publish my findings but I convinced him in the end with passionate plea.

Shortly after the story splashed across the front page: Navi Mumbai corporator embroiled in property scams stealing from the common man and in league with Bollywood producer-cum-organised crime boss. It was the talk of my city for many days consecutively. I waited for the call from the chief of police thanking me for alerting him to these shady goings-on and picture of the suspects in handcuffs being taken to justice finally.

No such call was coming. Instead the office of my newspaper was attacked with a small bomb causing damage to building. My editor fled to Dubai to avoid further trouble. Then came the attempt on my life. Leaving the office one day having delivered copy of my latest article I was beset by a dozen thugs on motorcycles and foot, all carrying lathis, chains, machete, etc. I knew that Rajesh Battacharjee had sent them to silence me. But it was too late for him. I had already revealed his deeds to the world and there was no chance for him to bury them again. I dispatched these twelve men sans hassle, very regretful that I must resort to violence to preserve myself bodily. It is always a sad time when one must strike one's fellow man down but there was no other option available to me. Hearing the cracking of another man's bones at my hand was a tough event but this is what I am trained for in order to resist the dangers of the world.

'Tell Rajesh Battacharjee that Bibhuti Nayak cannot be silenced,' I said to the stricken men as they lay at my feet. 'Tell Mr Karkera this also. The words I speak come directly from God and his mouth is bigger than all the seven seas, you cannot fill it.'

One fellow promised to convey the message and I helped him back onto his motorcycle after a quick examination revealed no broken bones except the jaw, which did not prohibit him from driving safely away.

I am happy to tell you that this message was delivered successfully, as no further attempts on my life were made before the police finally took an interest in my story. Rajesh Battacharjee, following extensive trial which became headline news throughout the nation, was sentenced to a hefty prison term. Unfortunately Mr Karkera escaped similar fate due to immunity purchased by bottomless pockets. But a different level of justice was served to him by the almighty when he succumbed only weeks later to hail of bullets fired by a rival Don.

I was given the duty of reporting on the trial for my newspaper and witnessed in person the sealing of Rajesh Battacharjee's fate. A careless threat to my life was uttered on passing of the sentence but he was in no position to act upon it from a central jail cell.

From this eventful segment of my life you will see how littered is the path of the righteous man. Mostly with the stones which wicked men are throwing to obstruct the journey to destiny's shore. Such men are only envious that their journey is not blessed by the guiding hand of God or illuminated by the talent he gives as a gift to his chosen few. Friends are changing to enemies at the drop of the hat and it is the righteous man's job to keep his eyes peeled for this eventuality.

Now a new friend has come to me from across the seven seas. His name is John Lock. I did not expect his arrival. It was a surprise gift from the almighty who sent him when I was most in need of his support. His commitment allows me to forget all previous betrayals. He is the first man I have known from England and also the first man I have met whose spirit matches my own. He has been tested very harshly since arriving with illness and unfamiliarity with Indian climate and he has sailed through each test with only minor complication. Soon we will embark together on ultimate test and my mind is very calm because I know he will protect me in the final time. When we have achieved our goal together our love will be sealed and I will wash my blood from him personally. Then we will live out the rest of our days as closest companions who share the sun and rain and all the food nature provides. This is our destiny and there is no force in the world which is strong enough to come between. Sometimes I wonder how so huge the earth becomes so tiny.

Thank you.

In the last days the women stamped their protest against us in silences and cooking. They stirred and chopped and whispered and tutted like twins conjoined in alliance against the hurtful outside world. They took slow morning walks together and rode to the market, Ellen precarious on the back of the scooter, trawling home bags of fresh ingredients to assemble skilfully while the men huffed and puffed in the courtyard below them. The scratches they left on the chopping board betrayed their own obsession. They would have made dolls to stick pins in if they'd had the wool and the stuffing.

I was back on Bibhuti's sofa. Ellen had only let me share her bed that one time, an act of mercy to mark our reunion. She couldn't stand to have me sleeping next to her again. She'd ask after my aches when she arrived at the apartment for a day of bearing crosses, and tell me off for leaving my socks on the floor.

We had our own alliance, the three men of the house. After a tireless campaign Jolly Boy had convinced his father he had what it took to be the third point of the triangle, the one who'd pass the fresh bats to me as each one was broken. Given the nod all his anxiety melted away. He showed his gratitude by turning his back on the women. He spoke to his mother only when manners demanded it and where once he'd found his calling in making her smile, now he found it in the stopwatch and the icepacks he applied to his father's multiplying bruises. When I broke my first bat in one strike Jolly Boy was there to pick the splinters out. He offered them to me as a souvenir, sensing their importance. We put them in a cup that we left in a safe corner of the courtyard, out of the rain but close enough to feel its spray. I said flowers might grow from them. He liked that idea.

Bibhuti ended each session more bruise than man but by the evening they'd disappeared. I began to suspect he was painting himself whole again when he locked himself in his room. I listened for the brushstrokes in his meditation silences.

All Ellen wanted to do was eat up the sun after too many years of cold weather. Suddenly the heat that once paralysed her seemed to draw out of her a vitality I thought long lost. I watched the Indian climate buff a shine onto her that I hadn't seen in half a lifetime, something rich and youthful and provocative. I watched her ripen and forget her disability, become red like an apple.

Sometimes I'd catch her looking at Jolly Boy with naked longing. She'd reach out for him whenever he passed too close, steal a stroke of his head. I felt the absence of children again. A small head of thick hair I could run my fingers through and an uncorrupted mind I could fill with the last thing I'd learned. A fact about friendship or the fish that lives in the lowest depths of the ocean, the one that comes with its own lantern to steer it through the darkness.

At the end of the day we'd all come together to bury our hatchets and eat. We talked economically about food and weather and the key differences between our two cultures, me feeling an affiliation to neither one. Adrift with Bibhuti above the pull of national customs. Citizen of nowhere, light-headed with the rare and shocking freedom that comes from giving up a flag.

The wives would clear the table and wash up and we'd draw into a circle to spin our myths, letting the imagined details of Bibhuti's happy ending swirl around our heads while the window blackened and the thunder growled. Jolly Boy saw all his friends crouching at his father's feet, pictured a national holiday in his honour. Bibhuti agreed that that was possible. I just looked forward to when it was all over and we were still standing, only bigger and surer than we'd stood before. Any thrill to be gained from the striking would be incidental. If it came it came. I wouldn't pretend not to feel it.

I went barefoot in Bibhuti's house and Ellen saw her nail polish on my toes.

I explained myself to her. I'd done it once when I was drunk and in the cold light of day it seemed wrong to stop. It would be disrespectful to her if I didn't keep it up.

'It's quite relaxing, isn't it?'

'You've gone over the lines,' she said.

I wasn't as steady as her. She agreed. It was a difference between us and it was too late to fix it.

I took my dose of cardamom and breathing, crossed my legs and closed my eyes in the living room and went through the motions of meditating. Bibhuti massaged me, his Ayurvedic fingers drawing my pain briefly to the surface where it could be examined and declared to be in decline. Ellen watched and pretended not to be uncomfortable with the sight of me arching for relief under the hands of a brown man with a vested interest in keeping me alive.

More than once she mentioned modern medicine and Bibhuti had to beat her down. Chemotherapy was pumping poison into the body and surgery was the slitting open of a body with knives and saws. Both acts of violence and obscenity. If I was to be cured only love and the wisdom of ages would do it. My doshas could only be pacified with his attentive care and the care of the God who worked through him. Ellen bit her tongue and I answered yes when Bibhuti asked if I felt better, wiping the sesame oil from his fingers. Admitting a weakness to him now would only disturb him and he needed all his fearlessness.

I'd walk Ellen back to the hotel through the swarming night, watching the path ahead of her for hidden dangers. Harshad would poke his shining head up from behind his latest project, wiring up a CCTV camera bought from the mobile phone shop next door in a moment of feverish speculation. That he was planning for a future where such things might be needed was an encouraging sign. But when he asked after my health it was with no care for the reply. His eyes were buttons and the furnace of his heart was down to its last embers. The glow it gave off was so pale that it failed to light all but the immediate space in front of him, so he had to bend close to the counter top to see the camera's innards and pick up the glass beside them.

A touch of cheeks and Ellen would pull the door shut on me. I'd hear the creak of bedsprings as she sat down to busy herself in autopsy of the day's miscarriages.

A dog followed me home in the dark. I sat down with him on the kerb outside Bibhuti's apartment and stroked his head until he fell asleep, his chin resting in the filthy groundwater.

It was coming back from our visit to the ape girl that everything nearly came undone. Her name was Rebati and she was Bibhuti's last assignment before he took his leave to break the bats. She lived in a slum on the mainland, in a house made out of reclaimed bill-board and packing tape. Her house advertised Bru coffee and smelt of shit. She was covered in thick lustrous hair and she was comfortable in her place. She wanted to be a teacher so she could tell the children all about tolerance and nature's various miracles.

Rebati's father had the same affliction as her. He invited us into his home with a smile that barely poked through the fur on his face. While Bibhuti interviewed his daughter he threw clay pots on a pedal-powered machine in the corner of the room. Every one of them came out smooth and flawless. Things of beauty that were destined to eat cigarette butts on the patios of franchise bars back home.

Rebati accepted her fur as a blessing from God and was only submitting to the treatment her father had campaigned for to soothe his guilt at having passed on his condition to her. He suffered extreme sadness for his daughter's plight but Rebati herself was a girl for whom life held no fears. She went to school and she walked the streets of her locality with her head held high. Throughout our visit a crowd of smaller children stood guard at the door, her protectors from the Turbanator's insensitive lens until she agreed independently to pose for a portrait.

I wanted to comb her arms. Her coat shone healthy and cared for and her overgrown lips jutted apelike, pinching her voice to a whisper that encouraged meditation in its listeners. She was something strangers tossed money at in return for divine favours and I was excited to be present in the same world that had made her.

Bibhuti told me how the doctors in her native place had tried to steal her blood.

'They wanted to sell it to foreign agencies for research. They believe she has missing link genes that could spell important news for the scientific world. Other scrupulous doctors insist there is no gene at work, only a disease which can be treated with surgery. They made a case for experimental treatment and after five years of campaigning a specialist in Mumbai has agreed to take her on. The first surgery will correct the unexpected growth of her lips and dental parts. Then a laser will take away the unwanted hair. She is hoping that the treatments prove unsuccessful so that she may continue in the life she has always known.'

'She's really happy like that?' I asked.

'God is making her this way for a reason. She believes it is to teach the world a valuable lesson. I understand this very well. God has chosen us both from among many. She has been given a special purpose just like me. She is asking if you would like to touch her.'

Rebati took my hand, peeled it tenaciously open, and ran it down her forearm. She felt like a dog. Less oily than I'd expected. She invited me to touch her face and I did, gently with the tips of my fingers. I pinched her hair between my fingers, played with her split ends. I used the palm of my hand to stroke her more confidently. She smiled at me serenely. Her eyes appeared very small behind the dense growth of hair. They sparkled with a kindness that could change the world.

The Turbanator lent me his Hero Honda to sit on when my legs started to buckle. I invited Rebati for a stationary spin but she laughed off the idea. Her amusement came from simpler sources, from the attaching of Hello Kitty clips to the hair on her cheeks and the farcical barking that startled the younger children into fits of delightful terror.

She wanted her photograph taken so she'd have a record of the girl she'd been born as, just in case the treatment worked and took her blessing away. She'd get the paper and pin the article above her bed. When she married, if the shedding of her hair ever made her a candidate for marriage, she'd carry the picture around with her in secret from a watchful husband. She'd steal away whenever the opportunity arose to look at her old self and remember that she was once a comet in the black of the Indian night.

Coming back to the apartment with Rebati's barks ringing in my ears the rain began to fall again. Bibhuti parked the car and went back out into the street to put on a show, one-handed cartwheels for the neighbourhood kids who'd grown tired of the storm's adventure. The smaller ones tried to board him as he passed them.

Jolly Boy ran to the badminton net and picked up a racquet to give me another drubbing. My attempts at converting him to football had failed miserably. Ellen sat by the wall on the neighbour's plastic chair, slitting banana skins for the butterflies' next visit. She waited to be amused by my sporting collapse. I took the receiver's stance.

I saw Bibhuti's wife straddling her scooter and walking it out into the road. On the way to the market, I supposed. Ellen asked if she wanted company. She didn't answer. The faces of both women were hard with the effort of keeping their grievances fresh.

At first he was just a man eating a dosa at the kiosk across the road. Watching Bibhuti for an entertainment as he sheltered from the rain. He ate slowly, nowhere special to be. His soft features save for the moustache made him look like a child, unwary of the world's attention.

Bibhuti was all over the road. His wife backed the scooter up to give herself the room to steer around him.

I bent to recover an ace. I straightened to serve and saw the man stepping off the kerb at the lip of the pothole. He traced around it in dainty steps and trotted out into the road. He stood there in the rain, as if unsure of what to do next. He scratched his head where the rain itched.

Bibhuti came to rest and became a tree. The children hung from him. He rose to meet the sky with a playful roar, and the children fell from him and scattered laughing. He pointed out the scooter and told them to clear the road.

Bibhuti's wife revved her engine. It mewed weakly. She lurched forward and stopped again. She wheeled back, much further than she needed to. A caution against the wet conditions. Her hands slipped on the slick handlebars. She gripped tighter.

The man reached into his waistband and brought something out. I thought it was a pen. He started running, his hand tucked in against his side. His tubbiness gave him a skittering gait that made him look hapless.

Bibhuti's wife revved her engine again and the scooter took off. She sped for Bibhuti where he stood at the edge of the road. There was room to pass him but her line towards him was true and unrepentant. Her face was blank. Bibhuti was facing away from her, taking pleasure in the rain. A twist of the throttle and she was on top of him.

Bibhuti saw the man approaching and his shoulders drooped as if the strings that held him upright had been cut. A sorrow came over him that sucked him to the ground. He raised a palm to the man in appeal. The man ran at him, his arm outstretched and poised to strike.

Bibhuti's wife swerved, passed Bibhuti and hit the man head on. He flew backwards and scudded across the road. Bibhuti's wife braked and let the engine idle. She watched the man squirm and flutter. She was solemn, unsurprised.

The man moaned softly. He was still holding the knife.

'Who's that?' I asked. The question was an involuntary one, aimed at nobody.

'It is Uncle Rajesh,' Jolly Boy said, his voice shrill and astonished. 'Why does he want to kill Baba?'

'I don't know,' I said.

Jolly Boy rushed to his father. Bibhuti was leaning over the man, his foot pressed down on his wrist to make him let go of the knife. He studied him for breaks and for a spark of humanity worth preserving. He kicked the knife aside and stepped away.

Bibhuti's wife became aware that the engine was still running and switched it off. A distance came over her, a separation from the physical world the rest of us were rooted to. She sat on the scooter looking only at the twitching man. Ellen hobbled over to her and rested a hand on hers where it still clung to the throttle. She was undisturbed by its touch.

The stricken man stirred like an infant in fever sleep, his legs running ahead of him on the wet road. An eye opened and sensibility flushed in. He moaned again and licked at the blood trickling from the corner of his mouth. I felt the acidic rush of wanting him dead. I couldn't quite bring myself to kick him.

I asked Bibhuti if he was okay.

'Not to worry,' Bibhuti muttered. 'I know this man. I should have predicted he would come.'

'Who is he?'

'Rajesh Battacharjee. A former friend of mine. He has been in prison. I sent him there for a good reason. Now he is free he has come to raise his dispute with me again.'

'He was gonna stab you.'

'Not to worry. My wife is saving the day.'

He turned to enquire of his wife's well-being. He spoke tenderly in his language. She replied with a drowsy tilt of the head. He was satisfied.

The kids stole back in to perimeter the scene, scuffling for a look at the dying man. The neighbours stepped in to ease them back to a respectful distance. The husband slid his phone from its holster and called the police.

Bibhuti sat down on the kerb and chatted with Rajesh Battacharjee while we waited for the police to arrive. He talked calmly and without anger. He rubbed the blood away from Rajesh Battacharjee's mouth and folded his arm gently over his chest to consolidate the bone where it had shattered on collision with the road. The two men spoke quietly, Rajesh responding to each question with a patience born of shock or maybe of a pain-induced epiphany. The thought of revenge had sustained him through six years of imprisonment and all the indignities that might involve. His failure to achieve it had left him humble and hopeless, knocked the hatred out of him. Now he was just an injured animal in need of mercy and deserving of it.

Rajesh Battacharjee sat up and looked around him, as if to convince himself by recognition of the things he saw that he was still alive. He reached for Bibhuti, who took him by his good arm and dragged him to the kerb. He sat beside Bibhuti, his legs pulled to his chest, his head lowered between his knees. He shuddered as if crying. The children fell away, streaming back to their homes to find other distractions from the summer washout.

The police came and processed the arrest with a petulance that suggested the chancing on a crime was the last thing they hoped for when they left for work each day. Bibhuti identified their prisoner and disclosed their history. His wife made orange squash while he gave his statement.

Rajesh Battacharjee sat brooding in the back of the police car, sideways with his legs dangling outside, cradling his broken arm and prodding with his tongue at the blood on his lip as it congealed under the heat of the afternoon.

Bibhuti's wife wouldn't look at anyone except Rajesh Battacharjee.

'You are very lucky I arrived when I did, Bhabhi,' he told her. 'One second more and you would be wearing these handcuffs.'

She spilled the orange squash in pouring from the jug. The officer drew his hand away, and the glass slipped from his grasp and smashed on the road.

'I am very sorry,' she mumbled.

The officer lashed out with his lathi, rapping Rajesh Battacharjee's knees. He yelped like a scalded dog.

Ellen looked at me and I knew what she was thinking. We'd both seen it, the true line Bibhuti's wife had taken towards him before Rajesh Battacharjee had got in the way. I shook my head no. It was an accident. She didn't have it in her to want her husband dead. She was only acting out a dark desire to burst his bubble and she would have pulled away in time.

His confession heard, the cops had only to return Rajesh Battacharjee to custody. He wished us good luck for tomorrow. He was tearful when he said it. He wanted Bibhuti to achieve everything he'd hoped for when he'd first arrived in the city of dreams. He wanted him to fly.

'I will not see it,' he said, 'but I am sure the news will reach me. God will be watching over you and so will I.'

I took this to mean that Rajesh Battacharjee planned to take his own life. I thought about warning the officers so they could take his belt and shoelaces away from him as a precaution. But I decided that his life was in fate's hands, just as everybody's was. The two men shared a final timid embrace and Rajesh Battacharjee was driven away.

I woke up frightened in the middle of the night by the sound of wings in the room. Whatever my good bird Oscar had come to tell me I was too proud to hear it. I got up and went looking for him but I gave up when I began to feel ridiculous. I didn't sleep again after that.

32

It was still dark outside when Bibhuti began his preparations, creeping past me and out the door to make his animal shapes in the quiet before the dogs woke up. His wife was up with him and she waited in the kitchen, keeping herself away from me. No rain fell and in the silence the house pinched at us, tugging at our sleeves for explanations. The time for explaining had passed.

When Bibhuti came back there was a timid conversation between them and she followed him into the bathroom and closed the door. She carried a pair of scissors with her. I thought maybe she'd heard about Samson's weakness and would make one last attempt at sabotage Delilah-style. I wondered if I should kick the door down and save him from a travesty. But no scuffles came from behind the wood and soon Bibhuti sauntered back into the room stroking his newly trimmed moustache, serenity draped over his shoulders like a cape for a vain superhero. The grooming was some kind of concession. He believed he'd won her approval and there was no more doubt in his eyes.

Then the sun rose with so many colours it nearly broke my heart.

Its light bled through the window bars and fell over us where we stood, warming our blood to fighting temperature. I heard a godlike voice calling me to generous deeds. Somewhere outside this room Ellen was stirring, waking up to her usual aches and a shortness of breath. She'd swallow her tablets and the electric shocks would subside, but before that she'd have to swim in a pain that had singled her out. This was how all her days started. My pain didn't matter anymore, it would end one way or another. Hers would last for ever. I resolved to make this day the one to end all pain. In surviving the bats we'd remove all pain from the world and Ellen would never wake up again to sharpness and desolation. I'd do it for her.

I looked at Bibhuti for a reflection of my own resolve. He tilted his head at me, caught in a fighter's cold swagger.

Jolly Boy wandered in from his sleeping and climbed on his father's back. He kissed his neck drowsily and asked a soft question of him.

Bibhuti told him in a raw monotone that he was feeling on top of the world.

Breakfast was eaten slowly, a show of calm for the spying demons when every muscle was straining for the door. I squatted over the hole in the floor until my knees locked up. The burning brought to mind a man on fire, wrapped in grieving cloth, ambitions peeling from him like dry petals in the flames. I wondered if Gopal Dutta would come in his new form to cheer us on. I'd look for a woman with belligerent goat's eyes and an inbuilt distrust of the ground. She'd be hovering three inches above it, her toes turned downward like the beak of a foraging bird to give the impression of standing. I didn't know how reincarnation worked.

Loading the bats into the car we were priests transporting holy relics, deferential and slow as if it were the blood of a saint we carried, gone dry and flaky in its ancient vials. Ellen came then and found us shuffling about in silence. She bowed her head involuntarily in respect of our sacred act. She looked tired and impatient. I knew she must have barely slept. Thoughts of my betrayal would have woken her up in the night. My betrayal of her and of the human law that read an outrage in the methodical striking of a man. I didn't tell her I was doing it for her now. I'd let her see it for herself.

She tousled Jolly Boy's hair when she passed him on her way upstairs, a premature gesture of sympathy. I distracted him with a plea for help before he could latch on to the implications. He ran to the backyard and came back with a single bat, carried casket-like with the same awe he saw in us. A butterfly flew at him and he stopped to let it pass before carrying on. He set the bat down in the boot where a blanket had been unfolded to make a lining that would protect them from scratches.

The butterfly made a quick inspection of the neighbour's washing line and found it empty, its appetite uncoiling too early for the banana skins. It flew away to the hills.

'Are you feeling strong today?' I asked Jolly Boy.

He rolled up his sleeve and flexed his bicep for me. A sparrow's kneecap. He dropped his arm and went looking for another bat, his hips rolling with his father's swagger.

When we'd counted fifty in it was time to leave. The boot was full and the back seat took the overspill. Jolly Boy was a boat on wooden waves. He rested his feet on the shifting bats and held the last one across his lap. He stroked it like a cat. It purred to him. A tiger tranquillised and made docile by his will.

Bibhuti's wife mounted her scooter cautiously, remembering the shameful use she'd put it to. She gave the throttle a twist as Ellen arranged herself behind her, her stick primed at her side while she reached her other hand behind to grip the pillion handle. Her lips pursed in corrugated wonder, surprising herself with her determination to bear witness to whatever horrors the day might bring.

The sun had burned the last of the night away and the street was stirring. Unseen dogs were marking out their day's intentions in defiant language and the birds were stretching their wings, making a plaything of the ripening sky. People spilled out of their houses, propelled by ancient instincts for heat seeking and the sniff of new money. The older ones washed themselves in weather after a night of confinement while the younger ones, interchangeable in their meaning-business suits, formed a convoy bound for the train station and office jobs that paid in commission and prideful glances from fathers wilted to tea leaves by a life spent trading in the open air.

Some waved to us and wished us well. Amused smiles and namastes and underneath each one the fear of being left behind. Bibhuti's passion was a timely reminder that everyone would die one day and there was hay to be made while the sun was shining.

The neighbours came out with their bananas ready to be slit and hung up. The husband gave us a thumbs-up. He asked Bibhuti when the attempt would start and if it would be okay to film it for his friend in Dubai. He'd told him all about Bibhuti and he sent his salaams. Another god to watch over us and another continent to sell our story to.

We drove slowly, a sober procession between the potholes.

'A/C, A/C!' came Jolly Boy's demand, but today wasn't a day for artificial comforts. Bibhuti needed his muscles to be warm, nothing would be left to chance. The air con stayed off and so did the radio. Bibhuti folded his songs into sleeping flowers that would bloom again once the storm had passed. Until then his only music would be the drumming of a blunt desire, somewhere deep down where men were first made.

I kept an eye on Ellen drifting in and out of the wing mirror, hanging on to the back of the scooter. I was glad she'd come to see what a danger I could be.

The barrel-bound priests on the road to the temple had stopped praying for the end of the national ordeal while a break in the rain allowed it. One of them was shaving his head while the other lifted his face to the sky to catch some sun. I imagined pleasant memories of boyhood cricket matches swimming behind his eyelids. A one-legged man attended them with a hand towel at the ready. His service would earn him favourable treatment in his next life. His prosthetic leg was a dead ringer for the one I'd seen on Bibhuti's stairs. Its foot was too small for him, the toes an infant's, like buds that would grow into the real thing given time and regular watering.

The temple was dedicated to Ganesh, the elephant-headed remover of obstacles. We entered his chamber with stilled breaths and strong minds. A pain came on fast and my blood left me and I fell at the feet of his statue. I had to be slapped awake.

The floor was cool. Bibhuti stood over me, his eyes wide with worry. I tried to tell him I was okay but no words came. Death was everywhere. I could smell it in the incense smoke curling up the statue's trunk.

Bibhuti gripped my wrists and pulled me up. My wrists felt as slender as a child's in his grasp and there was pity in the eyes of the rat that sat at Ganesh's feet. My time was running out on me again.

The priest looked at the fresh application of polish on my toenails and smiled to himself in private acknowledgement of some fact about me that I couldn't figure out myself. He dipped a finger into the bowl he was holding and painted a turmeric stripe between my eyes. He mumbled a prayer at me and I was anointed. Bibhuti already wore his stripe. He carried the marks of divine protection with confidence. He thanked the priest on my behalf and took me away to a smaller room where his God's soothing voice could be heard more clearly.

He sat down on the stone floor, folded his legs underneath him. He had me follow him down. He told me to close my eyes and breathe. I waited until his eyes were closed and he'd started to meditate. Still I didn't hear you. All I heard was Bibhuti breathing and the low hum of a friendship that had passed from obligation to something wilder. All I wanted was for him to be happy.

Bibhuti woke up, rubbed his eyes and grinned at me.

'I am ready now,' he said.

In the courtyard all lenses pointed at us. A steadycam from the sports channel and various press cameras jostled for elbow room at the spot where the first gob of blood would be spat. The Turbanator waved to us boyishly. The civilians raised their phones and snapped our walk to centre stage where the bats were waiting, arranged in neat rows to be got at quickly. On the other side of us was a space to throw them when they were broken, in the walled corner under the banyan tree. Children looked down on us from its branches, their hands full of themselves and rubbing their shins as if to knead the excitement evenly through bodies unused to the thrill of being hidden.

They cheered us. The air crackled and I got goosebumps. Someone was selling mango slices from a plastic bucket and a custodian was standing by with a mop to cleanse the sacred ground when we were finished.

Nobody was wearing goggles. Nobody had thought of it. I worried about stray splinters in eyeballs. It was too late to do anything about it.

Ellen and Jolly Boy and his mother hadn't been allowed inside the temple with us and instead they'd been practising their roles in the thickening air. The women in the crowd posed in shapes of grace, steadied their hands to catch the eggs from upturned nests when the sky started falling in.

Jolly Boy made a meal of checking the bats one last time, rolling them carefully so they all showed their faces. The duct tape covered B Pattni's embarrassment. The modification made the bats look more sinister. B Pattni himself peered out from the crowd, swaying from foot to foot, his massive frame trembling with the anticipation of some watershed moment in the history of violence.

The younger priests had to blockade the entrance, linking their arms in opposition to the latecomers. Meeting resistance the would-be spectators made ladders of each other and scaled the walls to sit in crowlike hope of throwaway bones.

The AXN reporter made an announcement. He told everyone who Bibhuti was and what he'd already done. He told them what he'd attempt to do today. He introduced me as the one who'd help. I had to remind him of my name.

I got him to namecheck Jolly Boy too. Jolly Boy prematurely picked up the first bat from the pile. I quietly told him to put it back. His wait for the clock was insufferable. Rigged to the trunk of the tree it showed zero. Another AXN rep stood by to press its buttons, an Olympic pretension for the glamour-hungry crowd.

Bibhuti took off his T-shirt. The scars on his back and the bruises I'd made shone livid. Bibhuti's wife turned her back on him. Ellen held her up.

On the announcer's cue the crowd fell silent.

A moment of realisation passed between Bibhuti and me, a look of delirious mourning. We both knew that the people we'd been before would be permanently lost when the breaking began. We both rued the time we'd spent as outcasts in a life before today. We were going home.

'I am only wishing Gopal Dutta is here,' Bibhuti confided. 'This will be the first record I have achieved without him. It is very strange feeling.'

'He'll be watching,' I said. I scanned the crowd but I didn't see any hovering goat women.

I asked Jolly Boy if he was okay. He tilted his head and offered me a bat again. This time I took it. I weighed it in my hands. I felt the grip and the heat in it from its exposure to the sun. I squeezed my fingers tighter around it to inflate the muscles that would make it murderous.

The air was still. Bibhuti gathered himself, a physical clearing and a shaking off of any last remaining trace of doubt. 'Don't forget, below the neck only,' he said, and he glanced to the sky for a final endorsement as the crowd drew in its breath. Everyone braced themselves to see a god being born.

I decided with a sense of quickfalling like stepping off a roof that I didn't have it in me.

'I can't do it.' I said it quietly so the crowd wouldn't hear. 'I don't want to kill you.'

Bibhuti's moustache drooped.

I felt the burn of crying behind my eyes. I felt you. The precious-ness of life was revealed to me in an urgent unfolding and the shock of it took all the lust out of me.

'I'm sorry.'

'You must do it,' Bibhuti said. His brown nipples were hairless and small in the stiffening breeze. He'd once been a baby. 'Please,' he pleaded.

'Go, Uncle, it has started,' Jolly Boy urged. 'Hit him!'

I looked at the clock. The numbers were already running ahead of me.

Bibhuti waved me impatiently in. 'Come, you must go now. We have no more time.' He spread his feet and tensed himself, his arms held out in appeal.

I felt you for the first time and I raised my hand against you.

The announcer counted the seconds aloud to hurry me on. The crowd started counting too.

'Go!' Jolly Boy hollered, enraged at me, and he picked up a bat and made to strike his father himself.

I pushed him aside and raised my bat. Bibhuti's eyes glazed over as he summoned the weird energies that would deflect the pain.

'Thank you,' he muttered, and he was already somewhere else.

I asked you to forgive me. I swung the bat with everything I had.

33

Bibhuti sleeps. His room's too small to breathe in now. The reporter has been called away to another story and me and Ellen sit in her seat. It's still warm from her. The corridor light stings my eyes and encourages confessions. Steam rises from the tea in Ellen's plastic cup. Her fingers curl around it, the knuckles wrinkled like walnuts, and the ring I gave her could do with a polish. She lets me confess, with the doctors buzzing round us. A scream of pain from somewhere behind thin curtains. She lets me confess because she sees the time has come to harvest my prior kindnesses. To bring them in for weighing and then have them argue for me at the last. I'll need every one of them to speak well of me.

I tell her I've heard your voice calling to me. That I've been going back over my life and filling all the holes in with you. The way we met, by chance in a dance hall in the dark, out of all those other bodies. It was you pinning me to the ground, I say, keeping me in the right spot so she'd find me.

It was you who made me iron-willed when her old man ran his rule over me and found me wanting, it was your voice telling him we'd made our choice and we were standing by it. It was you putting the words in my mouth when I asked her to make an honest man of me, even though the thing I feared most in the world was making a promise to someone and then having to make it stick.

When she needed kindness it was you who showed me how. What to say to soothe a toothache, where to put my hands to express sympathy or strength of character. It was you who made me believe in her piano dream.

'I took you, didn't I?' I say to her. 'To the music shop. I wanted you to play. I was good when I needed to be, wasn't I?'

'Of course you were,' she says, and her charity catches in my throat.

'I just need you to forgive me. Before it's too late. I'm scared and I need to know I was good. Tell me you forgive me.'

'Not yet.'

'When?'

'When he wakes up.'

Zubin wheels a trolley past us. There's a body on it covered by a sheet. The smell of charred meat laces the air. The old man's face is outlined under the sheet. I watch it all the way to the door to see if the sheet will move with the sucking in of a reanimated breath. It doesn't.

'I can't even remember how many times I hit him. How many did we break?'

'Enough.' Ellen shudders at the memory of what she'd seen me do. It must have been bad. All I can remember is the first hit. The sound of it, the vibration going up my arm when the bat met the resistance of Bibhuti's body. The instant release when it broke. Lightness. Looking down and seeing the bat dead in my hand, splinters hanging in the air. Disgust and exhilaration. Dropping it like it was hot. The announcer counting one.

Birds singing and the silver dragon on Jolly Boy's best shirt. His father's eyes glossed and cow-waiting. Just waiting for the next one to hit.

My God, I could feel your eyes on me. As death hovered at Bibhuti's shoulder you came to visit me for the first time. There was a scratching on the air, of new questions. I feel it again now. You're asking me to beg for your forgiveness. I think Ellen deserves it more than you. She has to forgive me first. Bibhuti has to wake up.

'I'm knackered,' I say.

'Have a sleep then.'

I let myself very slowly fall into her lap. She lets me stay there. The light's very bright but it's been a long day. Every day's long now. I feel her hand on my face but there's no stroking. Just her fingers resting on me, all done with dreams of music.

The holy men shove their way in before the nurse can stop them. When they see Bibhuti lying there they break into whalesong. Their prayers fill the room with the acrid bigotry of a smoke bomb. They must be the right denomination because Bibhuti's wife joins in with the song like she knows it, her lips making the words soundlessly. She glides over to them from the window, bathes herself in the light they throw out. Her shoulders rise as if she's shrugging off a heavy coat. Piety shakes the stiffness from her limbs. The nearest holy man invites her into the circle they've formed. They all peer down together at Bibhuti sleeping and breathe their spell over him.

From where I sit it looks like an act of violence. Leering over his lifeless body they're vultures eyeing up the choicest cuts. The whalesong grows louder. The rosewater comes out and is sprinkled on him roughly. It spatters his face. The nurse stands and watches, the needle still raised where she was about to recharge the morphine drip.

'Are they saying he's gone now?' Ellen asks me. 'Is this like the last rites?'

'I don't know,' I say. 'No, it can't be.'

I look around for an explanation but everyone's plugged into the ritual. Even Jolly Boy's caught up in it, sitting on the bed beside his father, watching the priests intently, a crouching animal keying itself up to strike.

Bibhuti sleeps. The singing stops and the holy men turn to look at me. This is how it happens, I think. They slip knives from their robes and cut me down in righteous retribution.

I grip the windowsill, something to steady me when the rush comes. I can feel the heat from the fires below. A lone voice shouts out that I'm a son of a whore. I don't think that's necessary.

The first one's on me and he takes hold of my shoulder and jabs a finger between my eyes. The turmeric is a familiar itch on my skin. The prayers start up again. I'm splashed with rosewater too. I blink it out. No one steps in to save me. They've got me cornered. One of them's got spit in his beard from so much arguing with God. His lips are wet with a desire for gift-giving. He wants to forgive me and make me clean. He doesn't know the first thing about me but he wants to save my soul.

For the first time in my life I feel my soul as a physical thing. It's a clawing in my chest. It has the weight of a prejudice. It feels like indigestion.

'They are blessing you,' Bibhuti's wife says. 'I have asked them for this.'

I ask her why. I tell her I've already been blessed.

'They have made my husband a guru. This is very big honour. He is teaching the world, this is what they say. I cannot have anger towards you anymore, it is not good for me. I ask them to bless you again for the rest of your life. Now you will be good. This is all I am asking.'

I thank her. There was never a time when I wasn't indebted to someone for something. I realise that it's his debts that keep a man clinging to life. I feel the weight of my soul drop. I swallow it in a moment of panic, like the stone of a fruit. Relief comes after.

Jolly Boy climbs onto his father and shields him from further intrusion. The holy men range their fruits and flowers on the bed, around Bibhuti's feet. Jolly Boy kicks out at them, sending an orange rolling off and across the floor. He kicks out at the holy men when they get too close. He's fevered, fighting for his life.

'He's not a god,' he cries. 'He's my Baba! Leave him alone!'

'They do not say he is a god,' his mother says, trying to soothe him. 'They say he is a guru. It is different. He is still your Baba.'

'They can't take him. Tell them to go.'

'They don't want to take him.'

One of the holy men raises his hands in a gesture of conciliation. Jolly Boy lands a foot on him. He backs off.

Bibhuti's body rocks under the motion of Jolly Boy's thrashing around. The nurse goes to insert her needle but the holy men heckle her away. They leave, taking the nurse with them. The air behind them is snagged with something horrific, an assumption that Bibhuti will wake up to his new calling and be neutered and lifted by it.

His eyes are swimming again. He's dreaming of a world without language, before there was a word for death.

I pick up my money and tell Jolly Boy we're getting out of here. 'You need a change of scenery, you've been in here too long. We'll come back. No one's gonna take him. Let's see if there's some trouble we can get ourselves into.'

A flicker of a smile but he hesitates, his hand on Bibhuti's heart.

'He just wants to finish the dream he's having. Let's leave him to it, we can ask him about it when we get back.'

He peels himself off his father and comes with me.

Jolly Boy stays close to me. I lead him under the buzzing lights and the blunt chopping fans. The amputated ghosts don't see us when we pass through them. Nobody stops us. Nobody feels what we feel.

We go down to the basement. The drums from outside fade away and the air closes in. We reach the orderlies' room. Zubin looks up from the card game and asks me what I need. I need a way outside. He takes us to the fire exit.

I push the bar and light breaks in. The drums and the screeching come back, but distantly. I peek out. In front of us is a patch of wasteland and trees beyond it. No fires. The sky is smoke-coloured and its consistency when I reach a hand into it is syrup. I'm asking a lot of my legs after days of sitting still.

We sprint for the trees, our breath loud around us. When we make cover we laugh at each other, a secret joining us at the heart. In the darkness of the trees I brush the wet hair from Jolly Boy's face. I can't tell him how sorry I am without making more holes in him.

There's a place down the road where we can get ice cream, he says, on the other side of the trees and then a walk away. He saw it when we were driving in. His favourite flavour might be there, chocolate. He leads the way. I stay behind him, pick through the footsteps he leaves in the earth still sticky from the last downpour. The mud ruins my shoes and I take them off and carry them at my side. The sight of me barefoot making friends with the filth delights Jolly Boy and he follows my example. Nobody chases us. We slow down, take our time in the shade of the leaves.

There's chocolate ice cream for Jolly Boy and vanilla for me. There are plastic tricycles hung by wires from the ceiling of the shop. Every shop like this must have them. I never saw them ridden, only hanging. They turn in the breeze above our heads as we sit on the kerb to eat. A stillness blows in and we let it enfold us, lick our ice creams slowly with shrewd insistence, like children do who know the world's waiting on them. Our muddied feet dry in the sun and silence comes. We sift it for fragments of gold.

Gold is woven into Jolly Boy's hair and when I look at him I see the man he'll become in his father's absence. A man made of locked doors and windows painted over. He'll be a room of dust and stale air, like I was. Maybe love will find him later and crowbar him open, maybe TV will teach him compassion. Maybe out of spite he'll follow different dreams to his father's and make a life's work in falling short of them.

Or maybe a quick end is in store at the point of a needle, a merciful deflation after grief's bloating. His mother a mountaineer in the landfill fighting the seagulls for his eyes.

He asks for another ice cream. I watch him go to work on it, something sweet to remember me by.

The clouds tussle and heave. Jolly Boy's shoulders sag and he ages. The ice cream falls from his hand. He's crying.

'I was too slow. I should give you the next bat quicker. There are too many. It is my fault.'

'Don't say that, it's not your fault. You didn't do anything. We shouldn't have let you anywhere near there. Don't ever think it was your fault. You're a good boy.'

His eyes claw for the sky and the peace to be found there in the brewing storm.

'You could do with a shower,' I tell him. 'You're smelling a bit ripe. I'll take you when we get back. I'll get you some new clothes as well.'

'Okay,' he sniffs.

'I smell worse than you do,' I say to appease him. I pinch my nose and wave a hand in front of my face. 'Pooey, what a stink. I smell like shit.'

Laughter dribbles out of him. He mimics me, pinching his nose and holding an exaggerated breath, his tear-streaked cheeks swelling like a hamster's.

The first rain spots the pavement. I hand him his shoes and we head back to the trees.

We go back to the fire-escape door and hammer on it until it's opened. Zubin promises a change of clothes in Jolly Boy's size. He takes us to the bathroom and locks us inside.

Jolly Boy makes me wait behind the wall of the shower cubicle, throws me his clothes once he's removed them. I wash them in the sink while he rinses five days of hoping off, scrubbing until the water runs black.

I catch myself in the mirror and think about growing the moustache again.

Zubin comes back with fresh clothes, taken from various small corpses. Jolly Boy recoils at the idea of stepping into a dead boy's shoes. Zubin reassures him that all is clean and death isn't catching. I turn my back while he changes. Zubin gathers up Jolly Boy's wet clothes and takes them away to hang somewhere. Jolly Boy is reluctant to be separated from his dragon. I tell him that dragons home, it'll find its way back to him.

When we get back to the room Bibhuti is wide awake and pulling at the drip line that dangles from his arm. It slithers from his vein, glistening with blood. His wife accepts it prudishly and lays it on the sheet. It dribbles the last of its shames onto the cotton and lies still. Bibhuti sees me and recognition floods his eyes.

'No more painkillers,' Bibhuti says, his voice garbled and rusty. 'They are trying to kill me with this poison. I am just now speaking with the fire-eater, he says we can still do it. Come, we must go home and practise. Eleven bats is poor number, we will come back tomorrow and improve on it.'

Jolly Boy is rooted to the spot, his hair still wet from the shower, unsure if what he sees is real or a ghost. His mother asks after his clothes and I tell her the story. She accepts my explanation without really hearing it, her attention flying back to Bibhuti and the terrible thirst he's woken to. She tips a water bottle towards his mouth. He tries to sit up to take a drink but the effort of it wipes him out and he falls back onto the bed. The sight of him helpless slaps me awake and I rush to his side. He bucks and slithers, impatient to test the honesty of his returning strength. I hold him down as politely as I can until the doctor comes. His skin where I can feel it is hot with life and his moustache tickles my ear.

'Thank you,' he says flatly. Nobody else hears it.

Bibhuti asks me how I'm feeling. I look ill, he says. He's calm, refreshed. Wherever he went while he was under and whoever he spoke to, his travels have stolen the memory of his ever being outwitted by the drugs. His only concern now is for me. Have I been following my diet? Have I been doing my exercises?

I've been sitting here waiting for him to wake up, I say. I've been remembering and trying not to remember. I've been scraping his blood from under my fingernails and telling myself it's just the storyless grime that comes from being in a foreign country.

I tell him I'm fine. Everything's fine. What he doesn't know can't hurt him.

The doctor has tested him, shone a light in his eyes and trailed a finger in a circuit around his nose and asked him the year and the date of his birth. He knew who 'The Little Master' was and who the opponents were when he made his last test century.

'Always cricket,' Bibhuti had complained. 'Why don't you ask me about floor gymnastics or karate? Ask me about my ninth World Record, I will tell you that on 14th October 2006 I successfully completed one hundred and fourteen fingertip push-ups in one minute. There is more to life than cricket.'

The doctor had smiled patiently and taken a blood sample. Bibhuti had flinched when the needle went in.

His wife and Jolly Boy cling to him, their fingers glued to his living skin. Now they've got him back they're not letting go of him. They plan to ride him home bareback.

I ask him what he remembers of the day.

Everything, he says, up until a blackout. Eleven bats lie broken. He stood up to them and they sang to his tune. There was no pain then. Everything went to plan. I did him proud, and Shubham too.

Jolly Boy coils tighter around his father, his relief a prehensile thing that pulls him to his beating heart.

'We found greatness,' Bibhuti tells me, his eyes glowing through the gauze of returning pain. 'I knew we would do it.'

'You're not disappointed we didn't get the fifty?'

'I have the record, this is the important thing. Nobody will match it. You have informed the Guinness people, they have ratified?'

'I don't know how. I was waiting for you to wake up.'

'It was never in doubt.'

His wife lifts her head from private thanksgiving and scowls at him. 'I doubted it. Every minute I am waiting for you to die. Shubham is afraid he will lose his father. Five days like this. Look at what you have done to yourself. Go on, look!'

Bibhuti looks down at himself. He takes in the plaster that holds him together and the bruises that intrude on his exposed flesh. Fear shivers through him. Then regret steals in to dull his eyes to ash.

'I will not do this again,' he says, his lips trembling as he speaks.

'You have promised this before,' his wife reminds him.

'I am very sorry. I will break no more promises.'

He's forgotten the revelation he shared with us when he first woke up. His conversation with the fire-eater is a dream that's lost to him. Now that the morphine is draining from his system he knows only pain. It's a bringer of clarity.

'I am finished. I cannot ask any more of myself. I have given everything. I will ask God to release me from this debt and show me an alternative path.' He examines the plaster on his arm, clucks his tongue disdainfully. 'This plaster work is very shoddy, the joins are too rough. I will change when I get home. Come, we must go. I cannot stay here, a hospital is not the place for me. I will die if I stay here, these doctors know nothing.'

He peels his wife's fingers from his neck and tries to move. A jolt of agony pins him down.

To know that he feels pain with me is a consolation. I want him to be human again and mortal. His time as a god only brought worry to the people who love him. To love him now is to convince him that his special properties are all exhausted. To save him is to remind him that he's just like me.

The nurse disapproves of Bibhuti's decision to bear his pain naturally. There's no talking him round. He's alive again and he wants to feel it, every spasm and firework. It's the price he must pay for his former arrogance. His prize for poking death in the eye is to spend the rest of his life respectfully running from it, as everybody else does. Milk and turmeric await him at home.

The nurse opens the door to leave with her tray of redundant painkillers. Ellen reaches for the tray and steals a handful of morphine vials, quick and nerveless. She hides them in her hand until the nurse has gone, then she slips them into her purse.

'Just in case,' she says when I look at her. Her daring fills me with admiration. I could love her all over again.

Vijay Five is waiting on the other side of the door. The TV news reporter cranes behind him for a look inside the room. She's heard the commotion of Bibhuti's revival and expects to see him bathed in a golden light, dispensing immortal wisdoms for the evening bulletin. She raises her iPhone to record his account of the afterworld.

Vijay Five shuts the door on her before she can follow him in. When he sees Bibhuti upright and talking a childish grin breaks out and the nights of vigil are forgotten. He slips Bibhuti's hand in his and the two men laugh together. The air in the room is charged with the levity of spring. It's only when Ellen makes the mistake of opening the window that the weight of consequences intrudes. Bibhuti cocks his head to the noise outside, an understanding blooming quickly of the gouge his actions have made in the ground of his city.

The crowd has been alerted to his comeback and their voices are raised in testament to the miracle of it.

'Are they for me?' Bibhuti asks.

'They have waited for you,' Vijay Five says. 'Everybody was there. You are big news.'

Bibhuti can't hide his excitement. 'What was the coverage?'

'Everybody. Local and national. Jai, Zee 24, TV9, ESPN, BBC, CNN, Live India, they were all there. All the newspapers. I have been in charge of the *Times* coverage, everything is passing from me. The city is full of you, BB, everybody wants to know you will pull through. When you are feeling better I will take an interview from you, everybody will want to hear your words.'

'You can take the interview now, there is no sense in delaying it.'

'You must rest, BB. I will take it later. I will keep the other press away from you, they will not disturb you. The Turbanator is downstairs, he will make sure they don't get in. This woman outside will not leave but I am looking for the right moment to take her phone,

I will destroy anything she has recorded. You are a *Times* man and we will take care of you.'

I hide behind the curtain and look down. The crowd is sparse now compared with its prime. The place looks like the site of a plane crash. The earth is scarred with errant fires and smoke hangs heavy in the air. The world came to a premature end while Bibhuti's life hung in the balance and now that he's awake it needs to repair itself. The hardcore followers have stayed behind to lend their hands to the restoration. The priests and the firebrands have nowhere better to be. The taste of war and its groping aftermath is salt on their tongues. When the soil knots again over the scalp of the earth they'll mark a new beginning in a splash of my blood. I raised the bats to Bibhuti and there should be redress. I meant to slaughter India and her sons will slice revenge from me as a warning to others who might come after.

I see the bobbing pink head of the Turbanator as he scuffles with an interloper at the hospital doors. He has the rival pressman in a headlock. His prisoner's arms are flailing behind him and his heels dig in to the mud. They caper in a dim-witted waltz while the rubbish fires flicker. Bibhuti commands a loyalty that turns men into happy maniacs and I feel no shame in counting myself one of them.

The constables prod me down the stairs, the heads of their lathis nuzzling the small of my back. Their inspector gives me a lazy shove to keep his hand in. Ellen takes offence at their roughhousing. The Inspector moves to help her down the last flight of stairs and she swats at him with her stick, catching him across the shin. He curses and shoves me harder.

We're taken out the front way so we can meet my public. Jeers warm my cheeks and placards are hastily raised above bedraggled heads. They've wilted and been humbled by the rain.

The kung-fu fighters freeze mid-air and snarl at me. A contingent from Bibhuti's karate class, I recognise some of the younger faces. A week away from the regimen of the dojo has made them restless. They've brought their twitchy limbs to the hospital grounds to parade their angst for the watching world.

I look for Kavita but she's not among them. I can only guess at the damage she would have inflicted on me in revenge for her sensei and wonder if adulthood's obligations will put a halter on her wrath or only provoke it into greater and more destructive feats. I think she'll become a nail bomb. I only wish I could be alive to see the hole she'll punch in the world.

The casual protesters have gone back to the relative comforts of concrete and dial-up internet, or to face whatever horrors the storms have visited on their loved ones in their absence. The police guard at the door has thinned in reaction to the decreased threat. The diehards who remain are kept in check by menacing looks alone. Word of Bibhuti's awakening has seeped like milk through the ranks of the abandoned, soothing their burns to itches that can be pacified with hateful remarks and the limp rattling of a fist.

The constables let their hands stray to the grips of their lathis, a challenge to anyone who might want to make a run at me.

Bibhuti has already cleared my name. He met the Inspector's interrogation with a steady insistence that I had no crime to answer to. We crossed the line of reason together, hand in hand. What I did in taking up the bats against him was an act of charity. The Inspector hadn't taken kindly to Bibhuti's version of events. He'd asked him to take a look at himself, broken and humiliated and writhing in pain.

'If I gave you a shake you would rattle like chipdya.'

'Then do not shake him,' Bibhuti's wife had suggested.

The Inspector had recited a summary of the record and the specifics of its execution. Those particulars had only brought a flush of excitement to Bibhuti's cheeks, provided stirring images that he could grip on to ride out the pain. The Inspector had pouted. There'd be no speedy incrimination or legitimate beatings to follow.

He leads me to the patrol car and a waiting cell. He's not finished with me yet.

'BB asked after you,' I tell the Turbanator as he steps aside to let us through. His arm still forms a doughnut at his side where his rival's head had been. The other man sits on the hospital step, smoking a cigarette and contemplating his feebleness. 'Go and see him, he'll tell you everything. I'll be going home soon. It was good to meet you.'

'Will you?' Ellen asks. She sounds disbelieving.

'I did what I came here for. There's nothing left to do. It hurts. I want to lie down in my own bed. Do you forgive me?'

'Yes.'

'Thank you.'

'It's not too late. They can still make you better.'

'It is too late.'

'How do you know?'

'I just know.'

'You don't know anything. What am I supposed to do on my own? You can't give up. I won't let you.'

I feel a bristle of something corrosive, like duty. It's been a long time since I thought of myself as subject to a word like that. Every sacrifice she's made for me has been repaid in counterfeit notes. I'll be gentle again and truthful. I'll believe in anything that brings her back home to me.

She falls silent. In the back of the car I hear her fart and I apologise for it before they can trace it back to her. She never was a fan of spicy food.

I can't stop them taking her away. It's the Inspector's retribution for the crack on the shin. They put her in a woman's cell that I suppose is no different to mine. They let me wonder at what's happening to her while I wait for the hands of the clock to creep to the moment when the Inspector will decide his honour has been satisfied.

He takes my money for safekeeping, locks the door on me and sits down at the desk that faces the cell on the far side of the room. He picks up a newspaper and starts reading. His lips move with the words. He wants to show me how unimportant I am.

I share my cell with a broken-down kid in a T-shirt that says 'Welcome to Fabulous Las Vegas'. He's coming down from something transformational and the tragedy of his return to earth is scratched into his face like a prayer gone cold. His eyes are empty and restless. He knows how close I came to killing a man. He can feel it coming off me and it's making him edgy.

I tell the Inspector I have to be somewhere.

'Where?'

'I have to go home. I'm dying. I haven't got much time left. You know I'm innocent. Let us go, we just want to go home.'

The Inspector mumbles something profane to himself and turns the page of his newspaper.

'You are dying?' my cellmate asks me.

'That's right.'

On hearing this he sways towards me, drawn in. I can smell the fight on his clothes. I know somehow that every day for him is a fight he can't win. His breath is hot and sweet and I need a drink.

'I also am dying,' he says. He looks very young when he says this. There's confederacy in his tone and it sickens me a little bit.

He puts his arms together as though he's handcuffed. The inner sides of his forearms are bitten and ravaged. He feels no disgrace in telling me he's a user of heroin. He says it's killing him but he can't stop.

I reach out to touch his shoulder but then I quickly pull back in case he doesn't want the intrusion. I'm not sure why but it's important to me that he thinks I'm a good man, sensitive to the needs of others.

I tell him God hasn't forgotten him. I surprise myself by believing it. But then I shouldn't be surprised, not after everything that's happened. I believe in you informally, like a recipe handed down. You're my bread now.

I've never been this hungry in all my life.

Then it's time to pay the fine for my release. Official reparation against the disturbance I've caused to the flooded city's peace. The Inspector digs in my bag and pulls out a fistful of notes. There aren't so many left and their denominations are generally high. He chooses a pleasing amount for himself and stacks his selection on the desk. He gets a logbook from a drawer and fills out a docket. I knew the shakedown was coming and I don't begrudge it.

'Just leave me enough to get home,' I say.

'I don't decide these things,' he replies. 'It is a fixed penalty.' He says this with sincerity. I pity him for having been sucked in to such a corrupting profession.

Ellen is brought to me dazed and dehydrated. I demand water for her. She takes her medication under the Inspector's impatient gaze, her senseless fingers struggling to open the pillbox with the tiny Klimt reproduction that I bought her for travelling. I never cared for art but she liked the colours.

The kid is curled up on the floor of the cell, slick with sweat and sleeping soundly. He twitches and whimpers, a dreaming dog.

I nearly drop Bibhuti in lifting him out of the wheelchair. My weakness comes as a shock and I can only watch as Vijay Five rights him and sets him down on the mud, his feet on our feet like a child dancing with his mother. We crabwalk him to the car, the doctor's complaints drowned out by the rain.

The Turbanator has brought Bibhuti's car round the back and it's his idea to bury Bibhuti under a blanket to throw the rubberneckers off our scent. He sits upright in the back seat, dust-covered and inert, our smuggled artefact. Jolly Boy rests his arm across his father's middle ready to pull the shroud aside as soon as they've cleared the hospital grounds.

'I feel foolish,' comes Bibhuti's muffled voice.

'No more foolish than you look,' his wife replies, smoothing herself into the seat alongside them. 'This is what happens when you break a baseball bat on yourself, I could have told you this.'

'Eleven,' Bibhuti says, but there's no defiance in the correction. It's a murmur that describes the mood of us all as we prepare to take our first steps into the world after the levelling storm. A simpler world, it will be, where the gaudy ambitions of men hang unworn on pegs and nobody looks you in the eye.

I'm ushered to Vijay Five's car. It's inappropriate for me to travel with the family. Ellen joins me in solidarity. We share the back seat, Ellen laying her stick down at my feet. The car smells like a single man who's yet to meet his match. When I catch Vijay Five's eye in the rearview mirror the loneliness I see provokes a twinge of pity. I press my hand down on Ellen's knee. I know how lucky I am to be one half of something bigger.

We ease past the fraying protest and out onto the road. When we're safely past the demonstration site the Turbanator floors Bibhuti's car and Vijay Five speeds up to keep him in sight. A lone boy runs behind us, his bits and pieces clanging joyfully against his thighs. He reaches out a hand to us. In his palm is a bright yellow ball of fur. His supply of chicks has been refreshed and his smile tells us the prosperous times are coming back. We leave him happy and cloaked in dust.

Navi Mumbai has drowned since we were last free. Its corpse has been dragged back out of the water and laid to rest on the bank in a tangle of weeds. Everywhere bears a tidemark. The trees have spilled their fruit. We slow down once we've stopped feeling the heat of the fires we incited. All the dogs have gone from the streets and I miss their enquiring faces.

The neighbours have been tipped off about Bibhuti's homecoming and they've arranged a welcome fit for a guru. Flowers decorate the apartment building's perimeter and a fresh swastika has been painted above the door, as much in praise of his promotion to spiritual middleman as in appeal against the unending assault of the weather. The evidence of a siege is scratched on every surface, a grime that's burned into the walls and spikes the air with the smell of clay and the spermy tang of the sea. It's in the slumped branches and the drooping power lines, the rutted axles and the football left stranded in the gutter when the tide stole in and swamped the street in mud.

Next door no banana skins hang from the washing line. The neighbour's wife wears gold and magenta to simulate the wings of migrated butterflies. Her husband is no longer the provider of beauty and all the starch has gone out of him because of it. He stands aimless in the road and watches our arrival, one foot poised at the lip of the flooded pothole as if he might give up his pretensions of buoyancy and jump in, sink to the bottom where weird inland fishes will lullaby him to a peaceful sleep.

He waves at us but the days of siege and scurf have taken his smile away.

Bibhuti sees the damage before any of us. He's lived through so many monsoons that he's attuned to the fine outrages they deliver. He looks sadly up to the roof of his building as our car pulls in.

'It is broken,' he clucks when I reach him. 'Look at this. It will have to be fixed.'

I look up and see the satellite dish hanging limp from the wall, displaced from its bracket by the storm winds.

'Baba, you must fix it,' Jolly Boy insists, scrambling from the back seat to see the devastation for himself. The sight of it unhinges him and he tries to pry Bibhuti from the car to make an immediate repair. Bibhuti sucks in an agonised breath and Jolly Boy lets go of him.

'It will be done,' Bibhuti tells him. 'Not to worry. As soon as I am on my feet again I will take care of it.'

'That will be a long time,' Jolly Boy complains.

'It will not be so long.'

Somehow I know I'll be dangling from that roof and I turn away from Ellen so she won't see my excitement.

The air in the apartment is gummy and dense with the gossip of the ghosts who took up tenancy while Bibhuti was away. Drowned children who've spent the last few days bickering over who died most stylishly and the best way to the afterlife. When they hear the key in the lock they bolt to the cracks in the walls. We walk Bibhuti in, sweating from the climb up the stairs. An anxiety enters the room ahead of us, a fear of the curse that might touch us should he find his home ransacked of its treasures. He scans the room suspiciously. He lingers at the sideboard and takes an inventory of its contents. His trophies and commendations provide momentary comfort. The ghosts evaporate.

He switches the TV on, watches the snow falling on screen until the pain becomes too much to bear and he allows us to sit him down on the zebra-print sofa.

'It must feel good to be home,' Ellen says.

He gives a shattered smile in reply. The rain beats against the window and makes a clock for Bibhuti to time his wasting by. Already he's desolate. The long healing ahead and the abandonment of his former creed have sapped the blood from him. He can't bring himself to speak or to look at us.

Jolly Boy runs to the bedroom to turn the air con on and there's a moment of tension while we wait for the system to expectorate and rediscover its breath. Cool air drifts in and Bibhuti's wife goes to the kitchen to be alone with her thoughts. A sour homecoming, everything in the house has been chipped or moved one step back from its rightful place by the knowledge we share of disasters weathered. Nothing has lasted. The neighbour, having followed us up, offers us his food until we get a chance to restock. Charity will be the fibre that stitches us back together.

We put ourselves where Bibhuti can see us, the men competing for his eye and the scraps of blessing he might toss our way. We all want him to know how committed we are to the cause of making him comfortable in his new obscurity. Being intimates with obscurity gives us leverage and wisdoms to pass on about how to walk in darkness.

We're asking a tiger to take up matchstick modelling.

He'll be writing again soon, Vijay Five assures him. The newspaper will always need him and the city will always have stories to tell. And there's the memoir to finish, new chapters to add. The world awaits his account with bated breath.

Butterflies on the wind, the neighbour says. He could use some help with the sanctuary he's been planning, when he's up to it. There's a patch of woodland he's had his eye on and he thinks he can get it for a good price. A butterfly man has peace and time to think. He has the friendship of nature and beauty is his companion. A blessed life, it could be.

Bibhuti thanks them for their help and asks them to leave. He's tired and he needs to rest.

When they've gone Bibhuti tears his plaster off. He's a child unwrapping Christmas presents, impatient to see the full extent of the disgrace the hospital bunglers have inflicted on him.

'Really they have done a very poor job,' he mutters as the casts are shed in eggshell pieces and more battered flesh is revealed, discoloured and creased from its quarantine. 'It is no wonder the pain is not leaving.'

His wife helps him out of the plaster sleeves, very careful not to touch him. Every suggestion he makes that his mastery of pain has left him is met with a sympathy cringe and a snapped retreat of hands. The rest of us sit and watch and let the second-hand tremors pass through us. To be touched even as an afterthought by the pain he feels is to wish myself in his place.

Everything I've wished for since I arrived here has come true. If only I could take it all back. I'm devastated by my own selfishness. It's a revelation that brings no pleasure or relief. I look at the family who took me in and see trees that I just had to climb. They're ruined now. I've carved my name in them and stolen all their fruit. My heels have scraped great gouges in their bark that will leave them open when I've gone to other parasites.

The last piece of shell is removed. Bibhuti appraises his wounds, moving his limbs very slowly to keep the bones in place. Shame comes over him again and his moustache droops. The effect has lost its comical allure.

'You should not see me like this,' he tells me, stripped down to his Y-fronts and fighting back tears.

'I've never seen a guru in his pants before. It's an honour.'

Bibhuti's wife seizes on his confusion and relates to him his new status. The news troubles him.

'Why did you let this happen?' he demands, stiffening. The tired muscles in his shoulders contract and he kicks out his legs, clattering his shins against the coffee table. The room jumps. He suppresses a howl.

'I do not want this,' he goes on, his anger rising. 'I did not ask for your priests. I did this for the love of one God only and for the love of the people. I am not a bearded man in saffron robes, I cannot teach others how to live. Look at me. This is not a good lesson. I have broken myself for twelve years and still the world is in pain. Planes are falling from the sky and my friends are expiring. My friend from England is unwell, I have not been able to cure him. His wife must walk with a stick. We have no television. Where is my lesson? You will get your priests here and they will reverse what they have done.'

Chastened, his wife slinks away to the kitchen again. She comes back with a plastic bucket, a jug of water and a packet of white powder. Ingredients for the new plaster Bibhuti is anxious to get into before his bones disintegrate under the strain of premature freedom. The inside of the bucket is crusted with the remains of past mixes, each new layer betraying another self-inflicted collapse. Under Bibhuti's trained eye she pours the water from the jug into the bucket. She adds the powder at his commentary, a little at a time. Its dust spills out in a plume that sandstorms our eyes before the air con wafts it clear.

'Air bubbles,' Bibhuti prompts, and she taps the side of the bucket with her spoon to disperse the powder and even out the mixture. When Bibhuti is happy with the consistency she gives it a stir and the water becomes a paste.

I think this is something I should be doing, but she has determined it her duty and besides, I'm still feeling the sting of Bibhuti's earlier comment. That my fragility should be so obvious to him when he's the one who's just come back from the dead. What a sorry pair we are.

Jolly Boy trots to the kitchen for the rest of the ingredients. He comes back with an armful of bandages still in their packaging and a fat spool of cotton wool. He drops the bandages and unrolls the cotton wool, cuts it to length for the first application. He holds Bibhuti's elbow delicately while his mother wraps the strip around Bibhuti's arm for padding. She dips the first bandage in the plaster solution and then winds it over the cotton-wool sleeve, her eyes darting all the while to her husband's for guidance. With great care she repeats the process until three layers of bandages clad his arm, smoothing the plaster down with her palm between each application to achieve a clean finish. Her sobriety throughout suggests many years of painstaking ministrations like this, of swabbing blood and smoothing matted hair, of binding fractured fingers and forceful reintroductions of ball joints to their sockets.

Bibhuti stays awake to watch, biting back the pain to remonstrate quietly with her over her fussy technique. She flusters to get the job done to his satisfaction while the room hums to a narcotic rhythm of muted industry. Before my eyes he's fixed and shielded again from my thrill-seeking bat. I've hit him for the last time. A pang of mourning. I'll end my life having never killed a man. I feel the consolation of it as I feel the cooling draught of the air con on my neck. Your mercy, that's what it is. If I feel saved from something, whether it's hell or an inescapable deed, then someone or something must have done the saving. That's what I'm thinking when I watch Bibhuti's other bones being dressed and then sit alone with him listening to the rain as the plaster sets.

'You didn't cure me, then,' I say. I try to make it sound breezy.

'I am very sorry,' Bibhuti says.

'It's okay. Not to worry. Thanks for trying anyway.'

'You still have plenty of time. You must use it wisely. Maybe there is another treatment for you at home. There is always hope if you listen to what your heart is telling you.'

I tell him I have to go soon. I hear him sobbing and I look away to spare his shame. His picture on the wall is crooked. I'll straighten it when I get up. He sits with his legs spread wide, three slabs of concrete between them. The sledgehammer poised in another man's hands. That should have been our record, it would have been so much easier. I should have found him years ago.

36

I hug the ladder tight and turn my face from the view of the ground. Rain shingles the back of my head. Somewhere below me Ellen calls out a spooked profanity and Jolly Boy trills a stiffener to his white uncle's nerves. I can't move. I want to sleep here, vertical and soaked to the skin. I want to forget all the new names I've learned.

I feel B Pattni's big hands on the ladder below me, anchoring it to the bed of the pick-up. The force of his grip fortifies me. That's the plan. The neighbour's ladder didn't reach on its own so an appeal was made and B Pattni answered with the bright idea of standing the ladder on the back of his truck. The extra height brings the broken satellite dish within an arm's length. A merry improvisation, in the Indian way. Safe as houses, as long as the handbrake holds.

B Pattni offered to climb the ladder for me and I had to stand my ground. It was my job. I had to suffer the spotlight glare of the crowd as I made my ascent, the neighbours come to see me make my amends and the reporters digging in for the first glimpse of Bibhuti on his feet and ever hopeful for the summoning to hear it all from the horse's mouth, how a man among them touched the sun and came back.

They all wonder at me, how a pasty Englishman became the hand of God. I free an arm to check the screwdriver in my pocket and take another step up, barefoot for bite on the slippery metal, the paint chipping off my toenails and my strength ebbing away. I'm barely animal enough to find my grip. I have to put everything into squeezing. My slowness shames me. I shake when I lift off and scrabble for the next handhold, an unmanly spectacle for the watching cameras. I keep going because I have to. I bet myself that my last act on this continent would be something charitable. Something useful to a friend. I haul myself up as far as I can go.

At the top it's just me and my breathing. I reach out and reel the dish in. It looks intact. Only the bracket's broken, sheared away from the wall. I shout out my findings. B Pattni steps away from the foot of the ladder to get the replacement bracket and for a moment I'm adrift. The wait for his return is an age without the ballast that comes from other people. I keep my focus on the prayer bracelet around my wrist. Its colour has faded and it slips loosely down my arm. When I feel B Pattni's weight engage again with the ladder I know I'll live beyond today.

I pick my way slowly back down the rungs to meet B Pattni at the bottom. He passes me the bracket and the screws and I begin my climb again. I hope I look determined and fearless and that he'll mention this detail when called to witness my feat to Bibhuti, who sits alone in front of a blank TV screen waiting for his connection to be restored. I lift my head to feel the rain slapping my face. It's still warm. Up I go.

Bibhuti is pleased with me. The screen throws a bold light into the room. The picture is clear. He clicks past the cricket, prodding tetchily at the remote control buttons. He shuffles through the channels to be reunited in little bursts of recognition with each of his favourites. He doesn't linger on the sports. The reunion is painful, a tactless reminder that the coming weeks will be spent idly and with terrible waste. To dull the torment while his bones recover he must banish all signals of the grace and power that live in the world beyond his walls.

He clucks his tongue and changes the channel. An American police procedural drama from a decade ago. His eyes glaze over and he slides back into the sofa, giving himself up to the indolence the doctor prescribed when we left the ward in a stumbling entourage.

'You should be in bed,' his wife chides him. 'You will rest much better there.'

He grunts in reply and fidgets with the volume control.

The floor is sand-shifting under my feet, my legs still think they're dangling in thin air. When I have time to reflect I'll recall how scared I was up on the ladder, it'll rush in like a tidal wave and sweep me away. But for now my thoughts are consumed with the logistics of going home. There are flights to book and a will to write. I have to choose which of my accumulated trinkets to bequeath and which to throw out, and that means listening again to the stories of each of them. The listening will take up most of what time remains. I'll have to go back and put a God to every one of them before they fade away. While I was sleeping you quietly filled me. Now I'm awake and responsible. I have to go and settle things. I have to leave the place where I woke up. I have to forget my friend.

I ask him if he's comfortable and if there's anything else I can do for him. He waves me away, his eyes fixed on the TV screen.

Jolly Boy senses his father drifting away from him and he has an idea. Does he want to see the record, the footage is on YouTube?

The life returns to Bibhuti's eyes and he sits up. He instructs Jolly Boy to get his laptop. Jolly Boy rushes to the bedroom, a bounce in his step, comes back with the laptop already open and whirring into start-up.

'Come,' Bibhuti says to me, 'we will watch together. Jolly Boy, let Uncle sit.' He watches with excitement as the browser opens up and the boy types a search into Google. Bibhuti Nayak baseball bat.

I look away before he hits enter.

'It's okay, I don't need to see it.'

Bibhuti is confused. 'We must enjoy these happy moments,' he says.

'You would not like to see what you have done?' his wife asks. It's a challenge. I have to face up to it. We all gather in close. Ellen takes my arm to console me. Jolly Boy hits play.

The footage is clean and crisp. The AXN cameraman must have leaked it to serve a greater good. It doesn't do me any favours. I look like a man possessed, chopping away at Bibhuti with indecent haste, my arms swinging apelike above my head. Jolly Boy is goggle-eyed passing me the fresh bats, his face sheened with shock and pride. Bibhuti is taking every hit with a shudder that could be mistaken for torture. My actions bristle with the anxious hunger of a bird trapped in tar. I look like someone discovering their superpower for the first time in the shadow of death.

'Lovely,' Bibhuti coos. He looks at me with pride, the son he never wished for.

'Uncle looks very funny,' Jolly Boy says. He studies his own image and finds himself an improvement on the boy his friends once poked and prodded, his puppy fat now wrapped around a skeleton of steel. An accomplice in great feats, he'll go back to class with a legend other boys will file to like ants to sugar.

'You must be very proud of your husband,' Bibhuti says to Ellen. 'He did very well.'

'I am,' Ellen says. 'He always tried his best.'

We could be a fever dream. I watch myself letting go on him and my skin prickles. Your eyes on me are pitying. I'm just another one of your children who lost his way in the race to see who could live the fastest.

Bibhuti crumbles and falls. The camera zooms in on his prone body. A moment of calm, then confusion sets in. A murmur winds through the crowd. Jolly Boy comes into shot and kneels down at his father's side. He strokes his arm, gives him a gentle shake. His mother joins him. Her shakes are fiercer and she's already gone hard as if she's been bereaved for years. Bibhuti won't move. The sky opens. A comment on the vain recreations of your children. Fat raindrops streak the lens, blurring Bibhuti into a memory in water of the man he was.

We stand there watching. No words come to us. We're all friends now and what's done is done.

Sleep comes too easily in Ellen's bed. I float away surrounded by the things she's brought from home. I remember the reassuring thrill when I first found myself among her laced and fragranced things, the woman-warmed garments that reminded me how I'd been chosen by another person to lead them through the dangers of the world. I feel that thrill again and yearn for those dangers. I go to sleep with the taste of her on my tongue. I sleep for us both, folding into a darkness that will flay the fat from me and leave me light enough for her to lift me on and off a fretting chair.

When I wake up the cases are packed, the little padlocks sitting on top ready for me to thread and snap shut. Ellen's numb fingers aren't up to the little things. I reach over to where she sits on the side of the bed and take her hand. I turn it round so the knuckles face out and run them down my cheek. It's supposed to be playful. The scrape of my stubble is an assault on the air. She looks sad. I think she's making a guess at how much she'll miss the touch of a man.

'You don't have to keep me,' I tell her. 'If you don't want to. I can go somewhere, they have places for dying in. The people there are trained, they don't take it personally. It'll be easier.'

'Don't be stupid,' Ellen says. And then she tells me a secret. It shouldn't feel like a secret but it does. She tells me she's never stopped loving me.

'I went to buy you a snowglobe once. You remember that's what I used to call you?'

I remember. I go cold. I haven't been her secret for such a long time.

She tells me there was a toy shop in town, with carousels in the window and snowglobes in different sizes, an old-fashioned sort of place that clung on to a handmade ideal for as long as it could. She went there to surprise me. It was the day I saw her, the time we never spoke about.

'I was looking for ages but I couldn't find the right one. There were so many to choose from and I didn't want to make a mistake. If I picked the wrong one it meant I didn't know you anymore. I thought it was such a good idea, I went there all full of myself and I pictured the look on your face when I gave it to you. Things had been hard and I needed to make it right again. You'd been trying so hard.'

She bites on something painful and she's so brave, I'm ashamed of myself for never seeing it and for everything she saw in me.

'I gave up in the end. None of them were you. But not because I didn't know you. They just didn't have yours there. I would have known it when I saw it. I didn't want to make do with something else.'

She reaches into the case and brings out a present for me, held in the palm of her hand like an offering. I take it and carefully peel the wrapping paper away. It's one of the snowglobes I helped save from the flood, the ones with the power station inside.

'I found it when I first got here, before I came to find you. It was in a little souvenir shop just by the hotel, you probably know it. The man had only just got them, it was the first one he put out. I don't know why but it felt right. Something about how random it was appealed to me. Go on then, see if it works.'

I give it a jiggle. The glitter falls unimpressively. 'It's perfect,' I say.

The tears fall out of her. I've won her back. I never lost her after all. I wrap my arms around her and let her shake. She's enough snow for the rest of my life.

The ghosts of man and cobra are peeking through the whitewash and Harshad has been in thrall to the radio since sunrise, the swoop of a favourite ballad drawing him away from the whisky bottle that stands near-full at the far end of the counter. Everything's working now. With nothing left to fix, his hands can be still at last. The bottle will be lifted and drained before the day is out but whenever the music plays it will soak up his sadness a little bit, insulate him against the slow crush of time passing unbrightened by a tactile and reforming love. Every day for him will be like this. I can only hope the radio keeps working so the music will come in rations enough to keep him afloat.

He stops singing when I approach the counter. He undermines me with a hateful look.

I ask him if he's heard, Bibhuti's awake and all is well.

He's heard. He's glad. But it changes nothing, I can see it in his eyes. It's luck alone that kept Bibhuti alive. It's luck that took his wife and his fingers and his best friend. And with luck he'll live to see his daughter marry into the happiness he never found. There's no telling. He just wants to be alone with his music now.

I offer my hand. I thank him, for everything. I have nothing particular in mind, I'm just being polite. I've been ungrateful in the past and I recognise the error of it. His mangled fingers are smooth as if from burns. I keep shaking for longer than I need to, just to let him know that nothing disgusts me anymore.

He comes out from behind the counter, picks up the cases and takes them outside. He stands on the spot where his friend used to sit and tests the weather. Hollowed out by his losses, he's a barrel for the rain. It pours into him, pastes the wayward hair onto his head. He stands straight, his face lifted to the sky, his eyes shut tightly. For a moment it looks like he might be taken up the way the old man with the gods had hoped to be.

The blast of a car horn pulls him back down to earth. It's Jolly Boy's hand on the steering wheel. Laughing, he blasts the horn again, startling his mother in the back seat. He looks small behind the wheel, a spoof of a grown-up. In the passenger seat Bibhuti winds the wheel towards the kerb. At his nod Jolly Boy brakes sharply. The jolt knocks Bibhuti against the dashboard, spilling his Ganesh. He recovers and looks up at me. He taps the dial of an imaginary watch, his new relationship with pain making him impatient. It's time to go.

37

My Final Glorious Victory (2010)

It is with great pride that I convey to you the latest record achievement which will also be my last as the almighty has decided. The attempt passed off with only minor hitch-up due to the extreme difficulty which cannot be matched by any other means. Memory of the event containing some holes but the important parts preserved on film and in the minds of all present, especially my great friend John Lock who pushed me to glory with undimmed spirit and determination which is second to none. Eleven baseball bats broken in one minute and thirty-seven seconds. Guinness ratification pending. My body is no longer the cage of my dreams. All my dreams set free to explore the world and come back to me with the news of seven seas and beyond. God is in everything and knows the best route to happiness. I followed always with sure steps until the path stopped at ultimate destination.

The pain is a gift from him. It is telling me that my work is done. There is no doubt about it. Typing this report with the fingers of one hand only is itself a test of my patience while I await further instructions for my next adventure as person of highest credentials.

You may be asking yourself why there is no regret that I did not reach my target of fifty bats. Really there can be no regret. The prize I received from the big record show and its lead-up is too much to kill time with introspecting on what might have been. This prize is a new friend in the shape of John Lock who will live in my heart for ever. We will share many beautiful moments to come when the almighty spares him from his present illness. He will teach me even more about the role of kindness than he has hitherto. Also there will be lovely times of humour in the vein of previous examples such as his first attempts at yoga and his defeats in the badminton arena which made Jolly Boy smile so frequently. And eleven bats is an impressive number which will never be outstripped by another man. Everything is walking in ideally as I wished it.

I could not hope to have the career I have enjoyed when first I landed on the extreme sports idea. This was now many years past as a young man with no wife or child and no money arriving in Mumbai from my native place. All I had then was belief in the promise of destiny to provide my bread and daily safety. Just twenty years later and I am the holder of some fourteen World Records under Guinness and Limca banner, with track record in training junior world-beaters and many more achievements under my belt such as beefing up security on Konkan Railway and bringing corrupt public officials to justice by exposing them in the pages of my newspaper. All for the benefit of my community and to preserve the respect for the common man. What a turn-up. How it has happened I am clueless. I am just the son of a farmer and social activist.

I intended to share my recollections of all the records I have broken over the years. This was my plan when first I hit upon the idea of a memoir. There are still many records which I have not yet featured such as one-armed knuckle cartwheels, fingertip push-ups, bicycles ridden over body, etc. But that was back in time when it looked as if my greatest feat would remain unfulfilled. I was at a low point with no financial support in the offing. Bats lay waiting with nobody to pick them up. Then everything changed unexpectedly with the arrival of John Lock. Now my stint has a fitting end with all footage linking up and there is no need to look back anymore.

Now I am only looking forward to when my bones have healed and I can stand again on the new path God will lay out for me. I am listening for the next time he will whisper in my ear and tell me what I must do. There is no hurry. I will be very patient and sure of myself before I take the next step.

Ram the fire-eater visited me again when I was sleeping. I did not know that I was in a hospital bed with broken bones and nurses filling me with poison. I thought I was back in my native place. It was very nice to be there. No strife of daily routine in the city and everybody much more relaxed instead of running hither and thither like rats. My father gave me my old duty of tending the goats. I watched over them in the field. Quiet all around and natural life in abundance. The birds called hello to me when they flew overhead and the snakes said good morning when they slithered past my feet. I was very peaceful and there was no pain, not within me or anywhere in the world.

I was just remarking to myself that the life is so good when out stepped Ram from the forest. He wore a big smile on his face for me and he came to shake my hand. It had been a long time since I saw him last but the joy I felt at being with him again made all the sadness of those years of waiting seem like nothing. They just flew away from me like another bird. I had grown older but he had not changed. His beard still glowed like fire and he was still naked except for the cloth around his loins. What is more he still carried the fire-eater's torch. I was very glad about this even though it remained unlit throughout our meeting.

Then another surprise when Gopal Dutta stepped out of the forest behind him. He had become a fire-eater also. He did not speak. Instead he ate the fire from his own torch repeatedly. He was covered from head to toe in spirit of total contentment and serene nature. This was a lovely sight and convinced me that all persons achieve the bliss when they expire.

I hardly dared to speak to Ram as I did not want to scare him away so soon after reuniting. The entire scene felt like a spell I did not wish to break. Finally I spoke to him. 'I have been waiting for you a very long time,' I said.

'I know,' Ram the fire-eater said. The wind became very still as he spoke so that the only things to be heard were his voice and my own. The sun behind him watching carefully as if we were actors in a dramatic plot.

'Why did you not return before now?' I asked him.

'You did not need me before,' he replied.

I pondered this and realised he was right. I was only needing him at the time he appeared. Between his first visit and this one I was able to carry the weight of my destiny alone.

He asked me how I was feeling. I told him I was fine. I asked him how he was feeling. He also was fine. He had followed my record-breaking stint with much interest. He heard all about my endeavours through the grapevine. Even on his most mysterious travels word had always reached him of my activities. He was very proud to be the one who had sparked this fire within me. He had not meant to. It was not a duty he had been given, he said. It was my work alone and he was a witness only. I did not believe him. I knew he was sent by the almighty. But I did not correct him as this would be disrespectful. Truth was revealed when he told me I must end my extreme sports career sans delay. He had received a vision that I would be seriously victimised if I carried on. He was worried for me and begged me to stop.

I did not want to accept this at first. I pretended I had not heard it. I pretended instead that he had urged me on to another attempt. But I was only fooling myself. I know this now. His message was clear. He insisted it was his personal concern only which prompted the visit but I know he was the messenger. I know finally that I am free of previous burden.

We sat together for a long time. We did not speak again. My heart was calm and a lovely tiredness settled over me like a blanket. Then Ram the fire-eater stood up and walked back to the forest. At the edge of the trees he stopped and waved at me. Then he turned around and was gone. I knew I would never see him again. This was fine as he left me with a certain feeling that the truth of my life had wrapped me in its arms.

Now I am back home in the bosom of my dear ones. My friend John Lock is preparing to leave. He will return to his native place and fix things there. Then he will come back to see me. I hope and pray for this.

John Lock has tagged my son Jolly Boy and now I call him this also. He likes it very much. While I am waiting for my strength to return he is keeping my spirits high with showings of the footage from my previous records. Presently it feels as if I am watching a different person instead of myself. But this will change as I grow stronger.

'I will help you choose the next record, Baba,' he said to me today. 'It will be the biggest of them all.'

'There will be no more records,' I told him. 'Your Baba has completed his journey. He will do something else now.'

The boy could not understand what I was saying. He looked very sad. Perhaps he thought his father would change too much if he did not have his exclusive outlet to fall back on. I had to put his fear to rest.

'Perhaps I will go back and try again to pull the locomotive with my hair. I think I know how to succeed this time. It is all about the method of securing the hair. A strong glue may work wonders if Guinness will allow this.'

Jolly Boy seemed happy with this outcome. My wife not so happy but I will convince her when it becomes necessary to protect the family bond.

I cannot wait to be healed and outside again breathing the fresh air. I hear the rain falling heavily and dream of making cartwheels through the streets of my city where they lie hidden by the water. Soon the monsoon will pass by and the everyday life will be restored to its former level. I will miss my friend but I will keep myself busy in giving thanks and setting a new goal. I am very lucky to be here at this time when God's love is freely distributed in the world. We only have one span of one hundred years or less and everything is possible with veg diet and positive thinking.

Thank you.

38

I've taken over the driving. Bibhuti wants me next to him. We're as close as brothers and I bring him comfort in his pain. Also it might be the last chance I get to drive a car and handing the wheel to me is an act of charity that seals his love inside me. I'll take his love with me. It'll keep me strong when the winter comes. These are his words and I believe them. He's heard about the English winter, how low the temperature drops, and about real snow. He wants to be a warming current from across the seven seas.

'When our prayers have been answered you will come back to see us. You must stay warm until then. Our sun will be waiting for you.'

'He's a good kid.'

'No, our sun. For the heat. This will restore you to full health.'

'Right.'

'Jolly Boy also will be waiting.'

I turn to look at him wedged impatient between the seats. 'Will you? Will you remember me?'

Jolly Boy smiles and tilts his head, asserting his devotion to me.

'We could go to Tadoba,' he says. 'We will find my tiger, he will let you stroke him too.'

'Sounds like a plan.'

Bibhuti grabs the wheel to steer us around a dead dog. We clip its bloated carcass and send it bobbing away on the shallow wave that nudges us towards the creek.

'Watch the road,' Bibhuti scolds me, the effort of wrenching the wheel sending pain whipping through him. 'We must get you to the airport in one piece.'

The traffic crawls across the bridge, fearful of treading too heavily on a world that has softened and become uncertain under the sustained assault of the rain. More people are walking, trusting their own lightness over the clumsy weight of steel and rubber, having made their peace through a season of erosion with the idea of being washed away. They weave between the bumpers with agility, umbrellas hiding their faces, wet hands sliding over bonnets and grasping for the momentary attachment of wing mirrors as the cars edge them out to the railings and invite them to jump.

The creek laps at our ankles, the grey water savaging the retreated land, and heroic swimmers are backstroking in the wake of a god come to life.

Down on the water Ganesh is taking a dip, sitting in silent contemplation on a deck of wood while the waves shake the teeth from his head. I imagine the delusions have kicked in as the mercenary cells take hold and the blood in my veins turns to mercury. Its elephant head tilts my way, and I see that its large painted eyes are unpanicked by its immersion. I see that it's lifeless and incapable of fear.

'Today is start of Ganesh Chaturthi,' Bibhuti says. 'It is big festival here. It is supposed to be the birthday of Ganesh. People all over are making statues of him to immerse in water. This is to bring prosperity.'

The figure spins wild in the current, a symbol of intervention against chance. The swimmers steal in to steady its hull and turn it towards the mouth of the creek. A sniff of the sea brings its many limbs to order and its journey is plotted by the men who turned the clay and painted the rings on its fat fingers and toes. There's no chance here, only the preordained outcomes of a thousand negotiations and an infinite number of fears fired to charm-size figurines in the kiln of meticulous faith. The swimmers make a band and tug their Ganesh by his flank to keep him pointed at the future. His face will charm diamonds from the mud when the rain has passed.

A man sets his umbrella down and jumps smiling from the bridge. He doggy-paddles to join the party. The swell rises to meet him with open arms. He disappears under the water. It looks like he's been lost. A moment later he's fished out to the jubilant cries of his new friends. He scrambles to the safety of the floating Ganesh, coiling a grateful arm around the statue's foot. Appeased by the offering of gods and men the clouds unstitch their fingers and blue sky leaks out, and I know I'll never see another morning as bright and crowded with fine noise as this one.

The airport palms are bowing in a satire of adulation as I eat up the Indian sun for the last time, stretching my legs on the Departures slipway. My last sniff of Indian air is a devoted one, drawn deep. Diesel and shit and blood and rain. Limes and sweat and the constitutional dawn.

Time embraces me. My thoughts run away. I close my eyes and breathe it in.

The hit comes from behind. A fist in the back of the head, I hear it before I feel it. I drop to my knees. When I look up my attacker is poised over me, wild-eyed and trembling. Bibhuti sticks his head out of the car and remonstrates with him. The man is young and muscle-bound. I recognise him from Bibhuti's class. Once I saw him take a flying leap at another man's head. I stay down, inch away out of range of his feet.

'What did you do that for?' Ellen demands of him.

He pays no attention to her. He listens to his sensei as he talks him through his mistake.

Bibhuti's wife looks at me on my hands and knees. She won't allow herself a smile but there's pleasure in her dark eyes, just at the edges. I've found my place. She couldn't have wished a better ending for me. I feel the back of my head. My fingers come back bloody. The blood is a gift and so is the pain. I'm a breathing bleeding fugitive of time. My life wasn't a dream after all.

Bibhuti sets the man straight and he rushes to help me to my feet, pulling me up one-handed as if I weigh nothing at all. He rains apologies. He'd thought I was his master's enemy. That's the way the footage and the press painted it. He didn't know the truth of it. Can I forgive him?

I spit out some blood. I've bitten my tongue. I tell him not to worry.

He dashes into the terminal building and comes back with a wheelchair for Bibhuti. We help him into it, and Jolly Boy sweeps in to load a trolley with our luggage and wheel it to the doors. The man offers to wait with the car. Witnesses to my attack surround him. He tells them who we are and they follow us inside, eager for a glimpse of their celebrity cripple and the man who took his legs.

Cool air. Inside is international. India is already behind me. The witnesses stop us and lay hands on Bibhuti's shoulders and arms, patting him like wet clay, leaving their finger marks in him for providence. A couple of them pose for photos crouching alongside their hero. They retreat at the sight of the security guards flexing their trigger fingers. We roll through the concourse, each of us pining in secret for the time when we can be alone to scratch at the various itches we've stirred in each other. Jolly Boy struggles to steer the misfit luggage trolley along a straight course. We laugh at the mess he's making of his attempt at swanlike self-possession. Knowing I'll never see him again prompts a dread that I cover up with idle talk.

'Will you carry on with your book?' I ask Bibhuti.

'Of course,' he says. 'My story is not yet finished.'

I thank him for letting me be a part of it.

'Not just a part. The biggest. When you come back it will be finished. You will read what I have written.'

His well-meaning lies make my heart ache.

The girl at check-in sees the blood dripping down my neck and offers me a tissue to wipe my wound. When the cases have gone through Jolly Boy takes control of the wheelchair and races me to the security line, his father's cries of alarm echoing off the sun-streaked marble. People are emptying their pockets and removing their belts, a nervous submission to an illusion of safety. I take out the last of my Indian money and give it to Bibhuti's wife. It's not meant to be a bribe and it's not her forgiveness I seek. I just want to leave her with an impression of a man who can settle his own debts.

She whispers thank you for bringing her husband back to her.

I bend down and kiss Bibhuti's neck, a scrap of brown between the plaster casts. I feel a tiny contraction as he recoils and then relaxes. I breathe him in and then I take Ellen's arm and lead her behind the security tape. I take off my shoes before I'm asked. When I've filled my tray I look behind me and my friend is gone.

The men with their guns walk in lazy circles and the lights above them make everything look older.

Over the tin roofs and Rebati the ape girl waves at us from her place of grand design. The smaller children pause from braiding her face hair to look up at the sky and wonder at the treasures a plane holds in its belly and where they're being taken. I think I see more Ganesh idols floating in the bay, the sun glinting off trunks raised in denouncement of the sea's irresistible pull. I'm a fruit that's missing its stone. The dark heart of me has been scooped out and without its unifying mass the flesh is falling in. What a sweet falling. Everything sings with a new sweetness and I'm more tired than I've ever been. I unbuckle my seatbelt and squeeze Ellen's hand.

One sleep will be enough if it goes deep. One sleep to undo a lifetime as we fly against the clock. Nothing to do now but remember and wait. The landing gear grinds back into its recess and my eyes drop shut without a fight. I see a flash of orange and hear a growling, a warning and then a submission. The last thing I feel is the tingle of fur at my fingertips. I stroked a tiger's tail and it didn't seem to mind.

AUTHOR'S NOTE

Bibhuti Nayak is a real person, and much of what you have read about him in this book is true. While his essence is embodied in the character who shares his name, and some of those character's exploits really happened – including many of the records – I have embellished or invented where necessary for the purpose of this story. Bibhuti himself was happy for me to do so; in fact he encouraged it. If you'd like to find out more about the real Bibhuti, please search his name online.

Stephen Kelman

ACKNOWLEDGEMENTS

My deepest thanks to Bibhuti Bhushan Nayak for gifting me his story and for blessing me with his friendship. This book was born of his generosity and his spirit inspires me every day.

My sincere appreciation to Smruti and Shubham (Jolly Boy) for placing their trust in me. Thanks to Jagatdeep Singh for doing likewise. I owe various citizens of Mumbai and Navi Mumbai a debt of gratitude for their kindness, encouragement and curiosity. Their lives infuse these pages and enrich me beyond words.

I first saw Bibhuti on *Paul Merton in India*, a documentary series for Channel 5. I'd like to thank Paul for accepting Bibhuti's invitation to kick him in the groin, an act of grace and bravery from which this book, and a life-changing friendship, eventually emerged.

My wife Uzma patiently endured with me every up and down that comes with writing a book, and I couldn't have finished it without her.

The same can be said of Jo Unwin and Clare Conville, agents former and current, and friends whose support and skill make the improbable a reality, and Helen Garnons-Williams, my editor, whose wisdom and sensitivity steer me past the vanities. Everything began with David Llewelyn, and I'll never forget it.

I am deeply indebted to my parents (Jagannath and Shanti) who have brought me to this beautiful world. Thanks to my journalist friend R. Ramesh for encouraging me to achieve several milestones and he has been my pillar of strength. Thank you Dr Vijay D. Patil, a visionary man and passionate about sports, who has always been magnanimous to me. I am gratified to my friend Charanjeet Singh Parwana for pushing me to limelight. Sincere thanks to my disciples D. B. Chand and Mahesh Vishwakarma for standing by me along the way of my arduous journey. My family friend Neelam Patil deserves special thanks for her impulsive and unselfish deeds. Thanks to my evergreen friends Hruday R. Mohanty, Abhishek Yadav and Narendra Kamath for being with me, their patience and unfussiness. My earnest thanks to Stephen and Uzma for bringing in cheers on my face after decades of my struggle, poverty and adversity.

Bibhuti Bhushan Nayak
Navi Mumbai
December 2014

A NOTE ON THE TYPE

The text of this book is set in Bembo, which was first used
in 1495 by the Venetian printer Aldus Manutius for Cardinal
Bembo's *De Aetna*. The original types were cut for Manutius
by Francesco Griffo. Bembo was one of the types used by
Claude Garamond (1480–1561) as a model for his Romain
de l'Université, and so it was a forerunner of what became
the standard European type for the following two centuries.
Its modern form follows the original types and was
designed for Monotype in 1929.

ALSO AVAILABLE BY STEPHEN KELMAN

PIGEON ENGLISH

Shortlisted for the Man Booker Prize 2011

Eleven-year-old Harrison Opoku, the second best runner in Year 7, races through his new life in England with his personalised trainers – the Adidas stripes drawn on with marker pen – blissfully unaware of the very real threat around him. Newly-arrived from Ghana with his mother and older sister Lydia, Harri absorbs the many strange elements of city life, from the bewildering array of Haribo sweets, to the frightening, fascinating gang of older boys from his school. But his life is changed forever when one of his friends is murdered. As the victim's nearly new football boots hang in tribute on railings behind fluorescent tape and a police appeal draws only silence, Harri decides to act, unwittingly endangering the fragile web his mother has spun around her family to keep them safe.

'A book to fall in love with: a funny book, a true book, a shattering book' *The Times*

'A gut-wrenchingly sad novel that makes you laugh out loud' *Guardian*

'Made me laugh and tremble all the way through … A triumph' Emma Donoghue, author of *Room*

ORDER YOUR COPY:

BY PHONE: +44 (0) 1256 302 699

BY EMAIL: DIRECT@MACMILLAN.CO.UK

DELIVERY IS USUALLY 3–5 WORKING DAYS.

FREE POSTAGE AND PACKAGING FOR ORDERS OVER £20.

ONLINE: WWW.BLOOMSBURY.COM/BOOKSHOP

PRICES AND AVAILABILITY SUBJECT TO CHANGE WITHOUT NOTICE.

BLOOMSBURY.COM/AUTHOR/STEPHEN-KELMAN

BLOOMSBURY